A holiday gift for readers of
Harlequin American Romance

Novellas from three of your favorite authors

Return of the Light

MAGGIE SHAYNE

Star Light, Star Bright

ANNE STUART

One for Each Night

JUDITH ARNOLD

ABOUT THE AUTHORS

Maggie Shayne lives on two hundred acres of lush meadows and woodland in central New York. She has published more than thirty novels and numerous novellas and articles, and has received many awards. Her longtime interest in the Shamanic religions of pre-Christian times led her to a study of modern-day nature religions. Several years ago she was initiated as a Wiccan priestess. She has now achieved the rank of High Priestess, and is legally ordained as Wiccan clergy, with all the privileges thereof, including the authority to perform marriages.

Anne Stuart has written over sixty novels in her more than twenty-five years as a writer. She has won many major awards, including three RITA® Awards from Romance Writers of America, as well as their Lifetime Achievement Award. When she's not writing or traveling around the country speaking to writers' groups, she can be found at home in northern Vermont with her husband and two children.

Judith Arnold is the award-winning author of more than eighty novels. She can't remember a time she wasn't making up stories. By age six, she was writing them down and sharing them with her teachers and friends. Today, with more than ten million copies of her books in print, she's happily sharing her stories with the world. A native New Yorker, she lives in Massachusetts with her husband and two sons.

MAGGIE SHAYNE

ANNE STUART

AND

JUDITH ARNOLD

Burning Bright

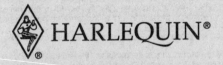

HARLEQUIN®

TORONTO • NEW YORK • LONDON
AMSTERDAM • PARIS • SYDNEY • HAMBURG
STOCKHOLM • ATHENS • TOKYO • MILAN • MADRID
PRAGUE • WARSAW • BUDAPEST • AUCKLAND

ISBN 0-373-75045-5

BURNING BRIGHT

Copyright © 2004 by Harlequin Books S.A.

The publisher acknowledges the copyright holders of the individual works as follows:

RETURN OF THE LIGHT
Copyright © 2004 by Margaret Benson.

STAR LIGHT, STAR BRIGHT
Copyright © 2004 by Anne Kristine Stuart Ohlrogge.

ONE FOR EACH NIGHT
Copyright © 2004 by Barbara Keiler.

This edition published by arrangement with Harlequin Books S.A.

® and TM are trademarks of the publisher. Trademarks indicated with ® are registered in the United States Patent and Trademark Office, the Canadian Trade Marks Office and in other countries.

www.eHarlequin.com

Printed in U.S.A.

CONTENTS

STAR LIGHT, STAR BRIGHT   11
Anne Stuart

RETURN OF THE LIGHT   81
Maggie Shayne

ONE FOR EACH NIGHT   169
Judith Arnold

STAR LIGHT, STAR BRIGHT
Anne Stuart

For BK and Mort—Romex rules!

Dear Reader,

Vermont was made for Christmas. Snow blankets the tiny villages and white-spired churches, with only the evergreens and the bright blue of the sky breaking the vast whiteness of it all. I've spent the past thirty-three Christmases in my little village in Vermont (a town that bears a striking resemblance to Crescent Cove) and the holidays just wouldn't seem right any other place.

It was wonderful writing a story in collaboration with two of my favorite people, Judith Arnold and Maggie Shayne. Judith and I are like the odd couple—she's the neatnik and I'm the slob—but we're great friends anyway. And Maggie is a force unto herself—a real treasure.

Getting the chance to share my Vermont Christmas with the rest of you was a pleasure, and I hope the holidays, whichever ones you celebrate, are glorious.

Merry Christmas!

Anne Stuart

Chapter One

First Week of Advent

It was snowing again. Angela McKenna navigated the icy roads with her usual panic, driving her old Jeep at a snail's pace. At least it had all-wheel drive. But even that wonderful invention wasn't foolproof when it came to ice. This was her second winter spent on the shores of Lake Champlain, and she would have thought she'd have gotten used to the driving by now. After all, she could navigate the heart of Chicago, the insanity of New York, the freeways of L.A. without breaking a sweat. But let a few flakes of snow start drifting out of the Vermont skies and she was swamped with a tightly controlled terror. It was a good thing she didn't have to go anywhere for work—she would have been hopeless. Except, maybe that would have forced her to learn how to drive in the snowy vicinity of Crescent Cove without courting a heart attack.

She usually avoided going out entirely when the weather was bad, but right now she was driving home from Burlington Airport after spending Thanksgiving with her parents in Chicago, and the sooner she got back the better. It was only going to keep on snowing.

They'd put the holiday decorations up in the middle of town while she'd been gone. Reindeer danced from every streetlight, and the big tree at the end of the main street was ablaze with lights. Wreaths were on every one of the white clapboard houses she passed. Just after four and already growing dark, the sidewalks of Crescent Cove were empty.

She had to get home and off these snowy roads, she thought as she made her way through town with single-minded concentration, past the stores and restaurants, heading north, breathing deeply as she listened to the New Age holiday music on her car's CD player, when for some reason she hit the right turn signal. She took the turn, half in a daze. In all the time she'd spent in Crescent Cove she'd never gone down this particular narrow road, never even noticed its existence, and why she'd do so in the middle of a raging blizzard made no sense at all. Nevertheless, that was exactly what she had done.

Well, it wasn't actually a raging blizzard—more a flurry or two. And maybe she'd just been daydreaming—forgetting where she was, and taken the wrong turn. It would be easy enough to stop and head back the way she'd come. She'd never been gifted geographically, and if she kept going in a strange direction, God knows where she'd end up. Her safest bet was to turn around.

The street was packed with the early snow, and she pulled into a driveway beside a small store, then backed out again. Not into the street, but into a parking spot just outside the tiny shop.

Crescent Cove was too small a place, especially in the winter, for Angie not to have known every single side street, every shop, every restaurant. Nevertheless, this tiny shop was entirely new to her, and the warm light spilled out onto the sidewalk.

On impulse she turned off the car and climbed out. She never could resist a mystery, and the appearance of a new street, a new store, was unimaginable. Of course the street wasn't new—that would be impossible. She just hadn't seen it before—the snow made everything look different.

And once she could read the faded gilt sign over the front door she breathed a sigh of relief. Christmas Candles by Mrs. Claus, it read. The very cuteness of it should have been cloying, but Angie was in a generous mood. No wonder she'd missed it—it was a seasonal business. No one would be buying Christmas candles in the busy summer.

The snow was falling gently on her shoulders, and she realized she should return to the car and get her butt safely home, but something kept her rooted to the sidewalk. After all, she'd decided this would be the Christmas she would go all out, and it was important to support local businesses. Buy Vermont First, they said, and she opened the old oak door, listening to the silvery laughter of bells as she stepped inside.

She was expecting to be assaulted by artificial perfumes, but instead the place smelled warm and delightful, like Christmas cookies. Candles of various shapes and sizes were arranged on a number of tables, decorated with festive tablecloths and sweet-smelling greenery, and Angie felt a surge of happiness that hadn't been there in a long, long time. Christmas always did that to her.

"Merry Christmas, dearie." The woman seemed to materialize out of the shadows, and Angie would have laughed, except it seemed so right. The owner of the shop had dressed the part—rosy cheeks, wire-rimmed glasses, a red-velvet mob cap atop her soft white hair.

"Merry Christmas," Angie replied automatically. "I don't really know why I'm here…"

"You're here for a Christmas candle," the woman said in a comfortable voice.

"Well, I suppose I am," Angie admitted. "I just hadn't realized…"

"We seldom do," the so-called Mrs. Claus said. "I've got just the one for you, Angie."

Angie was startled. "How did you know who I was?"

"This is a very small town in the winter, dearie. Everyone knows everyone."

Angie was about to point out that Mrs. Claus was a complete stranger to her, but she was polite enough to keep quiet. Besides, it wasn't strictly true. There was a familiarity about the old lady that was unmistakable.

"I'm not sure what I'm looking for. Whether I want some kind of Christmas scent or—the candles are unscented," she said suddenly, just realizing it.

"No, they're not. They only release their fragrance when they're lit. And I promise you, there's nothing artificial about the scent. If you smell cinnamon and apples, then that's what's in the candle."

"Well, maybe a nice big red pillar," Angie said, always a sucker for cinnamon and apples.

"No, dearie. I'll get yours." The woman disappeared into the back of the store with a swirl of her red velvet skirts, then reappeared holding a wide, slightly conical shaped candle. It was deep gold, with Florentine scrolling around the top and bottom, and a line of angels dancing. It was a work of art, undeniably beautiful, and not in Angie's budget. If she had any money to spare it was earmarked for presents, not her own pleasure.

"I don't think I can afford it," she said.

"Oh, you don't have to pay for it," the woman said. "It's already been taken care of. You notice there are three angels dancing on the side of the candle? One is for Christmas past, one for Christmas present and one for all the Christmases of the future. It will last just until Christmas morning, and when the candle burns down completely everything you need will be yours."

Angie would have objected, but the old woman put the pillar in her hand. It felt heavy, warm and oddly comforting. "But who…?"

"Does it matter? Think of it as a gift from Santa Claus. Or are you going to tell me you don't believe in him?"

She had been about to say that very thing but something stopped her. Certain things were meant to be accepted, not scrutinized, and she accepted the gift as she accepted the existence of Santa Claus. Unlikely, but very nice anyway.

"I guess I'll have to find out on my own," she said.

The woman calling herself Mrs. Claus smiled sweetly. "I guess you will, dearie. In the end, we all have to find out on our own."

Not until Angie was halfway down the town road to Black's Point did the oddness of the encounter hit her. The candle sat on the seat beside her, the rich colors glowing in the darkness. If all her wishes were going to come true when the candle burned down, then she'd better plan to burn it night and day. The old woman said it would last until Christmas Day, but Angie doubted it would make it halfway through Advent, the four weeks before Christmas. Still, it was a lovely thing, and its very presence in the car seemed almost a blessing, to ward off the danger of the snowy roads.

At least they'd gotten around to plowing Black's Point Road. Since she was the only inhabitant out there during the winter, and since the town road crew knew perfectly well that she didn't have to get out to a job, her road was low priority. She'd spent four days last winter trapped there, about to run out of canned soup, when her best friend, Patsy, had raised holy hell and gotten them to plow her out.

Had Patsy arranged for the candle? Unlikely—she and Ethan were saving every penny for their new baby, and besides, Patsy was a weaver. She made her own presents.

Angie was in luck this time—the plows had been through recently, and she only slid a little as she took the sharp turn left onto the narrow road. The snow was tapering off—typical that once she was safely home the driving would suddenly become safe once more. Maybe fate was trying to tell her she shouldn't have run away to Vermont when her marriage failed. Well, she had no intention of listening to such an arbitrary judgment. She'd had to rethink her entire life in the wake of Jeffrey's behavior, and she wasn't about to let a little thing like snow stop her from living the life she wanted. And there was no place in the world, not even the house she grew up in outside of Chicago, that felt like home the way Crescent Cove did. She was never sure why—it simply was.

She pulled into her narrow driveway. They'd kept plowing past her house for some reason—usually they just turned around in her driveway and headed back into town. Must be someone new on the road crew who didn't know the rules, she thought. There was no one else to plow.

Still, it would make walking easier. She no longer played

tennis or racquetball, and even though she now lived in Vermont, she'd decided that downhill skiing was vastly overrated. Particularly when you were skiing alone.

But walking in the silent woods that surrounded Crescent Cove was good for the body and soothing for the soul. She'd worked out all sorts of problems while she walked, and when the snow got really deep she even resorted to high-tech snowshoes. The weather wasn't that bad yet, though Vermont had had more than its share of snow already. And it wasn't even winter yet. Technically.

Weather-wise, winter in Vermont began around November 15. They'd already had two nights of below-zero temperatures, and caterpillars and the *Farmer's Almanac* had predicted a long, cold season.

The house was icy when she unlocked the door. She kept the heat down to sixty-two degrees most of the time, and augmented it with a cast-iron wood-fired stove. She shivered, closing the door behind her and flipping on the lights. Maybe she'd indulge in cranking the heat up, just until she had time to get changed and start a fire. Or maybe she wouldn't, and then her money would last her just a bit longer.

That was the problem with having married a lawyer, she thought, kicking off her soaked shoes and walking on the icy floors to the old farmhouse kitchen. Not only had she spent her marriage in a lifestyle well above what she was accustomed to, but her divorce settlement had been minuscule. It was her fault—she'd wanted to end her relationship with her philandering husband as quickly and neatly as possible, and land values in Crescent Cove had skyrocketed. The monetary value of the old farmhouse was impressive to any judge. The only problem was, she had no intention of selling the place, and it was the only thing she'd come away with from the failed marriage, while Jeffrey had kept the house, the car and most of their joint property.

She could always try to get a real job, but assistant professors of English literature were not in high demand, even with a number of colleges and universities nearby. And somehow the very thought of academia sent chills down her spine, colder than the Vermont winters. She wasn't in the mood for politics, students, or the Dead White Guys that made up most college curricula. The full professors got the fun stuff—the assistants were left with the same old crap. If she had to teach Charles Dickens one more time she would scream. Well, maybe not if she was teaching *A Christmas Carol*. But then, she'd always been a total sucker for Christmas.

No, she liked what she was doing just fine. Even loved it. She'd always loved to bake, and providing pies and breads and other goods to the local businesses kept her busy and brought her some peace of mind. Sister Krissie's Bar and Grill, Mort's Diner, even BK's Grocery provided enough standing orders that she stayed reasonably solvent.

The smell of the farmhouse welcomed her like an old friend. The place had been empty for years—Jeffrey's parents had acquired it as an investment and then forgotten all about it. Why they couldn't have bought her own family's house when finances had forced its sale was another question. Instead, the *über*-wealthy Jacksons had bought it and bulldozed it to make room for another tennis court, wiping out generations of love and memories. Typical of the new breed of summer people, she thought. Wipe out memories and traditions in favor of ostentation. The Jacksons had only been the first of the professional invaders. Their company, Worldcomp, made so much money that no one could figure out what they were doing in a quiet little seasonal community like Crescent Cove.

Except to tear down her family's home, she thought grumpily. And bring Brody Jackson into her life, someone she could have well done without.

She put the candle down on the scrubbed kitchen table and set to work. It didn't take her long to get a new fire going, and the heat began spreading through the kitchen. She lit the candle, and the scent was amazing. It smelled like cinnamon, and delicious enough to make her stomach rumble. She closed off most of the place in the winter—surviving nicely on the first floor with a bedroom, a bathroom and the parlor along with the huge old kitchen. In the summer she threw open the upstairs and invited everyone to visit, but the winters were hers, and she welcomed that season's approach with a sense of relief.

While the room was heating, she quickly put on some warmer clothes—jeans and a sweater and thick wool socks. She didn't bother with her indulgent silk long johns—those she kept for subzero weather. Today was comfortably in the upper twenties, according to her outside thermometer. A nice, brisk afternoon.

Five trips later, everything was in from the back of the car. One suitcase of her own, and four more that she'd borrowed from her mother. The first one was filled with Christmas presents from Marshall Fields. The other three were packed with family Christmas ornaments that her mother had finally decided to hand over.

Angie could never understand why her mother had held on to them for so long. Her academic parents had downsized when Angie had married, moving into a small apartment that overlooked Lake Michigan, and from then on they'd only had a tabletop tree, with no room for many of Angie's favorite ornaments or the Christmas tree house, an ornate tree stand made by her father's great-uncle Otto early in the last century. For some reason her parents had preferred to keep things in storage rather than let her have them, which was unusual, because her parents tended to dote on their only child.

Her marriage had ended Christmas Eve, and she'd spent the next few weeks huddled in a hotel room, not in the mood to celebrate a damn thing. By the next Christmas she'd been divorced for nine months and living in the farmhouse in Crescent Cove, and Jeffrey's new wife had just given birth. To Angie's surprise her mother had called, offering to ship the Christmas decorations east to her, but she'd politely declined, planning to spend the holiday alone in her farmhouse with nary a decoration or a Christmas carol to keep her company.

Big mistake, she'd realized. Fortunately, her old friend Patsy and her husband were living in town, and they'd dragged her out of her morose isolation and into the warmth of their large family holiday that had included Patsy's mother and her new husband, Patsy's father and his new wife, Ethan's father and his new wife, and Ethan's mother, newly widowed, plus five brothers and sisters and their spouses, countless children and even the ninety-year-old matriarch of the family, known to all as Aunt Ginny.

It had been impossible to stay depressed in such chaos. Impossible not to feel the faint, tentative rebirth of the Christmas spirit. And now that another year had passed, she was once more ready to celebrate the holidays with a vengeance.

She'd been half tempted to go right out and find the perfect tree the moment she'd come home from Chicago. A great many people in Crescent Cove put up their trees the day after Thanksgiving and took them down the day after Christmas. Since Angie had every intention of leaving her tree up until Twelfth Night, she decided it might not be smart to cut one so early, and besides, her mother was shipping the Christmas tree house stand to her. Time enough to find a tree when that arrived.

But she wasn't going to wait any longer to get the smell of pine in her house. She needed to make an outdoor wreath, an Advent wreath, a kissing ball and anything else she could think of, anything to start the season off properly.

She grabbed the clippers from the jumbled junk drawer, put on her felt-lined Sorrels, her down jacket, her turtle fur hat and her leather work gloves and headed out into the gathering New England dusk.

She knew just where she was going. The trees down by the edge of the lake were thick and cluttered—she could easily trim a boatload of branches off them and it would only help them flourish.

Tucking the clippers in one pocket and her flashlight in another, she headed down the freshly plowed road, toward the lake, with the vast, comforting silence of the Vermont winter all around her.

A little too silent. There were still the occasional bears

around, and fisher cats were downright nasty, so she began humming, then started singing. Loudly. "Good King Wenceslas" was an excellent song for tromping through the snow, and she'd always had a good strong voice. Patsy had talked her into joining the church choir for the Christmas season, and Angie had rediscovered the joy of singing. And on this deserted spit of land she could sing as loud as she wanted and no one was around to hear.

The edge of the lake was covered with a rime of ice, but beyond the crusty sheet it lay dark and cold and mysterious. She'd skirted the opulent Jackson compound, moving past the snow-covered tennis court that had once been her front porch, and ended up by the lake, where their rickety dock had jutted out into the water. She hadn't been down here since last spring—she did her best to avoid the flatlanders who spent their summers on Black's Point, particularly the robber baron Jacksons, who'd only been coming to Crescent Cove for the past twenty years. Rank newcomers compared with most of the summer population, whose grandparents and great-grandparents had settled in the cottages along the shore more than eighty years ago.

But things were changing, and she had to accept it. In the 1930s, Crescent Cove had been the summer colony of Ivy League professors, a few ministers and the occasional grudgingly accepted lawyer. Now the academics could no longer support the taxes and upkeep on second homes, and the very wealthy had moved in, buying up land and houses, and in the Jacksons' case, tearing down existing buildings to make more room for their extravagant and totally inappropriate taste.

She shook her head and began cutting branches, letting them fall into a neat pile on the snow, as she switched songs to "Silver Bells." She was so intent on what she was doing, so lost in her glorious solitude on the deserted tip of Black's Point, that she didn't hear anyone approaching.

"You're trespassing."

She let out a shriek, the clippers went flying, and she spun around in the snow, her heart pounding. "You scared me!" she said, breathless, too rattled to be polite.

"You're trespassing," he said again, patiently. She couldn't see him clearly in the gathering darkness, only a general outline. It was no one she recognized, and she knew most of the caretakers in town. He was tall, lean, young and not a local. There was something vaguely familiar about him, something about his voice, but she couldn't quite pin it down.

"I'm the only one living out on the point during the winter, and no one's going to mind if I take a few branches to make some Christmas decorations."

"You'll be sorry."

"Is that a threat?" A wiser woman would have been nervous, but her instincts told her that she wasn't really in any kind of danger. Then again, those infallible instincts had told her Jeffrey was her soul mate, and look how that had turned out.

"Not a threat," the man said in a calm voice. "You're cutting cat spruce. You put that up in your house and it'll smell like a litter box."

"Damn," she said, staring down at the pile at her feet. She'd forgotten about cat spruce, and it was too cold to notice the pungent smell. She glanced up at the stranger again. She couldn't see his face, and pulling out her flashlight and blinding him with it wasn't very polite. She knew that voice, somewhere far in the back of her memory, and it was driving her crazy.

"Listen," she said. "I don't know who you are or what business it is of yours, but I really don't think the Jacksons will mind if I pilfer some evergreen branches from the land that used to belong to my family. They may be greedy robber barons, but a little thing like this isn't going to matter to them—they won't even be aware that I've done it. Most of them haven't been up here for several years, so they're unlikely to notice. By summer everything will have grown back, and no harm done. Except—" she looked around her "—I lost my clippers when you startled me."

"Greedy robber barons? That's a new one." His laugh was without humor. "And believe me, they'll know."

She did believe him. Because it finally hit her who he was.

She didn't need to see his face—she was only surprised she hadn't realized right off.

"You're Brody Jackson," she said flatly.

"Yes." He didn't bother asking her who she was—it probably wasn't worth his attention, but she persevered anyway.

"I'm Angie McKenna. I live in the old Martin farm down the road. You probably don't remember me, but we used to hang out together when we were kids. A century and a half ago."

"Did we?" His voice was noncommittal. He'd forgotten her, of course. Why should he remember? Brody Jackson had been the golden boy all his life—beautiful, smart, athletic and charming, adored by all the girls, both summer and year-rounders, admired by the boys. For all that she'd been his next-door neighbor, after the first summer they hadn't had anything to do with each other. She was just one of a gaggle of girls at the Crescent Cove Harbor Club, and while she'd always been acutely aware of him, it was little wonder she'd passed beneath his radar. Except for two occasions, and she wasn't going to think about that.

"What are you doing here? I didn't realize your place was winterized."

"I can manage," he said. "And why are you here? Where's Jeffrey? I thought the two of you were America's sweethearts." His voice was faintly ironic—something new. And then she realized with a start that he knew exactly who she was.

"We're divorced. I've been living here for a couple of years."

"Another illusion shattered," he said. "I suppose I would have known that if we'd used the house in the past couple of years."

"I…"

"I'm not really in the mood to catch up on old times," he said. "You better go home."

The flat, weary tone in his voice made that clear, though it told her little else. Except that he didn't sound like the golden boy he once had been.

But she wasn't about to argue. She bent to scoop up the branches, cat spruce and all. "I'll just clean these up."

"Leave them."

No way she could argue with that, either. All she could do was aim for a dignified retreat. "Well, I'm, er, sorry I bothered you."

He said nothing, and she shrugged. She wasn't quite sure how to end the conversation. *See you around* was a possibility, but he'd probably come back with *not if I see you first.*

"Goodbye, then," she said. "Merry Christmas."

"Isn't it a little early for that?"

"It's never too early for Christmas," Angie said. "Sorry I bothered you."

"You already said that. Go home, Angel."

There was nothing she could do but leave, aware that his eyes were on her as she made her way through the snow to the plowed road. When she got there, she turned back to try a pleasant wave, but he'd disappeared.

"Hell and damnation," she muttered, tromping back down the road. Brody Jackson was the last person she needed around here, especially if he'd gotten mean in his old age, and he certainly behaved as if he had. At least he wouldn't stay long—there was nothing in the town of Crescent Cove for the likes of Brody Jackson.

Her house was toasty when she went back in. She kicked off her snowy boots, put another log in the stove and began to make herself some dinner. Not until she was falling asleep several hours later did she remember what he'd called her.

IF BRODY JACKSON STILL had a sense of humor he would have laughed. Angel McKenna had thought he wouldn't remember her. He remembered everything about her—her unflinching gaze, the freckles across her nose, the husky voice that he'd always found such a turn-on. Of course, as a teenager he'd found everything a turn-on. But in particular, Angel McKenna.

She didn't look that much different. She must be thirty now, and she wore her brown hair long, to her shoulders. Her eyes were the same rich brown that could have the most unnerving effect on a boy. And a man. And her slightly breathless voice was as familiar as if it were yesterday that he'd last spoken to her.

But that wasn't the case. It had been years, and he still hadn't quite gotten over her.

It wasn't arrogance to know that he could have had any girl he wanted in Crescent Cove. Any girl but Angel, who never went anywhere without Jeffrey Hastings by her side. They would have been prom queen and king, he thought cynically. Childhood sweethearts, teenage steadies, the perfect marriage that had been preordained by the Fates.

A marriage that had shattered. He wondered why.

It wasn't important. He hadn't come back to Crescent Cove to relive old times; he'd come to lick his wounds and keep a low profile. Softhearted people would say he'd come to heal. More realistic ones would argue he'd come to hide.

In fact, the house on Black's Point was one of the few things he had left, after the government got through with him. The penthouse apartment in New York, the house in Tahoe, the condo in Hawaii were all gone. As well as the cars, the money and any shred of reputation he might have once had.

And his brothers.

They'd wanted him to join them. They'd siphoned off enough of the money from Worldcomp to keep them very comfortable for the rest of their lives, while thousands of people had lost their life savings, pension plans had gone bankrupt and the very name of their company was becoming synonymous with corporate greed and treachery.

But he'd stayed. As only a junior partner, he stayed to face the music. Once his brothers had left the country he had no more allegiance to anything but the truth, ugly as it was. The Jackson brothers had ripped off hundreds of millions of dollars, covering up that the company was in desperate financial trouble, and they'd departed before it had all blown up in their faces. Leaving Brody behind with his inconvenient conscience.

They'd finished with him in Washington. He'd testified, answered questions, unearthed hidden records—and lost almost everything. He had the house in Vermont, an old Saab, ten thousand dollars and a law degree that he'd never used. And never would, given his reputation.

It was irrelevant that he hadn't known what his brothers were doing. That was no excuse—it had happened on his watch and he counted it as his responsibility, while his brothers enjoyed life in the Cayman Islands.

He kicked the branches that Angel had cut. She certainly didn't have much of an eye; these trees were sparse and spindly. He picked up the pair of clippers that had gone flying when he'd startled her and shoved them in his pocket. He'd have to find some way to return them, and the smart thing to do would be to avoid seeing her again.

He could pretend that he hadn't known she was in Crescent Cove when he'd made up his mind where he'd go, but he'd never been very good at lying to himself. He'd known she was here—the *Crescent Cove Chronicle* kept a busy social page for such a tiny town—and her presence had been a dangerous lure he couldn't resist.

He needed to resist it now, now that he'd come face-to-face with her. He hadn't realized she'd had such an effect on him. Even with Jeff Hastings out of her life, she was still unfinished business, and he'd be wise to keep her that way, at least until he had a better idea of what he was going to do with his shattered life.

At this point there was no room for Angel McKenna, no matter how much he wanted there to be. He'd thought maybe they could have a few laughs for old times' sake. But he was surprised to find his feelings for Angel were just too powerful. He needed to be smart for once and keep his distance.

Life was complicated enough.

Chapter Two

Angie slid into the booth at Mort's Diner, dumping her mountain of packages onto the seat beside her before she could meet Patsy's amused gaze from across the table. "Been shopping?" Patsy inquired in a dulcet tone.

"It's Christmas. What can I say?" Angie reached for one of Patsy's French fries.

"Weren't you the person who just last year said she was never going to celebrate Christmas again? It was all Ethan and I could do to drag you over to our house for Christmas dinner. You didn't even have a tree, for heaven's sake. And now you've gone all holly-jolly on me. What's the change?"

Before she had a chance to speak, Mort herself set a mug of coffee down in front of her. "Pie's almost gone," she said. "You gonna get back to work?"

"I'll bring you a delivery by this afternoon," Angie said, feeling guilty. There were four pies sitting on the counter in the old farmhouse, just a part of Mort's most recent order. She'd been halfway to Burlington before she'd remembered them, and she'd almost turned back, but they were talking about snow tomorrow, and she didn't dare wait any longer.

Mort departed in a dignified huff, shuffling in the run-down slippers she habitually wore in the old-fashioned diner, and Angie took a deep sip of her coffee, shuddering. "There are times when I would kill for a latte. This stuff could strip the enamel off your teeth."

"You could have had one in Burlington," Patsy said. "As a matter of fact, that's one of the best things about this miserable pregnancy—I can no longer tolerate the battery acid Mort calls coffee. If Junior ever decides to pop out I might just never go back."

Angie eyed her friend's huge belly, which was pushing against the table in the small booth. "She'll come when she's ready," Angie said, deliberately keeping up their ongoing battle. Patsy insisted her baby was a boy; she'd been so exhausted from morning sickness and so uncomfortable and unwieldy later on that she'd decided only a male could be oppressing her. Her husband had received this bitter pronouncement with his usual calm good humor. It was almost impossible to ruffle Ethan, and he had kept his volatile wife on a relatively even keel during most of her difficult, long-sought-for pregnancy.

But Angie had decided it had to be a girl, and she was hearing nothing else. Mort was running a pool on sex, weight and birth date, and so far most of the town was siding with Angie's pronouncement.

"There are things more important than lattes," Angie said.

"Name one."

"This!" Angie grabbed a brightly colored bag, opened it and whipped out a tiny red scrap of fabric. It looked as if it might fit a doll, but the red embroidery on the lacy collar said "Baby's First Christmas."

Patsy accepted the gift with feigned displeasure. "Junior's not going to like being in drag for his first Christmas."

"Any child you raise is going to be completely broad-minded about such things," Angie said. "Besides, he's going to be a girl."

"Humph," said Patsy, clearly not in the mood for fighting. "What else did you buy?"

"Lots of things."

"Like what?"

Angie took a deep breath. "Christmas napkins, Christmas glasses, soda pop with Santa on the can, Christmas pasta, Christmas paper plates, Christmas candy, Christmas towels. I even got enough fabric to make a Christmas shower curtain."

"Good God," Patsy said weakly.

"Plus, I got a baby's first Christmas tree ornament, a baby's first Christmas bib, a baby's first Christmas picture frame, even a pair of miniature red overalls on the rare chance that I'm wrong about your incipient offspring."

"You've gone crazy," Patsy said flatly. "Next thing you'll tell me is that you bought Christmas toilet paper."

"No. Christmas paper towels, and a Christmas toilet seat, but no toilet paper. Why, do you have some?"

"If I had such a revolting possession you can rest assured I'd give it to you immediately," Patsy said with a shudder. "As it is, I'm too busy being pregnant to think about Christmas. Ethan's already brought home the tree, and it'll be up to him to decorate. I never wanted this baby in the first place."

"Of course you didn't," Angie said in a soothing voice. "And all those trips into Burlington, all those painful procedures were what...? An excuse for a girl's day out with me?"

"Exactly," Patsy said, casting an accusing glance, daring her to disagree. "I want the last piece of pie."

"Of course you do," Angie said. She looked at the counter. "What's with all the flatlanders?" There were more than half a dozen strangers there, choking on Mort's coffee, talking in low voices among themselves.

"What do you think? The media have arrived. They think Brody Jackson is here."

Angie blinked. "Really? Why would they care?"

"Don't you read the newspapers, Angie? Worldcomp has gone bankrupt, and he and his smarmy older brothers hid the financial details until they could get their own money out of it. They've bankrupted hundreds of thousands of people. It's even worse than Enron."

"I gave up newspapers when I moved here," she said. "I had no idea. Why are they looking for him?"

"He's one of the most notorious men in America. His brothers skipped the country and are out of reach, but Brody stayed."

"Why?"

Patsy shrugged. "You remember Brody. Always the handsome prince. He's probably just living up to his self-image of nobility."

"You are so cynical," Angie said, taking another sip of coffee and shivering.

"Maybe he thought by coming clean he'd get off easy. He handed everything over to the special commission—all the records, everything like that. In return he didn't have to go to jail. Things won't go so well for his sleazy brothers if they ever set foot back in this country." She finished the milk shake with a noisy slurp. "As for Brody, he lost everything. Absolutely everything. The press love stories about how the mighty have fallen, and he used to get a lot of press, he and that model wife of his."

"He's married?"

"No, she divorced him before any of this came out."

"That's a shame," Angie said, wondering why she was feeling sudden relief.

"So," Patsy said, "are you going to warn him?"

Angie jerked her head up. "What do you mean?"

"I know he's here, Angie. Everyone does. You can't keep secrets in a town this size, though as far as I'm aware he hasn't left Black's Point since he arrived. You're the only one out that road. There's no way you wouldn't have seen him."

"He wants to be left alone."

"I understand that. And none of us will help these vultures. But it won't take long for them to find out where the Jackson place is. It's a matter of town record. Hell, if they went to BK's Grocery they could even buy a map of the area with everyone's house marked on it."

"I've got to go." Angie couldn't shove the table back any farther against Junior, but she slid out, grabbing her packages. "Tell Mort I'll be back with the pies in a few hours."

"Where are you off to? Or need I ask? You're going to warn him, aren't you? You always had a soft spot for Brody."

"I never had a soft spot for anyone but Jeffrey since I was a kid and you know it," she said stoutly. "I just happen to hate seeing anyone hounded."

"Sure you do," Patsy said with a smug smile. "Say hi for me, will you?"

The men at the counter watched her as she headed toward the door, and she forced herself to slow down, not scramble desperately. It was none of her business. If Brody and his older brothers had ripped off thousands of people—no, hundreds of thousands, Patsy had said—then he deserved everything that happened to him.

But she had a natural aversion to the tabloid press in all its various guises. Besides, she had to get home anyway, she reminded herself with a fair amount of righteousness. She had to make two more pies to go with the ones she'd already finished. And she found she was in sudden, dire need of a little exercise. A short walk down toward the lake would be just the thing.

There were still no tire tracks on Black's Point Road except her own. The town had plowed down to the Jackson compound, but so far she hadn't seen anyone else drive past her house. No sign of Brody Jackson at all.

Well, that wasn't strictly true. There'd been a sign, all right. The morning after her arrival back in Crescent Cove she'd found a huge pile of freshly cut evergreen branches on her porch, with her missing clippers on the railing. No note, but then, there was no doubt where they'd come from. She'd scooped them up and inhaled the fragrance. Not a cat spruce among them.

The whole house had smelled like Christmas ever since. He'd brought her more than she'd needed—she'd made the Advent wreath, setting the Christmas candle in the middle of it, a wreath for the front door, a wreath for the fence at the end of the driveway, and if she'd been able to figure out how to do it she would have made a wreath for the front of her Jeep. She made a kissing ball to hang in her living room—not that anyone would be kissing her in the near or even distant future, but she'd always liked them. She made boughs for her mantel and the arched doorway into the parlor, and she had still had enough greenery left to make one more wreath and kissing ball. The wreath would be a simple thank-you to her invisible neighbor, and the kissing ball would be for... Maybe sour old Mort might appreciate one in the diner. Anything was possible.

She jumped out of the car, leaving her purchases piled in the back seat, and grabbed the extra wreath off the front porch. She hadn't planned to deliver it in broad daylight—after all, he'd dropped his unexpected gift off when she'd been asleep. It would be easier if she didn't have to see him at all, but with the media hot on his trail she figured she owed him that much, if for nothing more than old times' sake, which he'd forgotten long ago.

She'd planned to walk down to the Jackson place, but at the last minute she got in the car again and drove the quarter mile down the road to his driveway. She pulled her car across the front of it, effectively blocking access, and climbed out, then headed down the narrow, snow-covered path to the house.

There was no sign of him, no sign of a car, but the snow on the front deck was freshly shoveled, and she knew he was still there. For a moment she almost chickened out—he was hardly her responsibility, and sooner or later he'd have to face what he'd done.

But then, Patsy was right. She'd always had an irrational soft spot for Brody Jackson, even though she and Jeffrey had been practically joined at the hip. For the sake of that long-ago, almost indecipherable feeling, she owed him this much.

She didn't even have to knock on the door. She was halfway across the snow-packed deck when the glass door opened and Brody stood there, a mug of coffee in one hand, an unreadable expression on his face.

It was the first real look she'd gotten—when she'd run into him a few nights earlier he'd been nothing more than a huge, dark figure. In the light of day he was startling.

He was the same man, yet entirely different. His shaggy, bleached-blond hair was now a definite brown, and didn't seem to have been cut in months. His eyes were still blue, but they were shadowed now, and his face was lean, drawn. He'd had the most remarkable mouth—smiling, lush, ridiculously kissable.

She should know—she'd kissed him. Twice.

But that mouth was drawn in a thin line. His blue eyes were expressionless and he only opened the door a crack. Enough for her to see the faded jeans on his long legs, the bare feet, the old flannel shirt with several buttons missing.

Oh, he was still gorgeous—there was no question about that. Bad luck and bad behavior couldn't change that much, and the scruffy stubble and shaggy dark hair only made him appear more real.

"Why are you here?" he greeted her in a wary, unwelcoming voice. "And what's that?"

For a moment she forgot why she was there. He was still distracting, even in his current downbeat state. "I made you a Christmas wreath. You were so nice to bring me all that greenery that I wanted to thank you."

"I brought you the greenery so you wouldn't come traipsing around my house," he said. "And I'm not in the mood to celebrate Christmas."

"Tough," she said. There was a cast-iron hook beside the door, one that held a hanging plant in the summer, and she dumped the wreath over it, against the house. "I've got more than enough Christmas spirit to spare. But that's not why I'm here."

"I assume you'll tell me sooner or later."

The cynical, world-weary tone was so unlike that of the Brody Jackson she'd once known that she was momentarily silenced. But only momentarily.

"There are camera crews in town, searching for you. I saw at least half a dozen of them in Mort's Diner, as well as trucks from CNN, Fox and a couple of the networks."

Brody's response was swift and obscene. "Why aren't they here yet?"

"They don't know where you are."

"And you didn't tell them? Why?"

She considered it for a moment. "I'm not really sure. It's not as if we've ever been particular friends. I guess I don't like people being hounded. Or maybe I just don't want a bunch of people crawling around Black's Point."

"I think you're too late." They could both hear the sound of the trucks and cars, noisy in the winter stillness, as they left the main highway and started down the narrow road.

"Not necessarily. I don't give up easily."

"And you're implying I do?" Brody said.

She didn't answer that. "Where's your car?"

"We have a garage, remember?"

"Then go back in the house and stay put. I'll get rid of them."

His expression was dubious. "You think you'll be able to accomplish something the best lawyers in the country couldn't? They're like barracudas—they won't be satisfied till they tear the flesh from my bones."

"Very melodramatic," she said, her voice brisk. "They're only trying to make a living. I just don't want them doing it in my backyard."

"And you imagine you can stop them?"

"Watch me." She thought twice. "I mean, don't watch me. Get back in the house and don't come out until they're gone."

"Fine with me, but I don't need you fighting my battles."

She wrinkled her nose. "It's my battle. I came here for peace and quiet, not *60 Minutes.*"

"Actually, I don't rate that high. I usually land on some tabloid show on Fox."

"How the mighty have fallen."

"Do you have a reason for disliking me? Apart from my charming behavior last week? I'd been drinking."

"How reassuring," she said sweetly. "If I have to choose between a drunk and the paparazzi I'm not sure—"

"I'm not a drunk."

The vehicles were drawing closer. "Go back inside, then, and I'll get rid of them."

For a moment it seemed as if he might argue, but he simply nodded and disappeared into the house, closing the door behind him.

She'd reached her car before the first truck pulled up, and she leaned against the back of it, arms folded across her chest, effectively blocking access to the driveway.

"Can I help you?" She used the tone that had always been effective on frat-boy athletes who thought they could coast through English lit, and the reporter who was approaching her hesitated. Probably a frat boy in his youth, Angie decided dispassionately.

The others with him were busy unloading the van, but she wasn't about to move, and there was no other way they could get down to the lake. The early snows were thigh-high in some places, the other driveways weren't plowed and the trees grew so thickly that anyone venturing down there would probably end up walking around in circles. It was a nice thought, but she couldn't take a chance on their stumbling across the Jackson compound.

"Rex Hamilton, Fox news," he said with a showy smile, and Angie kept a deliberately stony face. Brody had known exactly who his stalkers were likely to be. "We're looking for Brody Jackson…"

"I'm sure you are, but he's not here."

"Come on, miss. We know he is. He flew into Burlington eight days ago and he hasn't flown out. Passenger lists are simple enough to trace."

"I'm sure they are. He was here for one night, picked up a few things and then left. Driving, not flying."

Rex Hamilton didn't appear convinced. "Where was he headed?"

"I have no idea, and I don't care. Probably someplace warmer."

"That's easy enough to do," the man said, shivering. "Randy, set up a shot of this nice young lady and we'll go from there."

"You'll go nowhere but back into your van and on the road again."

"Do you know who I am?" the man demanded, affronted.

"You told me. Rex Harrison."

"Hamilton!" he snapped.

"Of course you are," she said in a soothing voice. "But you're not filming me, and you're going to get back in your truck and drive away. This land is private property, and posted against hunters, trappers and trespassers. I'm sure you fit in at least one of those categories."

Hamilton waved the cameraman off, fixing a disgruntled stare at her. "You the new girlfriend?" he asked.

She had to laugh. "Not likely."

"Because he goes through women like water. He's used and dumped supermodels and A-list actresses in the blink of an eye."

"Not really in his league," she drawled.

Hamilton tilted his head to one side. "Oh, I'm not sure about that."

"I am. Go away. If you're as good a reporter as you seem to believe you are it won't take you long to pick up his trail."

"Why are you defending the man? He and those brothers of his ripped off thousands of people."

"Then why isn't he in jail?"

"Because he can afford the best lawyers."

"Then why have his brothers left the country? Can't they afford the same lawyers?"

"You seem to know an awful lot about the case for an innocent bystander."

"Actually, I know very little. But as a gesture of goodwill I'll tell you what he was driving, and maybe you'll be able to track him down. He was in a Ford Explorer, dark blue or green, headed south."

"I don't suppose you have his license plate number."

"I don't even know which state issued it. All I can tell you is he drove out of here last week and I haven't seen him since. And as I'm the only person living out here in the winter, I'd know."

"And you are…?"

"Extremely tired of talking to you. Go away or I'll call the police."

"On what? Cell phones don't work in this godforsaken place."

"Where do you come from, Mr. Hamilton? New York City?"

"L.A. Why?"

"And you call this place godforsaken? Go back to the City of Angels, Mr. Hamilton. Or go chasing after Brody Jackson—I really don't care. Just go."

During their conversation three more vehicles had pulled up, blocking the narrow road. There was no place for them to turn around, and they were going to have a hell of a time backing out. Rex Hamilton looked at her for a moment longer, then shook his head in defeat. "We'll find him. I promise you that. He can't rip off the American public and get away with it."

"I don't care whether you find him or not. I just don't want you finding him here." Not the best choice of words, because Hamilton gave her one last, assessing stare.

Apparently, her innocent, self-righteous demeanor convinced him. She half expected him to make like The Terminator and say *I'll be back,* but he spared her.

By the time the last truck had headed south on Route 100 Angie was freezing. Two of the vehicles had gone into a ditch, and the film crews had shown a surprising spirit of cooperation in helping push each other out. By the end they were wet, tired, cold and frustrated, and it was evident that nothing short of a prearranged interview would get them back out there. Crescent Cove in the winter wasn't made for the faint of heart. She leaned against the hood of her car, listening to the sounds of the trucks as they faded into the distance, letting the peace of the snow surround her.

"How'd you manage that?"

She turned, startled. Of course the snow muffled everything, but she still thought some preternatural instinct might have warned her.

"I told them you were gone. It took some convincing, but they finally believed me. And you were supposed to stay put until I gave you the all-clear."

"I was curious. Maybe I should hire you as my bodyguard. You accomplished what few others have managed."

"I'm not interested in your body." That came out all wrong, and she could have kicked herself.

"No, I'm sure you're not," he said. "More's the pity."

She jerked her head around to stare at him. "What did you say?"

"You heard me." He walked past her to the end of the driveway, peering down the road. "You think they'll be back?"

"I doubt it. Once you get that badly stuck in the snow it pretty much ruins things." She could get a good look at him with his back turned to her. He was thinner than she remembered—instead of the buff golden boy she'd once been uneasily aware of, he was now wiry, almost tough, wearing rough winter clothes that had seen better days, and his unbleached hair was too long.

She'd had a crush on him—she might as well admit it. She and Jeffrey had gone together practically since childhood, and she'd never really noticed anyone else, believing in their fantasy of soul mates, but she'd noticed Brody. Who could miss him, with his easy charm and effortless grace? He'd dated just about every age-appropriate, halfway-decent-looking female in the summer population, except for her, of course.

And out of the blue, she suddenly remembered Ariel Bartlett.

Fate hadn't been kind to Ariel. She'd been plump, plain and hardworking, and had come from a family who'd farmed in Crescent Cove since the early 1800s. Her mother had given her that particularly unsuitable name, and she'd made her way through life, seemingly stolid and unimaginative, working as a waitress for Mort's Diner, working as a checkout girl at BK's Grocery, working at the Crescent Cove Harbor Club during the summers, while the teenage children of the vacationers played. She'd had a huge, embarrassingly obvious crush on Brody, and they'd all found it vastly amusing. Jeffrey in particular had taken to calling her Brody's pet cow, and he'd told Angie she was being a stick-in-the-mud when she'd tried to silence him.

Not that it would have done much good. Everyone thought her calf-eyed devotion was a riot. Everyone except Brody.

He'd never said a thing when people teased him, and he'd been unfailingly kind to Ariel. And at the Founder's Day dance, which always signaled the end of the summer, he'd brought her as his date, treating her with exquisite sweetness, much to Jeffrey's amusement.

That should have tipped Angie off to the fact that her intended was a snake, but she'd been too busy living up to expectations. And trying to ignore the fact that some tiny part of her, for the first time in her life, wanted to be Ariel Bartlett.

"Why'd you do it?"

Brody turned to look at her. "Do what? Steal billions of dollars from the unwitting?"

For a moment she was distracted. "Did you? Really?"

He shrugged. "I was a major executive at Worldcomp, and I should have known what was happening. I'm responsible."

"But you didn't do it, did you? Those slimy older brothers of yours did."

"Why would you care?"

"Actually, I don't. I was asking you about something else."

He didn't move. "I'm waiting."

"Why did you bring Ariel Bartlett to the Founder's Day dance?"

She'd manage to surprise him, but he recovered quickly enough. "Maybe I thought she deserved to have a night where she wasn't waiting on a bunch of spoiled kids who laughed at her. Or maybe I knew she had a crush on me and I decided to be condescending enough to give her the thrill of a lifetime. Why do you ask?"

"I don't know. I just thought of her."

"You'll be glad to hear she's a very successful chef in Philadelphia. She's happily married with two children."

"I know that. This is a small town, remember. Have you kept in touch with her?"

He sighed. "What the hell does it matter to you, Angel?"

She'd forgotten he'd called her Angel. The only one who

ever had, it had been both mocking and oddly affectionate back in those days. "It doesn't."

"Good. Thank you for your noble rescue of the fallen knight. I owe you."

"You don't sound very happy about it. If you care to, you can repay your debt right now and we'll call it even."

"What do you want, Angel?" He sounded wary.

"A Christmas tree." It came out of the blue, and it wasn't until she'd said it that she realized that was exactly what she wanted. A Christmas tree from the place where she'd spent her summers a lifetime ago. When she'd first fallen in love.

"There are fifty million trees on this spit of land," he drawled. "What are you asking me for?"

"I want a special one. It's near your tennis court. I planted it the year before we sold the house—I thought it was going to be there for my grandchildren. But instead my parents sold the house and it somehow escaped the bulldozer when you leveled the place. I'd like it."

"Show me."

It was tough going through the deep snow, especially with Angie breaking trail, but now that the idea had come to her she wasn't about to let go easily. If she'd had to walk barefoot in the snow to get her tree, she'd do it.

She circled the tennis courts, heading down toward the lake, ignoring the stab of pain that always hit her. She used to spend hours sitting on the porch, staring out at the lake, eating gingerbread, drinking grape juice, playing canasta with her friends. She'd probably miss it for the rest of her life.

The blue spruce stood there, where she'd planted it so many years ago. Now tall, thick, beautifully shaped, it was her last tie to this land that had once been in her family for generations. It was time to sever it.

Brody had come up beside her. "Too big," he said, looking up at it. "Unless you have cathedral ceilings, which I doubt. I suppose you could top it."

"Top it?"

He glanced at her. "I thought you'd been living here for a

while. 'Topping' means using the upper part of it for your tree. You could maybe use half the tree that way."

"Never mind. It was a stupid idea."

"There are lots of other trees around. Take your pick."

She shook her head. "Forget it. I'll just buy one when I get around to it. I don't need my main tree until Christmas Eve, anyway."

"Your main tree? How many Christmas trees do you have?"

She mentally counted. "Six. No, seven. One medium-size one in the kitchen, two small ones in the living room, one in the bathroom, one in the bedroom and two on the porch."

"You're crazy."

"I guess I am. And I guess you'll still have to owe me," she added with a certain amount of satisfaction. "I've got some baking to do. Let me know if you need rescuing again."

She half expected him to growl. After all, she was baiting him.

But to her amazement he smiled, a slow, reluctant grin that brought the memory of Brody Jackson back full force. "Yes, ma'am," he said.

HE WATCHED HER as she walked away. Angel McKenna was still a force to be reckoned with, as he'd always known. He wasn't surprised she'd managed to run off the news crews. She'd always been ridiculously subservient to Jeffrey Hastings, but when he wasn't around she'd been her own woman, vibrant, strong, enticing. Even when she was fourteen years old and he'd kissed her on her front porch, the summer Jeff's parents took their kids to Europe instead of Vermont.

It hadn't been much of a kiss, but then, they'd both been pretty young. And for all the innocence of it, it had lingered in his mind for years. Until he'd kissed her again—the biggest mistake of his life.

No, the biggest mistake of his life was trusting his older brothers with their elastic sense of morality. Second biggest was marrying Estelle when she had the intellect of a toaster and the warmth of a walk-in cooler. But she'd been decorative, understanding and inventive in bed. At the time it seemed enough.

Kissing Angel McKenna hadn't been a mistake. He just should have kissed her a hell of a lot more, and not given a damn about Jeff Hastings. Since in the end it didn't look as if Jeff had given a damn about Angel.

How could he have cheated on her, left her? Then again, Jeff had always been a dog-in-the-manger type. He wanted what everyone else had, and the more he suspected Brody's attraction to Angel the tighter he'd held on. Jeff would have done better with a party favor like Brody's ex-wife Estelle—he'd always been attracted to shiny objects. Angel was too deep, too multifaceted for a man like him.

And for a man like Brody. He'd been made for models and female tennis pros and debutantes. Not for women like Angela McKenna.

Except that there were no women like Angela McKenna. And he was old enough to know that and stop denying the truth. That all he ever really wanted in this life was the girl next door. And that was the one thing that was always out of his reach.

Chapter Three

At least there were no storms predicted for the next few days. Angie watched the local weather with all the intensity of a Greek sibyl trying to read the future, and while she trusted no one, she had a small margin of faith in channel three.

The back of her Jeep smelled heavenly, even after she'd dropped off thirteen pies, six tortes, two carrot cakes and one wicked concoction known only as Chocolate Suicide, and with each delivery she'd brought dozens of cookies. Her oven was on constantly, adding a nice dollop of heat to her drafty old farmhouse, and the smells of sugar and spice were divine. Almost as divine as the Christmas candle.

Angie had been unable to figure it out. It burned steadily, every night, but there were no drips—the flame glowed straight and true, and the fragrances were unbelievable, ever changing. One day it was bayberry, another pumpkin spice, then another day where it smelled just like cranberries. She'd given up trying to guess how the woman calling herself Mrs. Claus had done it—she simply enjoyed it.

She'd spent the afternoon with Patsy, drinking decent coffee while Patsy grumbled over her milk shakes, sorting through baby clothes, arguing about names. "This kid better not be born on Christmas Day," Patsy warned, taking a break and collapsing into the oversize rocking chair Ethan had found for her. "Nothing worse than having a birthday and Christmas all at once—you get shafted. Besides, I don't want to spend Christmas in the hospital."

"I thought you were planning on a home birth?"

"I am. But you and Ethan and everyone under the sun keep telling me I'm nuts," Patsy said. "The doctors say I'm strong as an ox, the midwives around here are the best in the country, and I think you're all fussing for nothing. This time I don't think I'll be my usual obedient self."

Angie laughed. "The day you're obedient is the day I learn to drive in snow."

"You drive in snow."

"Not if I can help it." She sat on the floor, folding the cloth diapers Patsy had insisted on. "I just wish I'd been able to get you a candle like mine. It's the most amazing thing. It smells like something different and wonderful every day, and the glow seems to fill the entire house. I wanted to buy one for everyone and I can't find her shop."

"Are you talking about that stupid candle shop again? I told you, there's no such place in Crescent Cove and never has been," Patsy said, putting a hand on her rounded stomach as Junior delivered a particularly powerful kick. "You must have been dreaming."

"You can't dream a candle into existence," Angie protested.

"Yes, but you brought back hoards of Christmas things when you went home for Thanksgiving, and you've gone out every clear day this month and brought back even more. Admit it—your back seat is filled with more stuff, isn't it?"

"Just a couple of new Christmas CDs," she said defensively.

"And…?"

"A Christmas sweater, green and red yarn to knit a scarf, a musical globe, a couple of Christmas mystery novels, cereal with red marshmallow stars and green marshmallow trees and—"

"Spare me," Patsy said. "At least they don't make Christmas diapers."

"They do! They're disposable, and, yes, they're against your environmental conscience, but I thought when you travel they might come in handy."

"Oh, God," Patsy said weakly. "Anyway, you probably picked up that candle in one of your insane shopping forays and just forgot where you bought it. And then you had some crazy dream about a shop run by Mrs. Santa Claus on some nonexistent street, and you don't remember where you really picked it up. Which is a shame, because it sounds cool, and I'd love to have one."

"I didn't dream it."

"Suit yourself. Are you staying for dinner? After all, you brought it. If you don't stay I'll worry that you don't trust your own cooking."

Angie looked out at the darkening afternoon. "As long as you promise it won't snow."

"Wuss," Patsy said genially.

Four hours later she regretted her decision. Channel three had betrayed her, and a few lazy flakes were swirling down under the moonlit sky. Angie crept along the bare pavement, clutching the steering wheel. *There's nothing to fear,* she told herself. *It can't turn into a blizzard until you get home—there isn't time.*

Though of course at the pace she was driving, she might not be home until midnight. She pressed her foot a little harder on the gas pedal, cautiously, and the Jeep moved with a bit more vigor. She had the heat on full blast, and the car still smelled like a bakery. She only slid a bit when she turned into her driveway and came to a solid stop against the snowbank.

The lights were on, and smoke was pouring out of the chimney. She never left that many lights on, and the fire should have died down by now. For a moment she considered putting the car in reverse and getting the hell out of there.

And then the snow started again, and she knew perfectly well that home was the safest place to be. Besides, if she'd imagined Mrs. Claus's Candle Shop, then she might very well have imagined she'd turned off the lights when she left.

She grabbed an armful of packages from the back of the car, trudged up the front steps onto the porch and opened the door. Then dropped the packages as she saw him.

"What do you think you're doing?" she demanded.

Brody looked up from his spot on the floor. The perfectly shaped Christmas tree towered over him, albeit at an odd angle, and he'd managed to assemble Uncle Otto's Christmas tree house, but the actual mechanics of it seemed to be providing more than its share of frustrations.

"What do you think I'm doing? Repaying my debt. And you might want to close the door before you freeze us both."

She kicked the door shut behind her, leaving her packages where they'd fallen. "By breaking and entering?"

"You don't lock your house, Angel. And you asked for a tree. I brought you one. Sorry it couldn't be the one you planted, but I have a certain affection for that one, and besides, it was too big. This, however, is perfect. If I can just get it to stand straight."

It *was* a perfect tree. "It needs two people," she said, stripping off her down jacket and gloves and kicking off her boots. "You hold it while I tighten the screws."

"I'm already down here. You hold it."

There was no way to avoid coming close to him—managing the Christmas tree required proximity. She kept as far away as she could, focusing straight ahead as she reached through the thick branches to grasp the tree trunk. The Christmas candle sat where it always did, in the middle of the table, shedding its golden glow, and she felt some of her tension begin to drain.

"I don't know why you need so many trees," he muttered, practically beneath her skirts if she'd been wearing any. Fortunately, she had on jeans, but his head was uncomfortably close. "Most people get by with one, and it's usually artificial."

"I'm not most people."

"And you should never leave the house with a candle burning," he said, looking up at her. "I don't care how safe you think it is, a cat could knock it over. We've even been known to have the occasional earthquake."

"Highly unlikely. I don't have a cat at the moment, and for that matter I didn't leave the candle burning. I'm not a complete idiot."

"It was burning when I got here," he said. "And anyone who marries Jeffrey Hastings qualifies as at least a partial idiot. You can let go now."

She released the resiny trunk and stepped back. The tree stayed where it was, straight and true. "What have you got against Jeffrey?"

He scooted back from the tree, making no effort to rise. "Same thing I've always had," he said. "I would have thought you'd learned your lesson."

"Our divorce was very civilized. And just because our marriage didn't work out doesn't mean he's a monster."

"No, not a monster. Just a total pig's butt. Always has been, always will be." He rose, in one fluid movement, reminding her with sudden, disturbing clarity how tall he was. "Don't tell me you're still in love with him. You spent half your life thinking he was God's gift. I would have thought you'd learned better by now."

"I'm not still in love with him. Though I don't know what business it is of yours."

"Don't you?" he said, his face enigmatic. "Where are your lights?"

"I beg your pardon?"

"Your lights. I'll put the lights on the tree before I go. I'm taller than you are, and I can reach higher. Unless you want to kick me out."

She wasn't sure what she wanted. Having him there was bringing back all sorts of memories, disturbing ones, confusing ones. But if he left she'd be alone with those thoughts and regrets.

She swallowed her protest. "That would be very kind of you," she said. "They're in the trunk under the table. Can I get you something to drink? Maybe some eggnog?"

"You don't have eggnog. I already searched your refrigerator. And why do you have light beer? You don't need it."

She let that pass. "I can make eggnog," she said.

He'd been rummaging through the trunk of Christmas lights, but he raised his head up at that, his dark hair falling into his face, and she found she wanted to push that hair away from his eyes. What the hell was wrong with her?

"How do you make eggnog? I thought it came from the grocery store."

"You use milk and whipping cream and raw eggs and brandy."

"Raw eggs? You're trying to kill me."

"I get the eggs from the Gebbie farm. They aren't carrying any disease."

"I think I'd prefer to go straight to the brandy."

"I can do that. I don't suppose you're hungry. I could probably make you something."

He grinned. "Don't sound so pained. If you really don't want me here just tell me."

She wanted him there. That was the danger. The Christmas candle cast a warm, romantic glow to the room, and he was reminding her of things better left in the past. At least she had the dubious relief of knowing he'd forgotten that night entirely.

"I want you here." She could have bit her tongue. It was his fault; he'd backed her into saying it, and it had come out all wrong. "That is, I don't mind."

"Don't spoil it, Angel. No one's wanted me around for a long time."

"I find that hard to believe," she said, managing to put a touch of asperity into her voice.

His smile was almost devilish. "Why, Angel. I do believe you don't hate me after all."

"Of course I don't hate you. I never have."

"Not according to your former husband."

"You discussed me with Jeffrey? When?"

"Relax. It was a long time ago. He didn't like the idea of anyone sniffing around you, particularly me. He was just warning me off."

"Don't be silly. I know that the two of you never got along for some reason, but it had absolutely nothing to do with me."

There was real amusement in his laugh. "Believe that if you want to."

"And no one was 'sniffing around' me, as you so elegantly put it. I was hardly a bitch in heat."

"More's the pity," he murmured. "What do you put on the top of the tree? A star or an angel?"

"What do you think?"

"Bring me the angel," he said.

The tree really was beautiful. And for some odd reason, she felt totally comfortable to be decorating it with Brody Jackson. He handled the antique glass balls with exquisite care, the ones that her mother would never let Jeffrey touch. He laughed at the string of nun lights, and he didn't laugh at one of her kindergarten attempts that her mother had refused to part with—a string of spools painted gold. The Christmas candle shone brightly, and she found herself loosening up, like a cat after a long nap. She sighed, a tired, happy sound, feeling better than she had for some time.

He turned to look at her. The tree was finished, the brandy was drunk, the candle light sparkled off the glass ornaments. "I suppose I'd better be going."

"Yes," she said, because she couldn't say anything else.

He reached for his old barn jacket and shrugged into it. He seemed a million miles away from the elegant executive who'd supposedly swindled thousands, he seemed a million miles away from the golden boy of summer she'd had a secret crush on. He seemed like a stranger, and the other part of herself.

And she must have had too much brandy. "Do you have a flashlight?"

"It's a full moon. I can find my way home." He had started toward the door, when suddenly she spoke.

"Would you tell me something, Brody?"

He stopped, turning. "Anything," he said simply, and she believed him.

"Do you even remember the Founder's Day dance?"

"The one I took Ariel Bartlett to? I thought we already talked about that."

"No. The last one. Ten years ago."

She examined his blank gaze and knew, as she'd expected,

that he didn't remember a thing about it. A few short minutes out on the deck at the Harbor Club that had shaken her to her core, and he'd been too drunk to even recall them.

"Not in particular," he said. "Should I?"

He seemed so innocent that she had to believe him. "No," she said. "It was just the last time we saw each other before this winter. Jeffrey had left early for college and we danced. I think it was the only time."

"Did we?" He shook his head. "Sorry. Did anything interesting happen?"

"No," she said. "We danced, you were drunk, you made a pass and I fended you off. I just wanted to make sure there were no hard feelings." It was sort of the truth. If one had a very broad definition where truth was concerned.

"Really? Funny that I wouldn't remember. What did we dance to?"

"I have no idea. It was some old-fogey dance band the club had hired, and I don't think they played anything written before nineteen-fifty. It must have been some old standard."

"I suppose so. You still haven't told me why you're asking."

She gave herself a tiny shake. "Just curious, I guess."

"Okay," he said slowly, sounding doubtful. "Lock the door behind me, Angel."

"Why? We're perfectly safe out here."

"Do it for my peace of mind."

"All right." She followed him to the door, holding it as he stepped out into the wintery night. He went down the front steps, then stopped.

"Lock the door," he said again.

"Yes, sir." She started to close it.

"And Angel…"

"Yes?"

"It was 'Night and Day.'"

He was gone before she could say another word.

SHE STILL DIDN'T know how she'd happened to find herself in his arms. She'd gotten along with almost everyone, but there'd always been tension between Jeffrey and Brody. For the first time in years she was there alone—Jeffrey had left early for college. She'd known Brody for most of her life, been to dozens of the same parties, yet she couldn't recall ever dancing with him. And suddenly she was in his arms.

"I'm very drunk," he'd told her with great deliberateness as they moved through the music.

"Maybe we should sit this out."

He shook his head. "This is my only chance. While the cat's away the mice will play."

She didn't bother arguing with him. He might be very drunk, but he could still manage to keep upright on the dance floor, holding her against him, not too tight, not too loose. "I hope you're not planning to drive home," she said severely.

"I'm hoping you'll take me home with you."

"You really are drunk, aren't you, Brody?"

"Very," he said. He'd managed to steer her over toward the French doors.

"Maybe you should get some fresh air," she suggested. He had a strong body, warm, lean, and he was taller than Jeffrey. And there was nothing wrong with a harmless little crush—everyone in Crescent Cove went through one sooner or later. It didn't mean that she didn't consider Jeffrey her soul mate and her future. It just meant she was human, and Brody Jackson had the most beautiful mouth she'd ever seen. And always had.

"Good idea," he said, steering her out onto the deck that hung out over the lake. They were alone out there—the night was cool, and a light mist was falling, and if anything would sober him up that would. But he didn't let go of her, and she didn't try to move away. He pulled her a little closer, so that she fit perfectly against his body, and she felt a huge knot of tension begin to dissolve in a pool of heat that the cool mist had no effect on.

Her face was tucked against his shoulder, her arms were around his waist and they were barely moving. She was suddenly, unaccountably happy. "You're not really going to marry that pig's butt, are you?" he whispered in her ear.

"Marry who?" she asked, moving her head to look up at him, smiling.

Big mistake. He kissed her then. He had to be drunk to kiss her like that, but she'd already known that he was, and she'd been playing with fire, coming out there with him. It was a shock of a kiss—openmouthed, hungry, and the biggest shock of all was that she kissed him back. And kept kissing him, as he pushed her into a dark corner where no one could see them. His hands touched her, his mouth promised her, and all she wanted to do was shut out the voices and the guilt and lose herself in Brody Jackson.

But they weren't inner voices; they were real ones, moving closer, and reality came rushing back. She pushed away from him, stumbling in her high heels, and she couldn't even bring herself to look at him. She'd run, down the steps to the street, and kept going until she reached her car.

It had taken her ten minutes to stop shaking. Fifteen minutes to pull herself together and start the car. Twenty minutes to realize he wasn't chasing after her.

"You okay?" It was Patsy's boyfriend, Ethan, peering into the car with a worried expression on his face. "Patsy sent me to check on you."

"I'm fine," she said briskly. "I'm just going home. I'm driving to Chicago tomorrow and I need to get a good night's sleep."

"He was drunk, Angie. He didn't know what he was doing. I doubt he even realized it was you, and he sure as hell isn't going to remember anything tomorrow. Are you sure he didn't hurt you?"

It had been too much to hope that no one had noticed. At least Ethan was trustworthy. "Of course not. I was just…surprised. Where is he now?"

"Passed out. I'm taking him back home and dumping him there, let him sleep it off. As long as I'm certain you're okay."

"Fine. I'm sure he had no idea what he was doing."

"None at all. You positive you don't want me to drive you home? He'll be out for hours."

She shook her head. "I'm fine, Ethan. Thank you." And she drove off before he could see the tears on her face.

"Is SHE OKAY?" Brody had been waiting, just out of sight.

Ethan looked at him severely. "All you did was kiss her, right? It's not likely to destroy her life. Just how did you manage to get that drunk that fast? If Jeff had been here you wouldn't have gotten within ten feet of her."

"Exactly," Brody said, turning his face up to the cooling mist. "What did she say?"

"She's leaving first thing in the morning. With any luck she'll forget this ever happened."

"Most likely," he said in an even voice. "Thanks, Ethan."

"Just how much have you been drinking?"

Brody gave him a calm, clear-eyed smile. "I'm just about to start."

ANGIE PUSHED the door shut and locked it in a daze. Everything she had believed to be true had just shifted, and she was on very shaky ground. He remembered. He knew. Those hurried, hungry kisses in the rain weren't some forgotten fantasy, fueled by drunkenness on his part and sheer insanity on hers. He remembered, he knew, just as she did.

She still wasn't quite sure what that meant. For him, or for her.

It was after eleven. The living room was lit only with the glow from the angel candle and the lights from the Christmas tree, and it was much too late to call anyone. Except that it was three hours earlier in L.A., and even if it had been three hours later she would have still made the phone call.

Jeffrey sounded the same—slightly self-important, oozing charm. How she ever could have believed in him so completely was still a source of embarrassment, but she'd had two years to come to her senses, and regret was a waste of time.

"What went on between you and Brody Jackson?" she said abruptly.

"And Merry Christmas to you, too, darling," Jeff said. "How lovely to hear your voice."

Angie sighed. Jeffrey would answer her questions in his own time, and the sooner she got through the formalities the sooner he'd be willing to talk. "Lovely to hear your voice, too. Merry Christmas, Happy New Year, how's Margaret, how's the baby, how's work, what went on between you and Brody Jackson?"

"Still my impetuous Angie. I thought age would have cured you of that," he chided. "Why are you asking me about that now? Brody Jackson has been out of our lives for years. He just missed being in jail by the skin of his teeth, and with luck he'll follow his brothers into exile and no one in Crescent Cove will ever have to see him again."

"He may be out of your life, but he's not out of mine," Angie said. "He's moved back up here, and I want you to tell me why the two of you never got along."

Jeffrey's lazy chuckle would have fooled anyone who hadn't been married to him. "Has he been putting the moves on you? Poor Brody—I would have thought he'd let go of that old rivalry. I've certainly moved past it."

"What rivalry? I know you two hated each other, but I never understood why."

"Jealousy," Jeff said. "He wanted what he couldn't have. It had nothing to do with you—he just wanted to score points off me."

"Why?"

"I have no idea. All I can say is he did his best to beat me at everything—tennis, sailing, golf. The one thing he couldn't beat me at was you, and it drove him crazy."

"Jeff, he wasn't out to beat you. He was just naturally good at all those things. Ridiculously so—he beat everyone. I don't think it was anything personal."

"Trust me, it was personal. You just happened to get in the way. Don't let him get near you, Angie. He probably thinks you're fair game since our divorce, and I wouldn't put it past him to try to score just for old times' sake, but he'd just be using you."

"My mother liked him."

There was a moment's silence at the other end of the phone. "What's that got to do with anything?"

"My mother didn't like you."

"And I blame her for the problems in our marriage," he said in a self-righteous voice.

"You blame my mother for you having a series of affairs? Somehow the connection escapes me."

"You're hurt and bitter. I understand, Angie, and I wish I could change the way things worked out."

"I'm not hurt and I'm not bitter, Jeffrey," she said patiently. "I just want to know what—"

"You were the one thing he couldn't beat me at, Angie. It's that simple. If you have any sense at all you'll keep away from him."

"I don't think I've ever been known for my good sense, Jeffrey," she said softly. And she hung up the phone.

Chapter Four

Brody kept his distance, but it didn't do Angela much good. The beautiful tree in the middle of her living room was inexplicably entwined with the presence of Brody Jackson. Her first instinct, after that troubling phone call with Jeffrey, was to march straight over to Brody's house and demand an explanation.

But it was dark, cold and snowing. And she wasn't sure she could handle an explanation right then.

It was really very simple, she decided. Some kind of midlife crisis as she was approaching thirty. She'd had a crush on Brody, one she'd never been able to admit to or even fantasize about, and it had stayed buried deep inside her. And without the restraining influence of Jeffrey, without anything to do on the long, lonely nights, it was flowering like a crocus after an endless winter. And she couldn't quite bring herself to squash it down again.

It hadn't been the only time he'd kissed her, of course. If it had been, it probably wouldn't have seemed so earthshaking. But that night on the deck of the Crescent Cove Harbor Club had simply been the culmination of something that had started five years earlier.

The Jacksons were newcomers to Crescent Cove, part of the new breed of summer people. The town was evolving— it had been a farming town for more than a hundred years before the first Princeton professor and his family arrived on the shores of Lake Champlain.

But taxes were rising, professors could no longer afford to take the entire summer off and wives worked, as well, and slowly but surely the big old cedar-shingled cottages along the lake were being sold in rapidly escalating bidding wars.

No one was particularly thrilled to see an industrialist like Walker Jackson move in, but he and his wife had been friendly and unpretentious, and their three young sons had blended in quite nicely. And fourteen-year-old Angela had been admittedly fascinated by her new neighbors, in particular the youngest son.

He'd been beautiful even back then—hair bleached by the sun, a tanned body, a dazzling smile. But that first summer he'd been lonely, spending his time out on the lake on his laser sailboat. When he wasn't spending time with Angela.

There'd been nothing romantic about it at all. She was fourteen; he was a year older. Jeffrey's family was in Europe for that summer, and for the first time Angela was at loose ends, free to do exactly as she chose. And then there was Brody. She'd read enough books, seen enough movies to feel the first forbidden burgeoning of romantic longing, but she wasn't ready to do anything about it. Jeffrey would be back, and Brody was nothing more than an increasingly close friend. They could talk about anything and everything— Brody's bullying older brothers and Angela's life as an only child. The stupidity of their relatively decent parents, how they wanted to live in Crescent Cove year-round as soon as they were old enough to do so.

The Founder's Day dance at the end of the summer had been a disaster. It should have warned her to avoid all such occasions in the future. It was the first dance she'd been to apart from the Wednesday-evening square dances, but the boys she'd known all her life weren't ready to cross the dance floor and actually ask a girl to dance. The best that could be hoped for was a sullen stride through the crowd, a silent appearance in front of the chosen victim and then off to dance with suitable grimness.

Brody didn't even go that far. He stayed in the corner with a group of boys, not even looking at her. It would have been miserable, except that most of her friends were lined up like ducks in a row, with no one wanting to pick them off.

By the time they announced the last song she was ready to cry, but she'd been experimenting with makeup and she thought it would run. So she lifted her head high as the kitschy sound of an Air Supply song filled the room, and then she rose and crossed the endless dance floor to stand in front of Brody.

He'd seen her coming, and he'd tried to ignore her. But they'd been best friends, and she wanted her first dance, the last dance of the summer, to be with him. She plastered a hopeful smile on her face. "Would you dance with me, Brody?"

She'd forced him to look at her. He was surrounded by his peers, all watching, waiting to see what he would do. She should have known it was a matter of teenage male pride and expected nothing less, but when he shook his head and turned back to his friends it crushed her.

She'd walked away, that same, endless walk, with remarkable dignity for a girl just turned fourteen. She'd walked out of the room, out of the building, and the two miles home on the moonlit path along the lake, wiping the tears and the makeup away from her face.

Her house was dark when she got there—her parents had gone to bed early. The Jackson house was still a blaze of lights, and she'd moved liked a shadow along the path. By that time tears and makeup and shoes were gone, and she wanted nothing more than to go curl up in bed.

She moved up her wide front steps quietly, reaching for the screen door, when she saw him in the darkness. He was there on the green wicker sofa where they'd spent hours talking, laughing, doing crossword puzzles or just sitting in a comfortable silence. There was nothing comfortable about the silence now.

He'd taken off his tie and jacket, and he looked as miserable as she felt. Her first instinct was to ignore him, go straight into the house and slam the door behind her. Her second was to demand what he was doing there.

She did neither. She went over to the creaky old sofa and sat down, curling up in her corner, wrapping her arms around her knees as she waited for him to say something.

He didn't say a word.

It was her first kiss, and it was a powerhouse. In itself it wasn't astonishing—just the soft pressure of his lips against hers. And then on her tearstained eyelids, and on her cheek, and on her lips again. He'd been good even back then, a natural, and it was no wonder she'd been ready to put her arms around him. But then the porch light went on, and he drew back as if bitten.

Her father stood there, rumpled hair, clueless. "Don't you think you ought to come to bed now, Angie? We've got a long drive tomorrow."

"I can sleep in the car." She didn't want to leave Brody. She wanted more kisses from his beautiful mouth.

"I should go," Brody said, starting to stand up. He had his jacket with him, and he held it in front of him. "Good night, Professor McKenna. Have a good winter. Goodbye, Angel."

It had been the first time he'd called her that. And then he'd gone, taking the front steps two at a time, disappearing into the moonlit night.

By next summer Jeffrey had returned, Brody had discovered he was irresistible to almost the entire female population of Crescent Cove and those chaste, almost dreamlike kisses had been forgotten. By Brody, at least.

But every time Angie sat on the green wicker sofa she remembered. And she spent a very large part of her summers curled up there with a book, trying not to think about anyone at all.

Oddly enough, she'd never kissed Jeffrey on the sofa. They'd necked on the steps, on the dock, in the boathouse, at the Harbor Club and just about everywhere else during their endless teenage years, but for some reason she'd never let him kiss her on the green wicker couch.

She never did find out what happened to the furniture after her parents sold the house and the Jacksons had it bulldozed. Probably gave it to Goodwill—most summer cottages were furnished with shabby hand-me-downs and secondhand furniture to begin with, and there'd been nothing of any particular grace or beauty. And she wouldn't have wanted the couch, really. She couldn't imagine it on Jeffrey's mother's freshly painted porch; the woman probably would have insisted on painting it a baby-blue if she'd allowed it there at all. Angie decided she would rather have it gone, over with, part of her long-lost childhood.

Of course she was thinking about it now. Brody had invaded her life, her thoughts, just as he had so many years ago. She could remember the faded cabbage roses on the cushions, the stain from the grape juice she'd spilled when she'd beaten Brody at canasta, the faintly musty smell as she devoured romances and ate homemade cookies.

Cookies. She surveyed the kitchen, the sheets of parchment paper covering every available surface, with Christmas cookies on each one. She'd finally run out of eggs and room, and she needed to give cookies away before she could bake some more. And she desperately needed to bake—it was what grounded her and kept her sane.

The snow was falling lightly, two days before Christmas Eve, and she'd already given cookies to everyone she'd ever met. She knew she wasn't going to be getting into her car in such suicidal weather, and she knew the one person she hadn't given cookies to yet was in walking distance. And he probably had eggs.

A simple, neighborly gesture, she told herself. So they had a confusing history together. They were both grown-ups, and that was in the distant past. She should go to show him she was entirely unaffected by it, and a friendly visit with a tin box of Christmas cookies would be just the excuse. If he wasn't there, even better. She would have made the gesture without having to actually talk to him and pretend it didn't matter. She blew out the Christmas candle, extinguishing its warm glow, and headed out into the night.

She walked past the snow-shrouded tennis court and the tree she'd planted so long ago. Funny that they hadn't bulldozed that when they'd wiped out everything else. She circled the house, only to discover where her Christmas tree had come from. He'd taken one of the three carefully landscaped balsams from the side of the driveway. His gardener would kill him.

The deck was freshly shoveled and his truck was in the driveway, but there was no sign of him. She could always hope he'd gone for a long hike. The wreath she'd made for him was still there on the side of the house, and smoke was curling out of the chimney. She couldn't see him when she peered through the French doors, and her knock was deliberately soft. If he was meant to hear her, he would; otherwise, she could just leave the cookies and head back to the safety of her house.

She should have known fate wouldn't make it easy on her. Before she could knock one more time the door opened and he stood there, barefoot and bare chested.

"Here," she said, shoving the cookies at him. "Merry Christmas."

He stared at her for a long, endless moment. She finally got a good look at the inside of his house—he'd brought a bed downstairs by the wood stove, the fancy kitchen was a mess and every surface was covered with books and newspapers. It was far too cozy, and she had to get out of there, fast.

He took the cookies, but he caught her wrist at the same time, and before she realized it he'd drawn her into the warm house, kicking the door shut behind them. "It's about time," he said, setting the cookies down on a nearby table. "Merry Christmas, Angel." And he pulled her into his arms, against his hard, lean body, and kissed her.

It was as if she'd been holding her breath, waiting for this, for the past ten years. Since the last time he'd kissed her. His skin was smooth, warm beneath the open flannel shirt, and his mouth was just as practiced as ever. He didn't give her time to speak, and she didn't want to. She just wanted to kiss him, touch him, let his hands strip the heavy coat from her shoulders and drop it onto the floor.

The house was dark with the oncoming shadows of early evening, and he hadn't turned on the lights. Maybe what happened in the dark stayed in the dark, she thought, as he gently moved her back, almost as if they were dancing again, until she came up against a piece of furniture.

He barely had to nudge her—she sank onto the sofa, still clinging to him, and he followed her down onto the cushions, his long hair falling over them both as he blotted out the light, and she closed her eyes, letting herself drift in the wonderful sensations. The smell of wood smoke and whatever soap he used, the feel of his hot skin against her hands, his hard lean body on top of hers, the taste of him, rich and dark and intoxicating. The muffled sound of the sofa as it creaked beneath their bodies, the distant sound of a phone ringing as he began unbuttoning her blouse.

He hesitated a moment, his hand stilled, and she put her hands over his wrist. "Don't stop," she whispered.

He smiled, a slow, sweet smile. "I wasn't going to," he said. "This has been too long coming." And he was reaching for the zipper of her jeans, when the answering machine clicked on and her ex-husband's smug voice filled the room.

She froze. "You haven't answered my phone calls, Brody. Too busy trying to steal my wife?"

She put her hands up and pushed, and Brody immediately released her, rolling off her to the side of the old sofa.

"It's a waste of time. I had her first and nothing can change that. I was her first and her best, and you'll just be an afterthought."

Angela got to her feet, fastening her jeans with shaking hands, buttoning her blouse crookedly. Brody lay on his side on the sofa, an unreadable expression on his face.

But Jeffrey wasn't finished with his long-distance monologue. "The only reason you might be able to get her in bed is that I warned her about you, and she's still so hung up on me that she'll do anything she can think of to pay me back. I didn't want to hurt her, but she didn't believe that, and hell hath no fury and all that jazz. Don't be fooled—she doesn't really want you. She just wants to get back at me."

Brody rose slowly, lazily, stretching as he ambled toward the telephone. Jeffrey's voice was getting edgier now, almost desperate. "I know you're there, Brody. It's a waste of time trying to avoid me. Sooner or later you'll have to face the truth. The only reason you want her is you never could have her, and you're a man who hates to lose. And all she wants is revenge. Brody—"

Brody picked up the phone, then set it down again, breaking the connection.

"Poisonous little son of a bitch, isn't he?" he said mildly, disconnecting the various cords from the telephone and the back of the answering machine. "He's been calling me for days now. You'd think he'd be ready to let go of you, now that he's got a new family, but he always was a dog-in-the-manger type. He may not want you anymore, but he doesn't want anyone else to have you. Particularly not me." He leaned against the counter. "But then that brings us to the question of you and your motives. Any truth to what he says?" He seemed barely interested. "Is that why you're here? For revenge against the man who dumped you?"

The room had been so hot, so cozy, the wood heat filling the high-ceilinged room. Now it was as cold as if he'd left the door open to the winter air. She turned her head to make certain it was shut, staring out into the darkness, but of course it was closed. It was only the ice in the pit of her stomach.

"Look at it this way," she said in a deceptively calm voice. "You finally got what you wanted, even if Jeffrey's phone call came at the wrong time. Consider me had. You've beaten Jeffrey. There is now no woman in Crescent Cove who wouldn't sleep with you."

"There are any number of women in Crescent Cove who don't want to sleep with me," he said. "Most of them, as a matter of fact."

"All of them," she said, picking up her coat and pulling it around her.

"Don't leave."

She paused by the door. "Why not?"

She would have taken something, anything. But he simply shrugged, and in the end there was nothing she could do but walk back out into the snowy night.

And in the distance she heard a crashing sound.

SHE SLIPPED on the icy road, sprawling in the snow, and the hard slap of the cold against her face was a salutary force. She scrambled to her feet again and ran the rest of the way, calling herself all sorts of names beneath her breath. What the hell did she think she was doing? All he'd had to do was touch her and she'd been ready to strip off her clothes and do anything he wanted. She'd done just what Jeffrey had warned her against, fallen into his bed without a second thought, and it had only been the phone call that had saved her from turning her life into a disaster zone.

Except that it hadn't been his bed. She'd been aware of very little but the man who was touching her, kissing her. In retrospect, she knew what had felt strange, wrong but right, familiar yet strange.

He had the old wicker sofa from her front porch.

She couldn't figure out why. Most of the furniture in the place had been broken-down junk, and the green sofa had been sagging badly, the wicker split and cracked. There'd been a few real Stickley pieces in the living room—the Jacksons should have saved those, not a worthless piece of porch furniture.

But it hadn't been the Jacksons. It had been Brody. She knew that as surely as she knew her own name.

And that was about all she knew at that point. She'd run, the moment she'd had a chance, letting Jeffrey do what he was so good at. Making her doubt everything.

Why had Brody kissed her, why had he saved the ratty old sofa, why had he done any of the unfathomable things he had over the years?

It didn't matter. If Jeffrey was right, then Brody had accomplished what he'd set out to accomplish.

Then again, why was she trusting Jeffrey at all? He said he'd been her first and her best. Oh, God, she certainly hoped not.

The house should have been dark when she opened the door. She'd left when it was still light, and she hadn't expected to be that long. She'd blown out the Christmas candle, but she hadn't bothered to turn on any lights.

But the Christmas candle sat in the middle of the kitchen table, the flame straight and true, filling the room with a warm, comforting light.

She stared at it. She remembered she'd blown it out—she was always very careful about such things, especially since Brody had warned her. She looked around her, wondering whether she ought to be nervous, whether someone had broken into her house while she'd been gone.

But no one had been there—she was certain of it. The place would feel different if there'd been an intruder. And no one would have come in, lit the Christmas candle and then left.

There was no question that the candle was unique—it burned forever with hardly any change in size, it didn't drip and the ever-shifting scents were a delight to the soul. Maybe the wick was made of some special substance that kept a dull glow, ready to flare back into life again when you thought you'd blown it out, like trick matches. Like childhood crushes. She needed to be more careful in the future.

She plugged in the lights on the Christmas tree, the extra glow filling the room. The woodstove was still going strong, and for the time being she didn't need to do anything but curl up on the sofa and pretend nothing had happened.

This was not turning out to be the Christmas she'd been determined to have. There were too many unsettled memories, too many voiceless longings.

And the time for denial was gone. Those longings all had to do with Brody Jackson.

Chapter Five

Christmas

He shouldn't have thrown his answering machine against the wall, Brody thought, but it had made such a satisfying crunch. Almost as good as if he'd slammed it into Jeffrey Hasting's smug face.

He'd said the wrong thing, of course. Once Jeffrey had begun to spew his nastiness, once she'd stiffened beneath him, pulling away, he'd known he'd lost her.

The question was, had he ever had her? Maybe Jeffrey was right—she was simply the one who got away. Except that despite Angel's flattering opinion of his irresistibility, there'd been any number of women who'd gotten away, including the first girl he'd had sex with, who'd dumped him for a football player; including his exquisitely beautiful, exquisitely shallow ex-wife and any number in between. He'd had his heart broken and he'd washed the pain away with a bottle of Scotch and emerged bloody but unbowed.

But he'd never gotten over Angel McKenna.

He was an idiot. He wasn't going to be fifteen again, stealing a kiss on a moonlit porch. He wasn't going to be twenty again, pretending to be drunk so that he could kiss her in the rain.

And he didn't want to be. He'd made countless mistakes in his life, lost just about everything, but in the end it had made him a halfway decent man.

And in the end, he still wanted Angel McKenna, and probably would until the day he died.

He ought to just get the hell out of there. Coming back had been a mistake, though his options hadn't been many.

But he had discovered that the perfect couple of Crescent Cove's summer population had split, and that Angela had moved up into a house on Black's Point. And invitations to stay with sympathetic friends in Hawaii, Aspen and Santa Fe had paled next to the chance to see Angel again.

To his shock, he still felt the same. No, scratch that. Not the same. When he was a teenager he'd mainly been interested in getting into her pants. What he was feeling now was stronger, deeper, surer. He wanted her on every level—as a friend, a lover, a sparring partner and anything else that came to mind. He wanted her, needed her, and he had the crazy hope that she felt the same.

He grabbed his coat and headed out the door. It was pitch-black—no moon that night, and snow was in the air. By the time he reached Angela's farmhouse he'd managed to build up a full head of steam, and his knock on the door was closer to a pounding.

He half expected her to ignore it, which wasn't an option, but after a moment the door opened and she stood there, looking small and wan, and some of his righteous anger vanished.

"What do you want?" she asked.

"We've got unfinished business," he said abruptly. Not the best thing to say—she immediately folded her arms across her chest in an instinctive defensive posture. "Not that," he said, irritated. "Though God knows that's been hanging fire for too damn long."

She didn't say anything. Behind her he could see a soft glow emanating from the living room, and the scent of bayberry mixed with the smell of Christmas cookies hanging in the air. Who would have thought Christmas cookies could be erotic? But then, that was his constant state of mind when he was around her.

After a moment she moved out of the doorway, holding it

open for him. "All right," she said. She kept well out of his way when he walked into the room, which was probably a good thing. He might have forgotten his noble resolve and kissed her again, and as long as Jeffrey Hastings didn't call they'd finish what they started. But he'd rushed it. Just because he hadn't been able to stop thinking about her for the past ten years didn't mean she'd spared him a thought. He had to take his time. Give her time.

He closed the door behind him to keep the winter air out, but he didn't take his coat off. She looked as if she'd been crying, and a pang of guilt hit him. Angela wasn't the kind of woman who cried easily—she never had been. The question was, was she crying over her lost husband or him?

"I think we need to start over. From the beginning again," he said. "The history gets too confusing, particularly with your ex-husband's little tricks."

"Start what?"

"Start us."

"I don't think that would be a good idea," she said carefully.

"Maybe not, but I don't tend to give up easily. I want to set a few things straight. The only reason I hated Jeffrey was that he had you. Oh, and the fact that he's a total moral vacuum. There's no rivalry between us. There's only you."

He couldn't read the expression on her face, but he persevered. "I'll tell you what, Angel. I'll leave you alone for now. Give you time to think about it. About whether you're over Jeffrey…"

"Over Jeffrey?" Her laugh was genuine. "I got over Jeffrey a couple of years before I caught him cheating. The worst thing about it was that I was relieved when I caught him and had an excuse to leave. One can't break up a perfect couple with no excuse."

He took a deep breath. "Okay. Then what's the problem?"

"I don't want to be another in your long line of summer conquests."

"Oh, for Pete's sake! In case you hadn't noticed, it's winter. The time for conquests is over. I'm in love with you."

He should have regretted blurting it out like that, particularly given the look on her face, but he couldn't.

"Go away," she said in a cold voice.

"For almost fifteen years, Angel. Since the first time I saw you, curled up on that green wicker sofa, crying over *Little Women.* You were my best friend, the first girl I kissed, and I want you to be the last girl I kiss. It's embarrassing, unlikely, and from the expression on your face I can guess that it's entirely unwelcome, but the fact is, I'm in love with you, and all the distractions in the world can't seem to shake it."

"You're lying," she said, but her voice was doubtful.

"If it makes you feel better you can believe that. You can spend the rest of your life missing Jeffrey."

"I don't give a damn about Jeffrey!" she said. "But I'm not about to trust your highly improbable declaration of love."

"Of course you're not," he said soothingly. "So we'll take it slow. Just promise me one thing. That you won't run. You'll keep an open mind, and we can see what happens."

"You don't love me."

"Just forget I ever said that," he said. "I promise I won't say it again. At least, not until I think you're ready to hear it."

"You don't love me," she said stubbornly, and she sounded close to tears. A very good sign, he thought. If she didn't care about him then his stupid-ass declaration wouldn't bother her so much.

He didn't bother arguing. "I'm going to leave this up to you," he said. "The ball's in your court, Angel. You make the next move. But I'll be ready when you are."

She bit her lip, and for a moment he thought she might be wavering. He took a step closer, just in case. But she took a step back, and he accepted the inevitable. For now.

"Don't take too long, Angel," he said. "And don't forget to blow out the candle when you go to bed. It's a fire hazard."

"I'll be fine."

She would, unfortunately. She didn't need or want him half as much as he needed her. But maybe that would change. It had to.

SHE WAS OUT of her mind, Angela thought. Totally and completely out of her mind. Brody Jackson wanted her, and he said it had nothing to do with Jeffrey. He even thought he was in love with her, though she had her doubts about that. But there was no doubt at all that he wanted her.

Almost as much as she wanted him. Which was the danger— she didn't want to risk that kind of cataclysmic relationship.

She needed time, she thought. He was right about that. He was right about a lot of things. He had no idea she'd spent seventh grade writing "Mrs. Brody Jackson, Mrs. Angel Jackson, Mr. and Mrs. Jackson" in her math notebook.

He didn't know just how pathetic she was when it came to him, and she knew she was going to have to tell him. Sooner or later. Preferably later. It was the night before Christmas Eve, her baking was done, her presents were wrapped, and maybe the safest thing would be to see if she could get a last-minute flight to Hawaii to have Christmas with her vacationing parents.

It would mean she wouldn't have to do anything about Brody for at least a week. She could just put him out of her mind, concentrate on the season.

And pigs could fly. Besides, Hawaii was no place to celebrate Christmas—Vermont was made for the season.

And if she made it through the night without going to him she was going to be amazed.

Did she believe him? Was she willing to risk it? There didn't seem to be any choice in the matter. Sometimes fate handed you a gift so powerful that you were afraid to grab it.

She went to the door, looking out the frosty pane of glass into the cold night air. It was a clear night, not a stray snowflake in sight. Nothing to keep her from going out, maybe discovering if he really meant what he said.

Her boots were already on when the phone rang, and she grabbed it, breathless, certain it was Brody.

"Get your ass over here," Patsy snarled. "I'm in labor, damn it."

And Brody would have to wait.

IF ANGELA HADN'T BEEN so exhausted she would have been highly amused. Patsy's manner of dealing with labor was to cuss everything and everybody, and even her husband's steady demeanor began to fray a little. Angela had had nine months of trying to talk Patsy out of a home delivery, but Patsy had strong opinions about everything, and Merline Kittredge was the best midwife in the Champlain Valley; plus, unbeknownst to the soon-to-be mother, the rescue squad was standing by, ready to whisk her off to Burlington at the first sign of trouble.

But there was no trouble at all. Harriet Patricia made her appearance after four and a half hours of very efficient labor, and she came out yelling almost as loud as her mother. Even Patsy was silenced by the sight of her perfect, healthy daughter.

"You're crying," Angela said.

"Am not," Patsy insisted, staring down in wonder at the tiny creature she'd just managed to deliver. "It just hurt."

"Pain's over, and you didn't cry during labor. You just cursed," Angela pointed out.

"Don't bother me. Can't you see I'm bonding like any good mother?"

"And I'm taking you to the hospital," Ethan announced. "You got to have your blissful crunchy granola back-to-nature home birth, and everything's fine, but we're going to check the two of you out and then we'll be right back. It won't take more than a couple of hours. Assuming the storm lets up."

"S-s-storm?" Angela stammered.

"Yup. A Christmas Eve nor'easter. They're figuring twelve to eighteen inches of snow, maybe more, with high winds and maybe even some freezing rain. If I were you I'd stay right here until we get back. We've got an extra bedroom."

"You think she'd drive in this stuff?" Patsy emerged from her rapturous examination of her infant for a brief moment. "She's the all-time wuss of the universe. Besides, she doesn't have to be anywhere. Her family's in Hawaii and there's no one else who matters. Is there?" She looked her calmly in the eyes.

"I should have never told you anything," Angela muttered.

"What the hell are you talking about?" Ethan demanded.

"Angie's in love."

"I am not!"

"With who?" Ethan asked, clearly bewildered.

"The same person she's been in love with since we were kids. Brody Jackson. The problem is, the only way she's going to get to him is through a blizzard, and she barely drives on cloudy days. And here it is, Christmas Eve, and there's never been a better time to admit it and be with him."

"Go to the hospital and get checked out," Angela snapped. "I'll be here when you get back."

Patsy smiled a catlike smile. "Sure you will."

They went off in the ambulance, driving slowly, the red lights flashing. They disappeared into the swirling snow almost immediately, and Angela closed the door behind them, leaning her forehead against the cold window.

Spending Christmas Eve with Patsy and Ethan and the brand-new baby was a perfect way to celebrate. It was safe and warm here, and people loved her, and there wasn't any risk of getting her heart broken, or driving off a cliff, or…

It was Christmas Eve, and she was too much of a Christmas slut to ignore it. She shoved her feet into her boots, pulled her coat around her and stepped out onto the porch. The icy snow whipped against her face like a cold slap, and the wind was howling down the main street, obliterating the lights and the town Christmas decorations. She walked down the steps, through the thick snow—they'd had almost a foot of snow since she'd first come to help Patsy, and it wasn't about to let up any time soon from the looks of things. The snow was mixing with pellets of ice, the kind that would probably cover every available surface and send her sliding into the lake. If she tried to drive in this stuff she'd die. It was that simple.

She managed to open one of the car doors, letting snow fall onto the seat, and grab the snow brush. She started at the front, moving around the car, brushing off the thick, wet stuff, and by the time she reached the windshield again another inch had piled up. She was going to die.

Maybe the car wouldn't start. She climbed behind the wheel, knocking the snow off her boots before closing the door, and turned the key. The damn thing started like a charm.

She took a deep breath. "You can do this," she said. "All you have to do is drive very, very slowly. You can do this."

Unfortunately, no one was listening, especially not her subconscious. She shoved the car into gear, put the four-wheel-drive in low, flicked on the lights and began to inch forward.

She could barely see five feet ahead of her. Visibility was slightly easier with the lights on dim, and when she tested the brakes she only slid for a moment before the reassuring chunk-chunk sound of the antilock brake system kicked in. She had her seat belt on, and she was clutching the steering wheel so hard her fingers were growing numb. She turned on the radio—there were nothing but Christmas carols playing on Christmas Eve and she figured that might help her to breathe. Or at the very least she'd die in a state of grace.

"'Sleep in heavenly peace,'" she sang under her breath, an octave lower than the thundering choir on the radio. They didn't sound as if they knew much about heavenly peace or sleeping, but at least she could sing all the verses, and it *was* a holy night, a silent night, no sound penetrating the thick blanket of snow.

She missed the turn onto Black's Point Road. Well, not actually missed it—she just failed to put the brakes on in time and went sliding past it, off into the ditch at the side of the road.

"Near enough," she muttered, turning off the engine and the lights, leaving the keys where they were. If someone wanted to steal the car they were welcome to it. After tonight she might never drive again.

Except that her hands weren't shaking, and she no longer had that sick feeling of panic deep inside her belly. It was almost a sense of elation.

She was afraid she might get lost in the snow—on foot the visibility was even worse, the snow lashing at her eyes in the inky darkness. Her sense of time, of direction, was shot to hell.

What usually took her five minutes to drive had taken her close to forty-five minutes. Her house wasn't far from the main road, but with her luck she'd stumble right past it and into the lake.

She hadn't left any lights on, not even her Christmas tree, but the faint glow was unmistakable. She knew what it was, and that it would lead her safely back home, and she no longer even thought to question it. When she stumbled in her front door the Christmas candle sat in the darkness, its warm glow filling the space.

If she had even half a brain at all she'd strip off her frozen clothes, build up the stove and get into bed. But she hadn't risked life and limb out on the roads because she had sense, or because she wanted to sleep alone. She picked up the candle and started back out into the stormy night.

The snow should have dowsed the flame. The wind should have blown it out. But it stayed, straight and true, leading her through the snow-filled woods to Brody Jackson.

The house was dark as she climbed up onto the front deck. He hadn't shoveled since the latest storm had begun, and she had a sudden awful feeling. He hadn't said he was going to be there for Christmas, had he? And she'd pretty much told him she didn't trust him and never would. Why would she think he'd be there that night?

It was too late now. The candle had led her there, through the storm, and this was where she was meant to be.

She pushed the door open, and the wind blew drifts of snow onto the floor. She shoved it shut behind her, then turned to look at the room.

He was lying in the bed by the woodstove, sound asleep. The covers were at his waist, exposing the long, beautiful back that she still remembered.

It would have helped if he'd woken up, said something, but he slept on, the rat. She set the candle down on the table. The only other light in the room came from the small white lights on the Christmas tree he'd brought in. There were no ornaments on it, but it was surprisingly beautiful.

She was soaking, weighted down with melting snow, and she'd come this far. And only good things can happen on Christmas Eve, right?

She pulled off her jacket and boots and left them by the woodstove. Her jeans were soaked halfway up her thighs, and they were cold, clammy and uncomfortable, when she took them off. She was shivering, but she stripped off her turtleneck and her sweater, too.

Colder still. She needed covers and a warm body. She peeled off her wool socks, but at the last minute couldn't bring herself to remove her bra and panties. She tiptoed over to the bed, but he slept on. She picked up the covers and slid underneath them, close to him but not quite touching, holding her breath to see if he'd wake up.

He needed a shave. His long hair fell over his face, his mouth had a stubborn, sexy look even in sleep, and she put her head down on the pillow, feeling suddenly, unaccountably peaceful. She should be nervous, climbing into bed with a man when she wasn't sure she was welcome, but she felt very calm. Safe. Home.

"It took you long enough." He didn't open his eyes, but reached out his arm and pulled her up against his warm, muscled body. "Your feet are cold."

"Everything about me is cold," she said with a little shiver. "Not for long."

It wasn't perfect. Sex wasn't meant to be perfect, graceful, elegant. But it was gloriously right. His hands knew just how to touch her, how hard, how gentle, how long. He did things with his mouth that she hadn't even imagined, and when he pushed inside her she climaxed immediately, unable to help herself.

He held her tightly as the spasms racked her body, an unending shimmer of delight, and when they finally slowed he whispered in her ear, "Hey, I'm not that good."

She cupped his face with her hands and smiled up at him dizzily. "But I am," she said with a mischievous smile. And she wrapped her legs around him, pulling him in deeper.

The night was too short, yet endless. They made love, slept, made love again, ate Christmas cookies and drank eggnog, then made love once more, and the light from the Christmas candle spread a soft, magical glow around the cavernous room.

When she awoke it was near daylight and she was sprawled across his body in a haze of total well-being. She could tell by the change in his breathing that he was awake, too, and when he spoke she lifted her head to see him.

"What the hell is this?" he said, holding up her discarded underwear. "Are there Christmas trees on your bra?"

She smiled at him. "Of course."

He groaned. "Oh, God. You're going to make me wear Christmas boxers next year, aren't you?"

"Absolutely." She put her head back down on his warm chest, closing her eyes as he stroked her shoulder. The early light of dawn had filled the room with a warm glow, almost like the candle. And then she opened her eyes, to see if it was still burning.

It was gone. The candleholder was still there, but the candle had burned to nothingness, not even a trace of wax left behind. Only the faint scent of cinnamon and cranberry lingered to remind her.

She closed her eyes again, letting out a deep, satisfied smile. "Merry Christmas, Brody," she whispered.

He put his hand under her chin, tilting her face up to his. "Merry Christmas, Angel," he said. "And a happy new life."

RETURN OF THE LIGHT
Maggie Shayne

For the Goddess, and those who serve Her

Dear Reader,

This anthology is the product of three women who have very different spiritual beliefs, three women who are friends and who have a deep and genuine respect for one another.

We don't waste our time trying to convert each other. Instead, we talk—we talk about the deepest, most meaningful things in our lives. And we listen. And we learn, because we each have a unique perspective and a depth of wisdom to share, and because we each know beyond any doubt that the path of the others is as valid and as sacred as our own.

At this special time of year, when we're in the midst of the darkest of seasons, this time when we rejoice in the promise of the light's inevitable return, wouldn't it be wonderful if the whole world could take a page from this book? Wouldn't it be nice if we could listen to each other's thoughts and ideas and beliefs without judging them?

My wish for each of you this season is that your hearts and lives be filled with light, love and peace. I hope that your beliefs will always be honored and respected, and your right to choose them will always be protected.

Happy holidays!

Maggie Shayne

Prologue

The candles were the only light in the room. They glowed from every quarter, painting the faces of the men and women in a golden light. Incense smoke hung in the air; sandalwood and myrrh, mingling with the seasonal aromas of pine boughs, holly and ivy.

In the center, she stood with her arms upward and outward, head tipped back as the High Priest knelt before her, completing the fivefold kiss by pressing his lips briefly to her feet.

She opened her eyes and spoke to the gathered assembly, spoke the words of the Goddess according to Leland, who said they were given to him by an Italian Witch named Maddalena more than a hundred years ago; and to Gardner, who adapted them from Leland, adding his own touches; and to Valiente, who made them beautiful and must have been truly inspired; and according to Dori, Lady Starfire, who had made them her own.

"Hear my words and know me! I shall be called by myriad names. I am the Maiden of the Moon, I am Mother Earth. And I am the Crone, who holds the keys of life and rest. I am an unknowable mystery and yet known to every soul!"

She lowered her arms to her sides, moving her most penetrating gaze from one face to the next, meeting their eyes so they would feel touched by the Goddess.

"Hear my words and know me! Whenever the full moon rises, come to me. Gather in some secret place, such as this…"

Not much of a secret place, though. Not really. Her pent-house apartment in Manhattan. Still, it served the purpose.

"And adore the spirit of your Goddess, who is Queen of all Witches."

Speaking the words of the Goddess felt a little phony to-night. Something was wrong; something was off. Dori wasn't sure what. And yet she felt that spirit wasn't speaking through her, hadn't in quite some time now. The Charge had become rote, recited from memory. And while those standing in a cir-cle around her seemed awestruck and mesmerized when she met their eyes with her own, she didn't feel the magic.

"I shall teach you the mysteries of Nature, and the ways of Magick!"

Not much nature, here. Not in the apartment, aside from her plants and her cat.

"All that is hidden shall be revealed. Even the secluded soul shall be pierced by my light."

She didn't really teach anymore. The priestesses she had trained did that, ran their own covens, taught bright-eyed be-ginners, organized social functions and rituals and performed weddings and funerals. But in this particular branch of the Pagan community, she was queen. The ranking elder, the most honored Witch in town, and a coveted special guest at many a Pagan function. She was even respected and a bit fa-mous in non-Pagan circles, having successfully worked with the police on several missing persons cases. The press loved that kind of crap. It was a damn good thing she saw no rea-son to be secretive about her beliefs. They wouldn't have stayed secret long.

"I do not demand sacrifice, for I am the mother of all living!"

She moved around the circle now, speaking to each indi-vidual.

"Create and heal!" she told one. "Be strong yet gentle," she said, touching the cheek of another. "Be noble yet reverent," she instructed a third. "Bring forth and replenish."

She returned to the center. "And just as the moon moves through her cycles, waxing and waning and beginning again, and just as seasons flow from birth in the spring to life in the summer, to aging in the fall and apparent death in the winter, so shall you—in both worlds.

"And you will say these words—I will love all, and harm none. For the free will of all, and with harm to none, as I will, it now is done. So mote it be!"

And with that, she moved to the seat of honor that had been placed in the North quarter of the circle and sat down to enjoy the rest of the Winter Solstice Ritual the priestesses had planned. She'd done her part, ensuring those gathered that the Goddess was indeed present to join in their rites. She sat and watched the elaborate procedure unfold. There were songs to celebrate the return of the light. There was a dance performed in its honor. The freestanding silver candelabras she had bought for ritual use really made it special, she thought. Each held seven candles—she'd spent a fortune on them, but it was well worth it. Some of the less-experienced priestesses still had to read their parts, and the light was extremely helpful.

The entire group began the circle dance, which usually generated such a rush of energy that Dori tingled from head to toe. Tonight it felt off.

Something was up this Winter Solstice. All week long, she'd been thinking that once again, she'd come through the darkest season without experiencing any real darkness at all. Her life was perfect. Tonight, though, she felt the sword of Damocles dangling overhead. Every nerve in her body was tensed as if expecting a blow.

She broke her train of thought long enough to wince when one enthusiastic dancer bumped into the altar. That was a Tiffany chalice, for Goddess's sake!

Luckily it didn't fall off, just wobbled dangerously.

The dancing grew faster and faster, until the High Priestess shouted, "Release!" Then all the dancers in the room went still, relaxing their bodies to let go of the energy they had raised, while the woman in the center lifted her hands to send the magic off to its goal. Its goal tonight was to bring back the light, to help it grow within every one of them and help them through their own dark times, whatever they might be.

The ritual was finished and the circle taken up as Dori rose again, lifting her arms in silence to bid farewell to the Goddess, then lowering them and crossing them over her chest, bowing her head.

As those gathered rushed into the next room, where snacks were piled high and wine was chilling, she quickly cleared her altar, lovingly wrapping each tool in silk cloth and tucking each back into the trunk in the corner. The Tiffany chalice. The crystal-tipped wand she'd had custom-made by an artisan in Greenwich Village. The statues of Pan and Diana, replicas of ancient artifacts. She'd bought them in the gift shop at the Met. The dagger, with its double-edged silver blade and onyx handle, slid neatly into its sheath. It was worth a small fortune. She was especially careful with the giant quartz crystal ball on its elaborate pewter stand. She rarely had time to use the thing, but it looked great on the altar.

She didn't relax until every item was safely tucked in the trunk and she had turned the key.

"Thanks so much for letting us use your flat, Lady Starfire." The voice was Sara's—could be no one else's, with that beautiful accent. She was new in town, but very highly regarded in the community. Had come straight from England with the equivalent of a Witch's pedigree—a long and distinguished lineage.

When Dori turned to face her, it was to see her dropping into a curtsy, her head bent low.

"We're not so formal, here, Sara. Ritual's over. It's okay to call me Dori. And I've never been all that comfortable with the genuflecting." She glanced into the next room, where there had to be at least forty people eating, talking, laughing. Someone had put John Denver and the Muppets on the stereo—which was sure to start an earnest debate about playing Christmas music at a Solstice party among those not yet far enough along their path to realize they were all celebrating the same thing.

Dori almost cried when she thought of the potential crumbs and spills on her carpet.

"I simply couldn't believe we had so many who wished to attend!" Sara went on. "Our open circles have only brought in eighteen to twenty people, up to now."

"I know."

"There just wasn't room in the back room of my shop," she went on. "And I couldn't bear to turn anyone away."

"I know," Dori said again, fixing the beautiful blond Witch with a serious look. "It's okay. Really, Sara."

The other woman sighed in relief. A little too much relief. So Dori quickly added, "And next time, you'll know in advance that you need a bigger place, so you'll have time to make other arrangements."

"Right." She nodded hard. "Absolutely. And we'll leave the place spotless, I swear."

"The cleaning service will take care of that."

Sara smiled. "Will you join us for the refreshments?"

Dori glanced into the dining room, at the smiling faces, young and old, dark and light, round and narrow. She didn't want to join them. They tended to fawn and fuss and treat her like a celebrity and she wasn't up to it tonight. Something was terribly wrong. But if she didn't take part, they'd be disappointed, so she lifted her chin and walked into the dining room.

Several of those present bowed in her direction when she did. One quickly vacated a chair and another brought her a glass of wine.

Dori sighed, sipped her wine, smiled a little. Every High Priestess in this room had been taught by her. Every coven had sprung from the little one that had begun around her coffee table when she'd first come to Manhattan from tiny Crescent Cove, Vermont, ten years ago. She'd really done a good thing here, she thought. Her Witches were busy, politically active, constantly working to educate the public about the Craft and debunk the widespread misconceptions that caused so many Wiccans so many problems. They provided services for the

Pagan community, raised money for the homeless, organized Pagan Pride events and voter-registration drives.

Yes. She'd done a good thing. And the Goddess had rewarded her. Her life was perfect. And she was sitting here in her penthouse apartment, petrified, waiting for the ax to fall.

In the morning, it did.

She showered and dressed for success in a burgundy Pierre Atonia suit—slender skirt, a little on the short side, tailored jacket that accentuated her narrow waist, matching designer pumps. She left a brief note for the cleaning service, asking them to spend extra time on the dining room carpet, and she took a taxi to work just as she always did.

But when she stepped out of the elevator into the reception area of Mason-Walcott Publishing, a grim-faced man was waiting for her.

"Ms. Stewart?" he asked. He didn't smile.

He was tall and dressed all in black. His face was pale and bony, his eyes deep set. He could have been the pop-culture version of the Grim Reaper, she thought. And a shiver went up her spine. Everything in her told her this was it, the thing she'd been feeling in the air.

"Yes?"

"I'm Martin Black, VP in charge of personnel."

She lifted her eyebrows. "Of Mason-Walcott?"

"Of Beckenridge."

Beckenridge. One of the largest publishers in the biz—and notoriously right-wing conservative.

"And you're here because…?"

"Because Beckenridge just took over Mason-Walcott."

She looked past him to see if co-workers were lurking, ready to laugh at her falling for such a lame joke. But her stomach had clenched into a knot that told her this was for real.

"I'm afraid we're…not going to be needing you."

She blinked twice, and for the first time she noticed the big cardboard box on the counter that separated the receptionist's desk from the rest of the area. It held her belongings.

She shifted her gaze back to Mr. Black's. "You're *firing* me?"

"Technically, we're laying you off. We took the liberty of clearing out your office. Everything's right here."

She nearly gaped. "May I ask the reason?"

He shrugged. "Does it matter?"

"Of course it matters. I'm not even convinced it's legal!"

"Oh, it's legal. The position of editorial executive director is being eliminated, to be sure it's legal."

"But that's not the real reason, is it?"

He shrugged. "Would you really want to stay, Ms. Stewart? Our titles fly in the face of everything you so openly believe in and practice." He handed her an envelope. "A month's severance. It's more than generous. Good luck, Ms. Stewart."

He scooped her box of belongings off the counter and shoved it into her chest, leaving her no choice but to take it or let it fall to the floor. Then he clasped her elbow, turning her toward the elevator, and reached past her to push the button.

"You can't do this," she said. Useless, but all she could come up with.

"I just did." The doors opened. He nudged her inside and stood there until they closed again. "Goodbye, Ms. Stewart. Have a nice life."

Chapter One

A few days before Winter Solstice, one year later...

"Hey, Dori, hon, you gonna get over here and fill this coffee cup, or do I have to climb over the counter and get it myself?"

"Keep your pants on, Bill." Dori set down the tray full of dirty plates, grabbed the coffeepot and hurried to fill the man's cup. Mort's Diner, in Crescent Cove, Vermont, was decorated to the max for the holiday season: wreath on the door, fake green garland looped everywhere, cinnamon- and candy-cane-scented candles burned and holiday music played constantly.

Jason was there, sitting in a corner booth, enjoying a sandwich and a cup of cocoa. Watching her. He was there a lot, more often than seemed reasonable. Then again, she didn't suppose there was much work for the police chief of a small, quiet town like this. Hell, maybe it was vain of her to think he came around just to watch her waiting tables. It had been more than a decade, after all, since he'd held her. Since he'd kissed her.

There was nothing between them anymore.

Dori sighed in relief when she heard the jingle bells over the door and saw Sally walk in. After setting the coffeepot back on the burner, she reached behind her to tug her apron loose as Sally came behind the counter.

"You're an hour late. Again," Dori said.

"I'm sorry, Doreen. Little Amy had a doctor's appointment

and I only just got her back home." She pulled her apron around her and tied it in place.

There was always a reason. Always. And it usually had to do with the woman's small army of children. "Whatever. I'm out of here." Dori tossed the apron down, snatched her coat off the rack and went into the back room to collect her sorry excuse for a paycheck from the owner.

But she paused near the door as she heard Bill say, "Damn. You'd think she'd have come down off that high horse by now, wouldn't you?"

Dori stood still, listening.

"It was a hard fall," Sally said. "Going from a penthouse in Manhattan to her uncle's log cabin on the lakeshore. From a high-powered job to slinging hash for lousy tippers like you. Hell, she probably used to earn more in a month than she's made here in…how long has it been now since Dori came running back here with her tail between her legs?"

Bill didn't answer. The grown-up version of the boy who'd been her summer fling as a teenager—for several consecutive summers—answered, instead. "Eleven months, three weeks and two days."

"Think she's gonna stay for good this time?" Bill asked.

"Wish to hell I knew," Jason said. And there was something in his voice—something kind of pained.

Dori moved to the swinging door, peered through its port-hole-shaped glass. He was still at his table in the corner, staring at the sheet of pink notebook paper he held in one hand. It was old, had been folded so long the creases were darker colored. It looked worn thin. As she stared at it, wondering, he lifted his gaze, and Dori backed away from the door.

"She belongs here," Sally was saying. "Don't you worry, Jason. She's gonna realize that by-and-by."

Now, why was she saying that? As if Jason had any stake in what Dori decided to do with her life. She'd broken things off with Jason ten years ago—in a Dear John letter….

Written on pink notebook paper.

Something knotted in her belly. She told herself she was

being ridiculous, snatched her paycheck from the slotted mail holder on the wall and decided to go out the back door rather than walking through the front of the diner again.

Tugging the hood of her parka up over her head, she trudged through the snow to her car and rolled her eyes when she realized she would have to spend a few minutes brushing snow off it before she could go anywhere.

She missed her Mercedes—the remote starter, the heated leather seats, the warm, snow-free garage where she used to keep it parked. But she pulled her mittens from her pockets and thrust her hands into them. She opened the door to start the engine, grabbed the snow brush and slammed the door hard enough to knock some of the snow off. Then she began brushing. A thin layer of ice lay beneath the two inches of snow, and that required scraping. She hated scraping ice.

An old woman walked past the parking lot, waved at her and called, "Cold enough for you?"

"Plenty," Dori replied.

"Ah, but cold means clear. It's done snowing. The stars are going to be beautiful tonight," the old woman said. And she continued on her way.

Fifteen minutes later, Dori had made a hole on the windshield just big enough to see where she was going, and she was heading out of Crescent Cove proper and toward Uncle Gerald's cabin on the shore of Lake Champlain.

The lake was moody today, dark and choppy except in the spots where it was beginning to freeze over. She drove into the curving driveway, past the big wooden sign with the image of a green sea serpent and the words Champ Tours: $20.00. She made a mental note to take the sign down. She'd dry-docked the boat and closed up the souvenir shop two months ago. No point leaving the sign up all winter.

Champ—Lake Champlain's answer to the Loch Ness Monster—had been her uncle's bread and butter for as long as she could remember. She used to come out here every summer as a teen and work for him as a tour guide, retelling the Champ legends until she knew them all by heart, taking people around the lake until she knew it by heart, as well. And spending every free moment with local boy-next-door Jason Farrar.

He'd been her first lover. It had been innocent and clumsy and wonderful. She would never forget that night. But at the end of her last summer here, she'd left him with nothing except that stupid note, telling him she would never be back, and to look her up in Manhattan if he wanted to. He never had.

She'd meant what she'd written in the note. She had never intended to come back here. She wouldn't have believed in a million years that she would be forced to revive the old business long after her uncle had retired to Boca Raton. But she'd had no choice. Goddess knew she couldn't survive on the pittance they paid her waiting tables at the diner.

Yeah, Goddess knew all right. She just didn't particularly care.

Sighing, Dori shut the car off and got out, hoping she wouldn't have to scrape the car off again in the morning.

She unlocked the front door and went inside, flipped on the lights, heeled off her boots, shrugged off her coat, tugged off her mittens. She went to the wall to turn up the thermostat, then padded into the living room and sank onto the sofa.

On the opposite wall was a tiny plaque. It depicted a Goddess in silver silhouette against a deep blue background, standing in the curve of an upturned crescent moon. Her arms were raised the way Dori's used to be in the midst of a circle when she was drawing down the moon. The plaque was the one ritual item she hadn't been forced to sell.

But she had found that out here in Crescent Cove, there was little use for her elaborate, expensive ritual tools. She was probably the only Wiccan within a hundred miles. She practiced alone.

That wasn't quite true. She didn't really practice at all, unless you counted all the spells she'd cast, all the magic she'd done to get her old life back. Nothing had worked. Nothing. And for about the millionth time she found herself wondering if any of it had ever been real.

She looked up at the Goddess on the wall opposite her and wondered why she kept the plaque hanging there. Did she even believe anymore?

JASON WALKED around the cabin toward the front door, but he stopped when he caught a glimpse through the side window of the woman he'd loved for as long as he could remember. She was standing, staring up at something on the wall. A single tear rolled down her cheek.

He couldn't take his eyes away. Why was she crying?

Hell, he hadn't been able to make much sense of Dori Stewart since she'd dumped him and headed off to the big city to make her fortune. She'd barely spoken two words to him since she'd been back. And he wasn't altogether sure that was a bad thing.

He still wanted her. Just as badly as he always had. But he wasn't ready to risk his heart again. She'd damn near crippled him when she'd walked away. He'd been seeing wedding bells, a house and kids in their future, and she'd apparently thought of him as little more than a summer sidekick. He wasn't going to let himself go through that again. So he'd stayed away from her, waiting to see what she planned to do, just about as long as he could stand to. For nearly a whole year he'd limited himself to a few words of greeting when they met in the diner, told himself to keep his distance for his own sanity, even while torturing himself by sitting in a booth every day, watching her.

He had asked her out once when she'd first come back to town. She'd shot him down cold. It was then he'd decided he owed it to himself to get over her. But getting over Dori Stewart was easier decided than done.

As he watched, she lowered her head, swiped an impatient hand at her tears and turned to walk out of his line of vision.

Jason went the rest of the way to the door, knocked twice, then stood there waiting.

It only took her a second to come to the door. She asked who it was, and when he told her, he heard locks turning.

Hell, she'd been living in the city too damn long.

She opened the door and stood there, looking out at him. "What is it?"

Friendly, she wasn't. Then again, he'd already ascertained that she wasn't in the best of moods. He offered a friendly smile. "I'd prefer to tell you from in there where it's warm. Save you letting all the heat out."

She met his eyes, but opened the door wider to let him in. He stomped the snow off his boots and came inside, and she closed the door behind him.

He liked the way she looked. He hadn't when she'd first come back. Her copper hair had been too tamed, too trimmed, too styled. Her skin had been as pale as porcelain and she'd been skinny as a rail.

A summer on the lake had improved things a whole lot. Put some color in her cheeks. She'd let her hair grow out just as it pleased, and she might have put on a few pounds, too. She was starting to look as though she belonged out here—even if she wasn't acting that way just yet.

"So what can I do for you, Chief Farrar?" she asked.

"Kind of formal, don't you think? Given our history?"

She shrugged. "It's been a long time."

"So long you can't even call me Jason anymore?"

She met his eyes, and he saw something flicker. Regret, maybe. Interest, perhaps, he hoped. Her tone softened, as did her face. He thought a little of the stiffness left her body.

"What can I do for you, Jason?"

"A cup of coffee would do for starters. If it's fresh."

"I stopped serving people at five, but you're welcome to help yourself."

"I'll take it." He tugged off his boots and then sock-footed his way across the kitchen, draping his coat over the back of a chair on the way. Then he took two mugs from the little wooden tree and filled them. He set them on the table, grabbed the cream from the fridge and sat down.

She sat down, as well. He poured cream into his cup, then passed it to her.

"Nope. I drink it black."

"You didn't used to."

She frowned.

"Two sugars and a good long stream of half-and-half. But only if no real cream was at hand. I remember."

She studied him for a long moment, her green eyes wide and searching. "I can't believe you remember that."

"I remember everything, Dori." He shrugged and sipped his coffee.

It seemed to take her a moment to stop staring at him and find something to say again. He took that as a positive sign and told himself that was because he was a pathetic sap.

"What are you doing here, Jason?"

"It's an official visit. You didn't think I was here to ask you out again, did you?"

She shrugged. "It crossed my mind."

"I'm not into masochism, Dori. You made it clear the first time that you didn't have any interest in starting anything up with me."

"With anyone," she corrected.

"Right. Because you would only be here long enough to decide which big-city offer to accept, and then you'd be out of here so fast we'd see nothing but a copper-red streak."

"Is that what I said?" She averted her eyes and drank her coffee instead of looking at him. He'd hit a nerve, he thought.

"That's what you said. 'Course, that was damn close to a year ago."

She sighed. "I get where you're going with this. I'm still here, right? So did you come to rub it in? Gloat a little that the snotty city snob got knocked down a peg?"

He swore softly, and that drew her eyes back to his again. He said, "Hey, it's me. Jason. Do you remember anything at all about me?"

She frowned for a moment, then nodded twice. "You're right. You'd never gloat over my failed life. You're not that kind. Never were."

"Well, thank goodness you remember at least that much. I'll tell you, Dori, city living made you cynical. Gave you a hard edge you didn't used to have."

"That's probably true."

He hadn't come here to insult her, but he thought he just had. "I was only asking about your still being here because it makes me wonder if maybe your plans have changed." He hoped to God she would say they had, but the misery in her eyes told him different even before she did.

Dori lowered her head. "My plans haven't changed. But what I plan to do and what I can do are turning out to be further apart than I imagined."

He held her gaze for a long moment. "So you still plan to take some big-time job and hightail it back to the city at the first opportunity?"

"I sent out a dozen more résumés last week."

He sighed. "Are you sure you don't belong out here, Dori? Hell, nobody tells those Champ stories the way you do."

She tilted her head to one side, averted her eyes. "You said you were here on official business?"

Jason sighed. If she was determined to freeze him out, there wasn't much he could do about it. "Yeah. Wanted to ask if you could help me out on a case."

She looked up at him fast. "Jesus, how do you know about that? No one out here knows about that!"

He was taken by surprise. "About what?"

"Look, Jason, I don't do that kind of work anymore, okay?"

He had no idea what she was talking about, but suddenly he wanted to. So he narrowed his eyes and watched her as carefully as he would watch an ex-con in town for the weekend, and he took a shot in the dark. "Why not? You did it in New York, didn't you?"

She lowered her head. "It's different in New York," she said. "A psychic or even a Witch helping the police find a missing person is so common there it doesn't even make the news every time anymore. Out here it would be the biggest headline to hit town in a decade."

He blinked three times. A Witch. She did say *Witch,* didn't she?

"You, uh, helped the police find some missing people."

"Helped. Past tense. Like I said, I don't do it anymore."

"And you used…uh…Witchcraft to do it?"

She shrugged. "I used whatever I could. The cards, the runes. My instincts."

"You're…psychic?"

"Everyone's psychic." She sipped her coffee. "Some people learn how to hone it, how to use it. I'm one of them."

"So you were successful?"

She nodded, but she was looking at him oddly now. "You didn't know any of this, did you?"

"I didn't have a clue. So you went off to the big city and came back a Witch, huh?"

She closed her eyes, irritated it seemed. "If you weren't aware of my history, then why were you asking for my help with a case?"

"I just need an extra pair of eyes. Some kids have been *borrowing* boats and taking them out on the lake to party. It's not safe—especially this time of year. I was hoping you'd keep a lookout and give me a call if you see anything suspicious."

She closed her eyes. "Oh."

"So tell me more about this…Witch thing."

She drew a deep breath, then shook her head. "No."

"No? Come on, Dori, you can't just leave me hanging like that."

"Yes, I can. It's not something I want to become public knowledge. Not out here—people wouldn't understand."

"What, you think I'm completely ignorant? I know what Wicca is. That is what we're talking about here, right?"

She nodded slowly.

"And as for not letting it get around, you know me better than that, don't you?"

"Do I?"

"You did once. You knew me well enough to make love to me, Dori. Or did you forget that, too?"

"Jason…"

"Knew me well enough to let me believe we had something

special, then left me in the dust, wondering what truck had just run me down."

She lowered her eyes.

"You trusted me then, didn't you, Dori?"

"People change."

"You sure as hell proved that." He sighed. "But I'm the same guy I was back then. A little older. A little wiser, maybe. But you can still trust me."

She sighed. "I haven't changed as much as you think I have," she said softly. "I couldn't be who I was. Not here. Not in this town."

"It wasn't the town holding you back, Dori. That was all you."

She sighed. "Maybe. Maybe I was just afraid."

"Maybe you still are."

She was quiet a moment, seeming to think things over. "I was thinking about reserving a table at the Holiday Craft Fair. Doing tarot readings for people."

He lifted his brows. "Yeah?"

"I wasn't sure what the reaction would be, though."

He shrugged. "As a rule, the word *psychic* doesn't stir up the same feelings as the word *Witch.*"

"I could really use the extra money."

"So do it. Give folks a little credit, Dori. Just 'cause this isn't a major metropolitan city doesn't mean we're all ignorant here. This is Vermont, for goodness' sake. Most open-minded state in the union."

She lifted her head. He saw a light in her eyes for the first time. Maybe she was a little excited about the idea of cracking the door of that broom closet where she'd been hiding, letting a bit of light shine in. He hoped so.

"Meanwhile, keep an eye out for those kids. Okay? They haven't done any harm so far, but that lake is no place for a bunch of rowdy teenagers."

"I'll keep an eye out."

He finished his coffee, got up from the table. "It was good talking to you again," he said. "It's been way too long."

"We've talked. At the diner."

He set his cup in the sink and went to the door, stomped into his boots. "I barely get a word in at the diner. They keep you too busy. Or maybe it's that you've been actively avoiding me."

She brought his coat from the back of his chair and handed it to him. "I guess I've been feeling guilty. About the way we left things."

"The way you left things," he corrected. "The way you left, period."

She pursed her lips, lowered her head. "I'm sorry I hurt you, Jason. It's long overdue, but—"

"But you're not sorry you left?"

"I had to leave. For me."

He nodded, looking a little sad. "I hope you found whatever it was you needed. I hope it was worth what you gave up to get it. 'Night, Dori."

Chapter Two

Jason didn't ask her out again, even though she'd been convinced it had been on his mind when he'd first come over. He would probably never ask her out again, now that he knew the truth about her. He just gave her the wisdom of his sound advice and left her with an unanswerable question niggling and gnawing at her brain.

Had she found whatever it was she had needed in New York? And had it been worth what she had given up?

She hadn't thought she'd given up anything, beyond a summer fling with a great guy and a part-time job with her beloved uncle. But now she wondered. Could it have been more? What was Jason thinking about their relationship back then? That it could be something…more? How could she weigh what she had given up when he'd never told her what that might be?

She knew what she had found in leaving. She'd found the freedom to practice her religion. A handful of other women to practice it with. A succession of willing teachers, each a master of some occult discipline; the cards, the runes, healing, meditation. She'd studied and learned and taught. Become a master in her own right. A leader of the community. A true High Priestess of the Craft.

And while she was at it, she'd worked her way up through the ranks at Mason-Walcott Publishing. First as an editorial assistant, then an associate editor, full editor, senior editor and, finally, as editorial executive director, with a clear path ahead to publisher. She'd been out and open about who she was at work, at home. Everywhere she went. She'd become the most in-your-face Wiccan she knew, with a Spiral Goddess on her desk and a huge pentacle hanging from a chain around her neck—to match the smaller ones on her ears, to match the middle-sized ones on her fingers.

Until Beckenridge bought the company. Beckenridge—publisher of inspirational novels and Christian self-help books and right-wing political commentaries. They didn't need an openly Pagan left-wing liberal giving them editorial input. Even she couldn't argue with that. It would make as much sense as hiring a vegetarian to edit books about butchering cattle and packaging the meat. It was ludicrous. She understood the new owner's decision, in hindsight.

What she didn't understand was why it had to happen. It was as if the Goddess were playing some great cosmic joke on her. And now all that she'd learned and done and become seemed to mean nothing at all.

Nothing. She was back where she'd begun.

Sighing, she turned from the window, headed back into the living room and flipped on the television.

"And the stars are going to be beautiful tonight!"

Dori stopped in her tracks, the remote in her hand, as she stared at the TV screen. The weather girl kept on talking, pointing to a map, discussing warmer-than-average temperatures that might be good right now, though they could be ushering in some serious weather later on. But those first words….

She flashed back to the old woman who'd passed the parking lot when Dori had been leaving the diner tonight. She'd said the same exact words.

Drawing a breath, heaving a sigh, Dori glanced up at the Star Goddess hanging on the wall. Then she went to the window and looked outside.

The stars were appearing in the sky already. How long had it been since she'd spent any time outdoors, in nature, or with her own spirituality? How long?

She'd given up. Why bother? It hadn't done her a bit of good. She'd lost everything. Every penny. She'd had to let the apartment go, liquidate her investments at a crushing loss just to pay her bills. She'd lost her job. No one else would hire her for reasons that defied explanation. And within a few weeks it had become clear the beautiful British Witch, Sara, was after her position in the Pagan community. Before long she'd taken it, and all those women Dori had guided and trained and mentored turned to the newcomer, instead. And Dori refused to believe any of that had been due to her own withdrawal from them. She had lost everything.

And here she was, in the middle of nowhere with nothing and no one.

Maybe it was time—

Her thoughts were interrupted by the telephone ringing. She was still musing as she answered it.

"Ms. Doreen Stewart?"

"Yes?"

"Jen Stevenson, Turner Books. This is a courtesy call to let you know that the position you applied for last week has been filled. Your résumé looked very good, but in the end…"

The woman droned on, her message the same one Dori had already heard from ten other companies this week. They hadn't all given her the courtesy of a phone call. She'd been the one to make the call a few times. Others had sent letters. But the dozen résumés she'd just bragged to Jason about having submitted last week had generated eleven rejections. And she had no reason to believe the next would be any different.

She'd been a high-powered executive with a six-figure income, had had wealthy lovers if and when she wanted them, a Mercedes and a bright future.

Now she slept alone, waited tables and depended on tips from strangers in order to survive.

She had been a revered holy woman within her spiritual community. Now she didn't even wear her pentacle in public.

"What did I do to deserve this?" she asked the Star Goddess. And then she felt her heart darken. Why was she talking to a hunk of plaster and paint, anyway? What was the point? It wasn't real.

Nothing was real.

She yanked the plaque off the wall, carried it into the kitchen and dropped it into the garbage can. "I'm done with you. Do you hear? I'm finished. I'm not your priestess anymore."

THE WOMAN AT THE DESK leaned over Dori's application form, her eyes zipping along the lines from behind black horn-rims that looked great on her. Dark hair, short and fluffy. Black eyeliner and violet eyes. Pretty woman.

There were other desks in the little room at the town hall. Christmas songs jingled merrily from a radio on one of them, and white holiday lights, twined with silver garland, dipped and draped from the windows.

The woman looked up, smiling. "You're Gerald's niece, aren't you? The one who used to come out summers and help him run the Champ tours?"

"Mmm-hmm."

"Well, that makes more sense, then." She slid the application back across the table. "This isn't gonna do, hon."

"I'm sorry?" Dori wasn't sure she'd heard the woman correctly.

"Well, see this is a holiday *craft* fair. The tables we rent are for folks who want to sell arts and crafts. You know, quilts and afghans, homemade candles and centerpieces, floral arrangements, jewelry."

"I know what crafts are." Dori pushed her application back across the desk. "Reading tarot cards is a craft."

"That's all well and good, but it's not what this craft fair is about, Ms. Stewart. This isn't some New Age freak show."

"Well, then we're in luck, because I'm not some New Age freak. And there is nothing in the list of rules and conditions you have posted that precludes me telling fortunes at my table, so long as I pay the fee and am a resident of the town.

I'm paying the fee and I'm a resident of the town. So you can't deny me a table."

The woman picked up the application form this time and handed it to Dori. "*This* is not in keeping with the holiday spirit on which our event is based."

"Seeing the future on the night of the Solstice is one of the oldest holiday traditions around."

"According to whom?"

"Dickens, for one."

"Dickens who?"

"Charles Dickens, you illiterate twit."

"I…I…" The woman rose from her chair, her face reddening.

"It might interest you to know the police chief thought it was a great idea that I buy a table at this stupid little show." Yeah, the police chief she'd been thinking about all night. Having him in her kitchen had been like throwing a switch—powering up feelings she'd buried long ago. She'd dreamed about him!

Clearing her throat, she continued with her rant. "But if you insist on discrimination, I'll be happy to organize the noisiest, most un-Christmas-spirited protest march outside this event that you could ever hope to see!"

They stood facing each other over the desk. The entire room went silent as everyone stopped to stare.

Then a heavyset man came trundling over to the two of them, his cheeks as red as Saint Nick's. "Now, now, ladies, what seems to be the problem here?"

"This *woman* refuses to process my application for a table at the Holiday Craft Fair," Dori accused.

The man's eyebrows shot up and he turned to the woman. "Mrs. Redmond, is this true?"

"She wants to set up a Gypsy fortune-telling booth, Thomas."

"A tarot-reading booth," Dori corrected.

"It's ungodly. Un-Christian. We can't have it."

"Oh, now, Mrs. Redmond, it's not up to us to decide what's

godly or ungodly. This isn't a church-sponsored event. It's for the whole town."

"But…but—"

"Now, Miss uh…oh, say, you're Gerald Stewart's niece, back from New York City, aren't you?"

"Yes. I'm Doreen."

"Ah. Well, that explains a lot." He reached to take the application from the black-haired demoness with one hand and patted Dori's shoulder with the other. "I'm Thomas Kemp, town supervisor. Now I want you to rest assured that I'm going to handle your application personally, Ms. Stewart."

"Th-thank you."

"Did you leave your check?"

"She wouldn't take it." Dori pulled the folded check from her pocket. Seventy-five hard-earned dollars. But she would make several times that much if her table was busy.

"I'll call as soon as everything has been processed, Ms. Stewart," Thomas Kemp, town supervisor, said, taking the check from her hand. "Don't you worry about a thing. You have a nice day now."

Dori took only a moment to send the demon spawn a smug look of triumph before heading out the door. She felt good when she hit the streets. She hadn't had a spirited battle like that since trying to get a parade permit for Pagan Pride Day in Manhattan the first year they'd held it. Damn, she missed being in the thick of things.

She reminded herself that that part of her life was over. She wasn't backtracking; she wasn't "priestessing." She was just going to tell fortunes to make a few extra bucks.

She sucked in the crisp, fresh air as she strolled along the sidewalks. It was snowy in Crescent Cove. Snowy enough to make it as beautiful as a Currier and Ives Christmas card. It wasn't too cold, either. Cool enough so her breath made little steam puffs, but not quite enough to numb her fingers or burn her nose. She actually enjoyed her walk down the block and across the street to the diner to begin her day's work.

When Jason came in around noon, wearing his black

leather cop jacket, he sat at the counter, not at his usual table. She tried not to assume it was because he wanted to be closer to her, that maybe he'd changed his mind and was finally going to ask her out again.

She was still attracted to him. She'd been nursing a bad crush ever since turning him down the first time he'd asked, and she was beginning to detect those old feelings stirring to life deep down. He'd always been so good-looking, so attentive, and goodness knows, she hadn't found a better lover since. Even though it had been his first time, too.

It had been in the summer, in a secluded cove near the shore, the moon riding high. He'd brought a blanket, a bottle of wine and a condom. Everything needed for teenage romance. And it had been incredible.

She smiled at him for a change, unable to banish the memory from her mind, and brought him a cup of freshly brewed coffee. "On your lunch break?" she asked.

"You guessed it." He moved his gaze over her face in a way that made it clear he liked what he saw. He'd always been able to flatter without a word. But he hadn't looked at her like that in a long time. Why now? she wondered. Or was it all in her mind? Her inner thoughts manifesting in an overactive imagination?

"What'll you have?"

"Ham and cheese on potato bread. Side of fries." His voice stroked her nerve endings. She'd been better off when he'd basically ignored her existence.

"Mayo on the sandwich?"

"Let's go with the honey mustard today. And no cheese."

"Don't tell me you're dieting."

"Real men don't diet. This is strictly preventative."

She smiled and turned to shout the order through the window into the kitchen.

When she turned back, he said, "You sure seem cheerful today, Dori."

"Do I? Well, I suppose I have you to thank for that."

"Yeah? Why?"

She smiled and thought about last night's extremely pleasant dream. But she wasn't going to confess that. "I took your advice. Applied for a table at the craft fair."

He didn't smile back. He frowned, instead. "When did you do that?"

"This morning. Oh, it wasn't at all pleasant at first. Some little twit of a female—a Mrs. Redmond—tried to say I couldn't have a table, but then this Thomas something or other—"

"Kemp?"

"Yeah. He stepped in and said he'd handle it personally."

"I...see."

"What?" The bell rang behind her and she moved to pick up his sandwich, then brought it back to him.

"Uh, I'm going to move to a booth. Do you have a break coming up?"

"No."

"You do now. Join me."

"But—"

"Mort, cover the front," he called. "I need your waitress for five minutes. It's official."

Mort emerged from the kitchen, grouchy as always. She was old, tough and mean, dressed in a purple warm-up suit, with her silver hair in a long braid down her back.

"Five minutes," she snapped. "And it's coming out of your lunch hour, Dori."

Dori sent Jason a scowl that faltered as soon as he clutched her hand in his and drew her around the counter. He hadn't touched her in ten years, and the impact of it now was damn near stunning. That warm hand, so strong, closed around hers, holding it...she remembered it cupping her cheek, cradling her head while his mouth made love to hers.

What was wrong with her?

She was lonely, she realized. She'd been painfully lonely since coming back here—no, no, that wasn't quite right. She'd been lonely in New York, too.

She let him lead her across the diner, then slid into a booth across from him. He released her hand and she managed not to weep for the loss. "What?" she asked.

"Kemp. I had a visit from him this morning, and I was afraid it had something to do with you. Now I'm convinced of it."

She lifted her brows. "Go on."

"I know I told you we're not all ignorant in this town—and that's still true. We're not all ignorant. But that doesn't mean we're all enlightened, either. There are still a few narrow-minded idiots around, and I'm afraid Kemp is one of them."

"Jason, what on earth are you talking about?"

He sighed. "Kemp was poring over town statutes this morning. Old ones. Turns out there's still a law on the books making 'fortune telling' illegal."

"You've got to be kidding me."

He pursed his lips, shook his head slowly. "Nope, it's there. He showed it to me, asked me if it was enforceable."

She lifted her eyebrows. "Is it?"

"It's easily worked around, Dori. You're going to have to post a disclaimer in plain view on your table, stating that the readings are for entertainment only. A game, not a real prediction. You do that and his hands are tied."

She blinked twice. "So I'm supposed to put up a sign saying I'm a fraud."

He shrugged. "Only if you're charging for the readings. You could do them free…."

"That would defeat the whole purpose. I need to pad my income a little." She pursed her lips and sighed. "So I put up a sign that says I'm a fake. Well, what the hell, at this point I'm not sure it would be all that inaccurate, anyway." She pressed her palms to the table and stood up.

Jason stopped her, covering her hands with his. They were firm and strong and they sent all those old feelings spiraling up her arms and into the center of her chest. "What's that supposed to mean?" he asked.

She looked down at his hands on hers. He didn't move them. Experimentally, she turned hers over, palms up against his palms now. His eyes shot to hers, but he didn't take his hands away. The intimacy of his palms on hers almost brought tears to her eyes. "I don't know anymore," she told him.

"Sit back down, Dori," he said. His voice was rough, as if he needed to clear his throat.

"I have to work—"

"Not for another two minutes. Sit." He closed his hands on hers, squeezed.

Sighing, she sat down, because when he squeezed her hands her knees went weak.

Still holding her hands, he said, "After we talked last night, I did a little…snooping."

She lifted her head and her eyes as one. "Into what?"

"Into you. Into what you've been up to these past ten years in the big city."

Her eyes narrowed, and she tugged her hands from his, feeling as stunned as if he'd slapped her. "You investigated my past? Jason, why would you do something like that?"

Chapter Three

"Oh, come on, Dori, I was curious. You spring this Witch thing on me, tell me you've helped the police find missing people—I've never believed in any of that stuff. I had to know more."

"Why? It's not your business."

He shrugged. "Maybe I want to make it my business."

"You can't—"

"I contacted a friend of mine. He did some checking, faxed me some information. Turns out you've located seven missing people. Seven."

She shrugged. "So what?"

"I read the files. Figured it could be explained away. Coincidence. Lucky guesses. Inside info. But none of it fit. Then I spoke to Detective Hennessy."

Dori blinked at the familiar name. She'd worked with Mike Hennessy on every one of those cases. He'd never ridiculed her, had always taken her seriously.

"He convinced me—this thing you have, it's for real."

She moistened her lips, lifted her eyes to his. "Again I ask, so what?"

"So I'd like to know why you're suddenly questioning it. You just said labeling yourself a fraud wouldn't be inaccurate. So what happened?"

"What happened?" She lifted her hands, palms up. "Look around, Jason. Look at my life. I've lost everything." She lowered her head, shaking it slowly, feeling bereft, empty. "I don't know how many times I've thrown the cards, asking why this happened, what's the purpose. But I get nothing. No answers. I didn't see any of this coming, and I can't see when it's going to end. Or if it's going to end. I don't know what I did to deserve this, much less what I'm supposed to be doing about it."

"Maybe you're supposed to be doing…this."

"What? Waiting tables? Taking people on Champ tours?"

"Why not?"

She sighed. "You just don't understand."

"Sure I do, Dori. I think you're the one who's confused here. It's all about the journey, isn't it?"

She blinked and lifted her head.

"That's what you said in that letter you left me. 'It's all about the journey, and my journey is leading me somewhere else.'"

"I did not say anything like that," she told him. Not because it was true—she didn't remember what she'd written in that letter to Jason. But because it sounded far too wise for the girl she'd been when she'd set out to seek her fortune.

"You said something exactly like that." Jason yanked something from his pocket as he spoke. And then Dori felt the breath leave her lungs in a rush, because he was unfolding the old piece of pink paper, smoothing it flat on the table, pointing at the lines she had written. "It's right here."

She didn't say anything, and after a heartbeat of silence, he looked up at her slowly. She was staring at the letter, her eyes filling. "You kept it," she whispered.

He shrugged and lowered his head, quickly refolding the letter and tucking it back into his jacket pocket.

"All this time, you…you've been carrying that letter around with you like some kind of…"

"Memory," he said softly. "It's just a memory. That's all."

She met his eyes, not sure what to say.

"Maybe that part of your journey is done, Dori. You lived in a big city, you experienced big money, big success, learned whatever it was you were supposed to learn from all that.

Maybe this is a new phase for you. A new journey. Maybe you're not supposed to know why just yet. Maybe there isn't any why. Maybe it just is because it is. And maybe if you stop fighting it so hard, you could enjoy it a little."

She sat there staring at him. He might claim he hadn't changed, but he clearly had. "What have you been doing the past ten years, Jason, studying with a Tibetan monk?"

He shrugged. "You didn't lose as much as you think you did," he said. "You still have a home. You still have a car. You still have a job. Change your perception a little. I know you Wiccans are all into being in control of your own lives, but fate isn't gonna be cheated out of playing a role. Can't you take a page from another book? Let go and let Goddess or something?"

"Five minutes are up," Mort called. "C'mon, Dori, we have customers."

Dori got to her feet, though she felt her head spinning. Five minutes with a small-town cop, and suddenly she was questioning everything.

Everything.

"Here's a tip for you, Dori," he said. "At the craft fair, bring something to sell. Mark it up the same amount you usually charge for a reading, and give a free reading away with every purchase."

She frowned at him. "So I wouldn't be charging for the readings."

"And you wouldn't have to use the disclaimer." He gave her a wink, picked up his sandwich and dug in.

Tilting her head, she studied him. She had never seen this side of him before. Open-minded, accepting, even…spiritual, though she doubted he would call it that. "Thank you, Jason."

"My pleasure. Now, go. Mort's glaring at you."

She glanced at her employer, sighed and got back to work.

Jason finished his sandwich and left, but his words stayed with her all day. She *had* been fighting this; he was right about that. But since when did a small-town cop spout wisdom like a spiritual guru? It was as if he'd looked right inside her soul and diagnosed the problem. Was it possible she'd missed something so simple?

And God, he had kept her letter. She must have meant so much more to him than she had ever realized. And she'd walked away, left him with barely an explanation. He should hate her for that. But he didn't.

When her shift ended, she stepped out of the diner and into the cold air. Christmas carols wafted from every store and business she passed. Sister Krissie's Bar and Grill, the best restaurant in town, was filling up with hungry customers, and every time the door opened, strains from Manhein Steamroller wafted out into the streets. As she passed BK's Grocery, a stream of bundled children came out with foil-wrapped chocolate Santas in their mittened hands, as their harried mom tried to herd them toward the car while juggling grocery bags.

Dori hurried across the street and down the block to where she'd left her car. She swept off the snow, started up the engine, and sat behind the wheel rubbing her hands while it warmed up.

"A car is a car," she said softly, trying hard to see things from a new perspective, as Jason had suggested. And this wasn't a bad one. Only two years old, with a good heater and working AC, a radio and a CD player. It wasn't rusty and it ran well. It even had studded snow tires and front-wheel drive.

She didn't *want* just a car, though. She *wanted* her Mercedes.

She sighed, pulled into the road and began the drive back to her cabin, only to find that the road out of town was blocked by road crews hoisting holiday lights. Damn. A small Detour sign pointed left onto Evergreen. Dori turned, and realized she'd rarely been on this side street. It meandered among small homes and a handful of shops.

Then out of the blue, her car—which she was working very hard on believing was as good as a Mercedes—spit and sputtered and quit.

"No." She turned the wheel, coasting to a spot near the curb, then put it in Park and tried twisting the key. Nothing. Dead. And no onboard assistance button to push for help. No cell phone. She'd let it go, to eliminate the extra bill.

"Damn." Her mood—which had been improving—took a nosedive. She wrenched open the door, got out and looked around.

The building in front of her, nestled on the corner of Evergreen and Hope streets, looked for all the world, to be a haven. White lights in the windows surrounded the words Burning Bright. The window display had candles of every imaginable shape and color. And the sign on the door read Open.

Well, she was going to have to use a phone somewhere. Call a garage. A tow truck. Something.

She opened the door, and a bell jingled as she walked inside.

And then she just paused and breathed. The place smelled of sandalwood incense, and dragon's blood oil, and the hot melted-wax smell that always transported her. It smelled like a sacred circle. It smelled like her religion and her craft. It smelled like magic, and the scents hit her hard, like a fist to the gut. Tears burned in her eyes and she wasn't sure why.

"Well, hello, dear."

Dori looked up, startled because she had thought the place empty. But it wasn't empty at all. A woman stood there, an old women with a face that was craggy and lined yet somehow beautiful. Her eyes were huge and ebony, and her jet-black hair was streaked with vivid white and hanging loose, halfway down her back. She wore a black caftan, printed with rich gold swirls, that reached to the floor, long dangling earrings that were silver spirals, and a strand of huge beads around her neck, amber and jet.

Amber and jet!

In her hand, she held a broomstick.

Dori stared, stunned to her bones. The image of the Dark Goddess, the Crone, stood before her, so vivid and so real that she bowed her head and very nearly fell to her knees. Those black eyes sparkled, and the Crone said, "I've been waiting for you."

Chapter Four

"My goodness, child, don't look so frightened."

The Crone set her broomstick aside and brushed her hands against each other. "I'm Helen. This is my candle shop. Every candle, handmade."

"He-Helen?" Not Hecate or Holda or—but she'd said she was waiting for her.

"I saw you sitting in the car out front," the old woman said as if reading her thoughts. "I was wondering when you'd get around to coming inside to get warm." She smiled and offered her hand.

Dori took it, surprised that it was warm and entirely human. "I'm Dori," she said.

"Good to meet you, dear. My but you still seem rather distraught. Is anything wrong?"

Everything was wrong. Including the fact that she thought she'd just had a visit from the Dark Goddess Herself. "I…my car broke down. Do you have a telephone I could use?"

"Of course." She reached for the broom again, bent to the dustpan Dori hadn't seen before and swept up a nearly invisible pile of dirt. "I'll be right back with the phone. Feel free to browse around. You never know, you might find just what you need—even if you didn't know you needed it!"

With another smile, she carried her dustpan away through the shelves and shelves of candles. She jingled when she walked, and Dori glimpsed bracelets adorning her wrists and her ankles. Dori blinked and tried to give herself a mental shake. But it didn't work. She felt the way she did when she was in an altered state: very relaxed and open, her heart and pulse thudding slowly, her body heavy, her vision slightly out of focus. Part of it was this place; she knew that. The smells, the candle glow—these were triggers that told her body it was time for spiritual practice, for ritual, for magic. But there was something more about this place that was working on her.

She'd spent a lot of time in this town, yet she didn't remember a candle shop here. She'd been back for nearly a year, and never heard of or seen it.

Every shelf held candles and holders and snuffers. Tapers and pillars glowed from every windowsill and stand.

When Helen returned, she wasn't carrying a phone but a candle, the most unusual candle Dori had ever seen. It was as if three strips of wax—silver, gold and white—had been braided together to form a single piece. "I have something for you," she said.

Dori looked at the candle the old woman held out. "It's the most beautiful candle I've ever seen," she said. "But I couldn't…"

"It's a special candle. Waiting for just the right person to come and claim it. I think you're that person, Dori."

Dori smiled, lowering her head. "I couldn't possibly—"

"Why not? Not celebrating the Solstice this year?"

Dori looked at her sharply. How could she know?

"You see, child, the silver is for the year that's about to pass." As she spoke, she stroked the silver parts with a long, gnarled finger. "And the gold is for the new one, the one about to begin. And the white is the bond that connects all things, every ending and every beginning, every death and every birth. It's the perfect candle for you, especially at this time of year. Here, smell."

She held it closer, and Dori inhaled its scent. Hazelnuts and cedar and cinnamon. She closed her eyes.

"Take it, child. There's a little magic in this candle. And it's meant for you, I'm sure of it."

Opening her eyes, no longer sure this wasn't a visitation from the Goddess after all, Dori clasped the candle in her hands. How could she have doubted, turned her back on her own faith? she wondered. Surely this was proof…this was a sign…this was—

"That'll be five-ninety-five, with the tax."

Dori's eyes popped open wider. "Huh?"

"Now, where did I put that phone?" the woman said, turning again in a slow circle and searching blankly around the shop. "Maybe it's in the back."

"I'll just try the car again," Dori said quickly. If she let the woman out of her sight, she'd no doubt find something else to force her to buy. Visitation from the Goddess, hell. Helen was sly and ultra-observant. Nothing more. Dori dipped a hand into her jeans pocket, even though she knew there was no money in there, and came out with a five and a one. She must have shoved some tips into her jeans and forgotten about them, she thought, and handed the cash to the woman. "Thank you, Helen."

"You're welcome, Doreen. Don't stay away so long next time."

Dori was out the door before she processed any of that. She'd never told the woman her name was Doreen. She'd said Dori, not Doreen. And what did that "Don't stay away so long next time" bit mean? She looked at the candle in her hand. Its scent teased her senses, and called out to her like a lover calling her home.

She got into the car, wondering which place on this street would be a better bet for finding a phone, and twisted the key just for kicks.

The car started without a sputter, and ran perfectly all the way home.

JASON RETURNED to his office, glanced at his desk and frowned. "Uh, hey, Sheila?"

The receptionist peered in through the open door.

"There was a folder here, just some uh…Internet research I was doing."

"Oh, you mean all that stuff about Doreen Stewart being a Witch?"

He bit his lip to keep from swearing.

"Who'd have guessed, huh?"

"Sheila, that stuff was private."

Her smile faded. "It was?"

"Where is it?"

"I took the folder to my desk when I gathered up the others. I was just filing stuff, Jason, I didn't mean to…" She licked her lips, lowered her head.

"What happened to it?"

"Some of the guys saw me reading through it."

"Which guys?"

"Joey, Frank…and Mr. Kemp, he was here."

Jason closed his eyes.

"I tucked it in my desk drawer. But…well, if it was supposed to be a secret, Jason, I'm afraid it's not anymore."

"Kemp knows."

She nodded.

"Hell, Sheila." He lowered his head, shaking it slowly. Now what? He sighed. "Get me Kemp on the phone."

"I'm really sorry, Jason."

"Yeah. My fault. I shouldn't have left it lying around."

He went to his desk when she left, waiting for the phone to ring, picked it up. "Kemp?"

"Jason. Wanted to call you anyway, thank you for that research you did on the Stewart woman."

"That research was not meant to be public knowledge."

"No? Well, kind of late now."

"What did you do, rent a billboard?"

"Tipped off the local press. Reverend Mackey, too. Figured he ought to be aware of what was brewing. Get it? Brewing? Witch?" His hearty chuckle made Jason's stomach knot up.

"Got it. Not smiling. This is her personal business, Kemp. What earthly good is it going to do to spread it all over town?"

"Might show her who she's dealing with. We're a God-

fearing town, Jason. We don't need her kind coming in trying to corrupt the youth."

"Corrupt the—Jesus, Kemp, she's a decent woman."

"Best brush up on your scriptures, Jason. And trust me, law
or no law, there's no way in hell she's getting a table at our
Christmas Craft Fair."

"Holiday Craft Fair," Jason corrected. "Remember you
changed the name for the sake of political correctness?"

"Name or no name, it's the Christmas Craft Fair and everyone in this town knows it. That's the way it's always been, and
that's the way it will continue to be. Period." The decisive
click told him when Kemp had hung up.

Jason sighed, unable to argue with dead air. Now he'd
messed things up thoroughly. Dori was going to be furious.
This was the last thing she wanted. He hit the flash button,
got a dial tone, and reached to the keypad to punch in her number—but then he thought better of it.

This kind of news ought to be delivered in person.

Or maybe it was just that he wanted to see her again. God,
he wanted to see her again. When he'd touched her today in
the diner, held her hands, it had been like…like taking his first
breath after too long under water. He hadn't breathed like that
in ten years. She was his air. He needed her. But now…now
he'd probably blown any chance he'd ever had.

DORI WALKED into Uncle Gerald's cabin and shucked her winter clothes. Then she took the candle from the little bag in
which the mysterious old woman had packed it. A year ago,
she wouldn't even have questioned the significance of the encounter. A year ago, everything in her life had made sense.
Everything mundane had spiritual implications and everything spiritual affected the mundane. Her life had been inte-
grated, or she thought it had been.

But she'd changed her mind about all of that. Decided
she'd been deluded. There was no such thing as magic, or if
there was, it had abandoned her. Just as the Goddess had.

So why was she questioning this now? Why was some

doubting voice in her mind telling her it had all been more than just a coincidence? The detour, the car breaking down, the woman looking the way she did, the shop that had never been there before, the candle.

Had she really stopped believing in magic? Or had she only told herself she had?

Sighing, she went into the living room, to the mantel. The glass-enclosed candle holder there resembled a lantern and had always been her favorite because she could use it indoors or out. But a long time had gone by since she'd done either. It held a long since burned-out stump. She swallowed, feeling guilty.

She lifted off the glass chimney and plucked the old stump free. Then she carefully placed the new candle in its place and lowered the glass over it again. She spent a moment, staring at it, reviewing the feelings that had rushed over her when the old woman had first appeared in front of her. She hadn't felt that way in a long time—that surge of certainty that she was in the presence of the Divine. Not really. And now that she really thought about it, her spirituality seemed to have been flagging long before she lost her job and all her money.

She went to the wastebasket and looked down at the Goddess sculpture that lay, face up, atop a banana peel and some coffee grounds.

Someone knocked. She lifted her head and went to the door. Why did her heart jump just a little when she saw that it was Jason? Okay, so she was attracted to him. What woman wouldn't be? But did she have to react like a teenager with her first crush?

Yes. Because she *felt* like a teenager with her first crush. Hell, he had *been* her first crush.

"You came back," she said, and in spite of her best efforts, her voice sounded breathless.

"You didn't think I would?" He was doing that thing with his eyes, again. Looking at her in that way he had. He focused on her toes first and then her face.

She shrugged. "No, I really didn't."

Jason sighed. "I'm afraid you're not gonna be glad I did. And you can't believe how sorry I am to say so." He stomped the snow off his boots and walked inside. He was avoiding her eyes.

She pursed her lips. "So this isn't a social call?"

"Not really." He was in the process of prying off his boots as he said it, but he stopped and looked up quickly, as if to gauge her reaction to that. "Did you want it to be?"

She shrugged, and avoided his searching look. She wasn't surprised. His learning the truth about her might have cooled any notion he might have had about starting things up again with her. He might be open-minded, but being open-minded and dating a Witch were pretty different things.

"I owe you an apology, Dori."

"Don't be stupid, Jason. I'm the one who walked away. You don't owe me a thing."

He licked his lips, shrugged out of his coat and draped it on a hook inside the door, next to Uncle Gerald's old hurricane lamp. Then he stepped away from the snowy entry rug, leaving his boots behind. "I'm not talking about what happened ten years ago, honey. I'm talking about what I did today."

Dori frowned at him. His tone was so gentle it frightened her.

"I mean, not that I don't *want* to talk about our past—I do. I'd love it, it's just—"

"What did you do today that requires an apology?"

He lowered his head, walked across the kitchen to the stove and turned on a burner. Picking up the teakettle, he gave it a shake, heard enough splashing to satisfy him and set it on the burner. He glanced over his shoulder at her. She was standing in the doorway between the little kitchen and little living room, leaning against one side, watching him, arms crossed over her chest.

"You have cocoa?"

"It's in the second canister."

He nodded and took out a couple of packets of hot cocoa mix, snatched two mugs from the wooden mug tree on the counter and emptied the packets into them.

"Spoons?" he asked.

"Middle drawer. What is it you came to apologize for, Jason?"

He located the spoons, removed two of them. Then he wadded up the empty cocoa packets and spotted the wastebasket. He went to toss them in, but paused as a deep frown etched itself between his eyebrows. "What's this?"

"It's nothing. Jason, don't—"

Too late. He bent and snatched the sculpture out, rising with it and brushing coffee grounds off it. He held it up, staring at the nude female form standing atop the crescent moon.

"Looks old," he said.

"The figure is a reproduction."

"Of?"

She sighed. "The Goddess. It's one of the older images of her, known as the Nile Goddess, I believe. The modern artist added the moon and the starry backdrop."

He lifted his eyes to hers. "So what's she doing in the garbage?"

"I don't know." She lowered her head. "I don't know anything anymore." That tears sprang into her eyes angered her, but she managed to keep them hidden. She heard water running, and when she looked up again, he was rinsing the sculpture clean, holding it almost reverently, his hands sliding over her to brush the coffee grounds away. Dori brought him a towel from the rack. He took it from her and patted the figure dry.

"What happened, Dori? You decide to stop believing in magic?"

She pursed her lips. "I decided to. I tried to. But I don't think it took."

He smiled. "Let's hang her back up, hmm?"

"Not yet. I should do a cleansing first."

He frowned, a little furrow in his brow that made her want to smooth it away with her finger—or maybe her lips.

"I…thought that's what I just did," he said.

She smiled. "A ritual cleansing. It's a little different."

"Will you show me?"

"Oh, come on, Jason. You aren't really interested in seeing—"

"I really am."

He sounded so sincere. The teakettle whistled. Dori found herself conceding. "All right. If you're sure." He nodded. "You make the cocoa, then," she said. "And bring a bowl of snow from outside. And I'll get the room ready."

Chapter Five

The minuscule amount of reading Jason had done since learning the truth about Dori didn't prepare him at all.

She had surrounded the room with candles, and converted her coffee table into an altar by draping a white cloth over it. It held ordinary items. A wineglass with some of the snow in it, rapidly melting. A bowl with something in it that appeared to be sugar or salt. A stick of incense. A small candle. An old iron cauldron in the center.

When he entered the room, he found her kneeling in front of the coffee table, holding her hands over each item, whispering words too softly for him to hear. He stood in rapt silence, watching as she lit the incense, the candle. She sprinkled some of the white stuff into the water and lifted the glass high, bowing her head. Finally, she set the glass down and rose to her feet.

"I used to have the prettiest tools," she said. "My athame—that's a ritual dagger—had a sterling blade and a hand-carved onyx handle. My wand was tipped in the biggest quartz crystal you ever saw. My cauldron was a replica of the Gundestrup artifact."

"I don't know what that is," he admitted.

"Oh, it was a beautiful piece. Found in a peat bog in Denmark. It dates back to around one hundred BCE. It was Celtic, maybe used by the Druids in their rites, and has images of more than a dozen gods and goddesses engraved on its sides."

"Sounds like something special."

"It was."

"What happened to all those…tools?" he asked.

She looked at him and he thought her eyes were sad. "Had to sell them. Even the crystal ball."

"When you were first learning all of this, did you have fancy gadgets then?"

She shook her head. "No."

"But you managed fine without them, huh?"

She met his eyes. "Yeah. I did. I used to tell my students, 'It's not about the tools. It's about you.' Come here."

He came closer. She reached to the table and picked up the wineglass. "The cup is the female. The womb of life. And the dagger is the male. The phallus. To bring our rituals to life, we lower the dagger into the cup. The combination of male and female—force and form—creates the spark of life. The source of all things, and magic."

"That's kind of sacred and sexy at the same time."

"Sex is sacred in the craft. We call this ritual the Symbolic Great Rite."

He was liking this side of her. Deep and intimate. Mystical and wonderful. "That would imply there's a…nonsymbolic version?"

She smiled mysteriously at him. "I don't have my dagger anymore. Will you help me?"

He nodded, all but holding his breath wondering what she was going to do next. She scooped some of her water into her palms and held them cupped loosely. "My hands can be the womb."

"I get it." He lifted his own hand. "Mine can be the phallus." He slid his fingers between her hands, over her skin, sinking them into the water in her palms. She closed her eyes and he thought she shivered. For melted snow, the water she cupped seemed awfully warm. Her hands felt downright hot. And he was burning up.

He withdrew his fingers slowly. She opened her eyes, and they glistened. Then she held her palms over the wineglass to release the water back into it. "You're a natural," she told him.

It had *felt* natural, he thought. About as natural as pulling her into his arms and kissing her senseless would feel.

But he didn't do that. Instead, he stood quietly watching as she walked around the room. She moved in a circle, carrying the water with her. Then she did it again, carrying the smoking incense and wafting it around the room. The third time, she lifted the candle. When she finished, she moved back to the altar and picked up the Goddess sculpture. She held it over the smoking censer, so the spirals of smoke wafted around it.

"I cleanse and consecrate you by the powers of Air, emblem of the Goddess."

She moved the sculpture over the flame of the candle. "By the powers of Fire, I burn away all negativity."

Then she dipped her fingers into the water and sprinkled the sculpture. "All malignancy I wash away by the powers of Water."

She picked up the salt—he was sure it was salt now that he'd tasted it on his fingers—and dusted the sculpture with it. "By the powers of Earth, be you cleansed, purified."

She lowered the sculpture into the cauldron, then held her hands over it. "By the power of Spirit I…" And there she faltered. "I…I'm sorry."

Frowning, Jason moved closer to her.

She dropped to her knees, her hands still over the cauldron; trembling now, she said, "I'm so sorry. I remove every negative emotion I sent to you. I cleanse you of my anger. Of my fears. Of my doubts. I…"

Tears slid silently down her cheeks. This was a powerful thing that was happening here, he thought. More powerful, maybe, than even Dori realized.

Jason lowered himself to his knees behind her. He folded his arms around her, stretching them out alongside her arms, his hands sliding over hers above the cauldron. His fingers extended the length of hers, his thumbs bending around to her palms.

"I cleanse myself in you," she whispered. "Goddess, take

this darkness from my soul. I so want to live in the light again." Her head bowed, and she cried softly.

Moved beyond words, and unsure what to do, Jason felt her relax back against him as she wept. He wrapped her in his arms, held her there. Then, without knowing why, he reached for the incense. He brought it close to her and used his hand to waft the smoke over her. He couldn't quite remember her words. "Cleansed by Air," he said softly. "Let it blow away the darkness, Dori."

He saw her head rise, her brows bend. Sitting on the floor with her legs folded under her, she slid around to face him, searching his eyes. He set the incense down and picked up the candle, moved it under her chin, up and around her body. "Cleansed by Fire, everything bad is burned away."

She closed her eyes, and more tears spilled over. Her shoulders trembled. He put the candle down, dipped his fingers into the water, then drew them out, dripping, to her face and wiped the hot tears from her cheeks. "Cleansed by water, everything sad is washed away."

Then he reached for the bowl of salt, gathered a bit in his palm. "Cleansed by…" He hesitated. "Salt?"

"Earth," she told him.

"Right. Earth. Cleansed by Earth—solid, dependable Earth—everything that hurt you in the past is gone. And you're starting over, right here, tonight." He grinned as he sprinkled some of the salt over her head.

"You're amazing, Jason."

"Yeah, we'll get to that." He sat down, glad to see the tears had stopped welling up in her eyes. "Finish this first."

She nodded, and then she got to her knees again to remove the sculpture from the cauldron and bring it to her lips. She whispered thanks to the powers of the Universe, and then walked around her circle, in the opposite direction this time. When she finished, she knelt and pressed her palms to the floor, eyes closed, and sat silent for a moment.

Finally, with a deep breath, she lifted her head, opened her eyes. "It's done."

"It was something," he said. "No eye of newt or testicles of a righteous man."

She smiled slowly. "I'm saving those things for your second ritual."

"Right."

Her smile died. "What you did for me, that was—"

"That was nothing. I haven't got a clue what I'm doing. I'm not even sure what made me try."

"It was perfect. It was…wonderful." She leaned closer and pressed her lips softly against his, for just a moment.

Jason thought his insides were going to shake themselves apart. Somewhere deep down a little voice was warning him not to let himself fall too hard, too fast. She could easily walk away and destroy him again.

"Thank you for that, Jason."

He drew a deep breath. "It was the least I could do." He reached for the cooling cocoa and handed it to her, just to put some distance and perspective between them. Otherwise, he was going to sweep her into his arms and—

Best not to think about that.

"Are you feeling better?"

She nodded. "A little."

And now he had to tell her what he had come here to tell her. "I hate to bring you down," he said. "I can't believe how much I hate it. I felt like we…oh, hell." He closed his eyes.

"Jason, what's wrong?"

"I have to be honest with you, Dori." He opened his eyes, gazed into hers. "That research I did on your background?"

"Yeah." She looked worried now.

"The secretary found it on my desk and took it to hers to file it. She was looking through it, and some other people read over her shoulder. Including the good town supervisor, Thomas Kemp."

She blinked. "You mean everyone in the police department knows I'm a Witch?"

"Yeah. And pretty soon everyone else in town will, too. Kemp called the newspaper, and one of our local ministers,

Reverend Mackey." He prayed she wouldn't hate him for this. "I'm sorry, Dori. I'm so sorry. I never meant to spread your secret like this. I…if I could undo it…"

"But you can't. Oh, Jason, what's going to happen now?"

"I don't know," he said. "I don't believe people are as narrow-minded as you think they are. Give Crescent Cove some credit. Have a little faith."

She narrowed her eyes. "It's a good thing you're telling me this today and not yesterday."

"Yeah? Why?"

"'Cause yesterday I didn't think I had any faith left."

He sighed in relief. She hadn't thrown him out. Yet. And if she was feeling she had a little faith left after all, then hope wasn't lost. He reached for the sculpture they had just cleansed. "Can I hang her up for you?"

"You'd better. I'm going to need her."

So he hung the plaster image up for her. And he thought about kissing her before he left, but in the end, he didn't. In fact, as she stood there at the door, saying good-night, it was all he could do not to. But the night had been an emotional one for her. He didn't want to scare her off or send her into a panic, much less convince her that his motives were less than decent. And he was scared; he was still damn scared that the minute he let himself fall head over heels, she'd get the job offer she'd been waiting for and walk out on him again.

Because despite all that had happened—she still hadn't told him she wanted to stay. And damn, he couldn't risk his heart until she did. And then that little voice inside him asked him if he really believed it wasn't already too late.

THE TELEPHONE WAS RINGING by the time Jason left, and Dori picked it up with a sigh.

"Doreen Stewart?"

"Yes."

"This is Grace Merrill from the *Crescent Cove Chronicle.* I'm doing a story about you and I was wondering—"

"I don't want a story done about me."

There was a brief moment of silence. "You don't understand. You see, I'm a—"

"This is my private business here, and I don't want it spread all over the pages—"

"Some of it's a matter of public record, Ms. Stewart."

"Maybe I can't stop you then, but I'm certainly not about to help you." She hung up the phone, feeling just a bit guilty for having been mean. The reporter had seemed respectful enough, been decent on the phone. But she did not want this. And she knew the press well enough to know anything she said could be twisted around and used against her.

She cleaned up the living room, skipped dinner because her stomach was roiling, and went to bed early. But she barely slept. That morning paper might very well have the entire town talking and she did not want to deal with the gossip.

But she didn't think she had much choice.

All those worries paled in comparison, though, to the big issue on her mind. And that was—she thought she just might be falling in love with Jason Farrar. All over again.

THE NEWSPAPERS WERE STACKED on the end of the counter for the customers, just as they were every morning, when Dori went in to work. She avoided looking at them as she tied on her apron, put on three pots of coffee, filled the sugar dispensers and cream pitchers and set them along the counters and on the tables.

The bells over the door jangled, and jangled again as the morning crowd came in. "'Morning, Dori. Got my coffee ready?"

"'Morning, Sam," she said, not meeting the old fellow's eyes, afraid of what she might see there. Instead, she filled four foam coffee cups, added fixings, snapped on the lids and stuck them into a cardboard carrier. "Here you go. Four large, two cream no sugar, one sugar no cream, one black. Three-fifty."

He dropped a five on the counter. "Keep the change, hon. Have a good one."

She looked up only as the man took his standing order and

headed for the door. That was odd. He always read the paper before he came in, always knew about the day's news.

Bill tapped his cup on the counter. "Hey, Dori, you gonna top this up with coffee, or just wiggle your nose?"

She frowned at him.

He grinned and sent her a wink. "Hell, I've done it now. I'll be a toad before the day's out."

She carried the coffeepot over and refilled his cup. "You were a toad to begin with, Bill."

"Yeah, but I'm still your favorite customer," he said.

Then he went right back to work on his breakfast. Nothing negative, nothing dark. He didn't seem the least bit upset about the newspaper's revelations.

A throat cleared. She glanced up and saw the Reverend Mackey sitting at the counter. Great. He never came in here. Pasting a smile on her face, she walked up, grabbing a heavy mug and bringing the coffeepot. "Coffee, Reverend?"

"You bet," he said. "I read your article in the paper this morning."

"Wasn't my article," she said as she poured. "I didn't really want my private life plastered all over the front page, but I didn't have much choice in the matter."

"Really?"

"Do you need a menu? Breakfast, or just coffee?"

"No, no breakfast. Mainly, I came in to talk to you."

She met his eyes. They were kind and blue. He had a blond crew cut and looked more like a marine than a minister. "Please tell me you're not here to try to convert me."

His brows went up high. "I imagine you're expecting that. Might get it, too, from some folks, including some clergy. Nasty mail, phone calls, a protester or two. Are you ready for all of that, Dori?"

"I guess I'll have to be."

He nodded, sighed. "I assumed you could handle it. You handled New York, after all. Besides, you're clergy, according to the newspaper. Quite highly placed clergy at that."

She stared at him, half expecting some kind of a trick. He

reached a hand to hers, and she realized she was still pouring his coffee and damn close to flooding the cup. She stopped and took the pot back to the burner. "I used to be considered an elder," she said. "But it's hard to be highly placed when you're one of a kind."

He smiled slowly. "That's why you were against the article? You think you're the only Wiccan in town?"

She lifted her brows. "I am."

"No, Dori, you're not. You might be the only Wiccan clergy in town, though. Which is why I'm rather glad that article ran. There are people here who need you. Now, I admit I'd prefer they come to me, but my beliefs don't fulfill the needs of every person in Crescent Cove, and I've learned to accept that and recognize there's more than one way to find God."

"I can hardly believe what I'm hearing," she whispered.

"Aha!" he said, and pointed at her. "You, of all people, giving in to preconceived notions and expecting me to come in here threatening you with eternal damnation for your beliefs just because I'm a Christian minister?"

"You're right," she said. "Shame on me."

"It takes all kinds to make a world, Dori. Now, here. Take this."

She picked up what he slid across the counter to her. A card with his name, address, phone number. She flipped it and saw a date and time scrawled on the back. "What's this?"

"Next meeting of the Crescent Cove Interfaith Council. Every pastor, priest and rabbi in town is a member." He gave her a wink. "You'll be our first priestess."

"You really think they'll let me in?"

"I'm the president and founder. If I let you in, they'll let you in. Vermont is a very open-minded state. Now, don't be offended if some are hesitant. They won't be once you explain the difference between what your faith really teaches and the ever-popular misconceptions."

"You say that as if you already know the differences."

"That's because I do. A man in my position can't afford to

be ignorant or uninformed." He tapped the card in her hand. "We meet in the rec center out by the lake. Neutral ground."

"That's walking distance from my place."

"Perfect," he said. "Be there, okay?"

"Okay."

He slugged down his coffee and reached for his wallet.

She held up a hand. "It's on the house, Reverend Mackey."

"Thanks, Lady Doreen."

He headed out, and she felt herself smiling. It wasn't the end of the world after all. People were not looking at her as if she'd grown another head. Maybe she'd underestimated the open-mindedness of Crescent Cove. Or overestimated the shock value of being Wiccan. Just because she'd run into a couple of narrow-minded bigots didn't mean the whole town was that way. After all, there were Wiccans in every town these days. Why shouldn't it begin being accepted as just another religion?

As she was serving a platter of sausage and eggs, Jason walked in and slid into a booth. She filled a fresh coffee mug and carried it to his table.

"Did you read it?" he asked.

She shook her head. "No. My day got off to a pleasant start and I don't want anything to ruin it."

"It won't ruin it, hon. It's good. Approaches the entire story from the angle of you having helped solve those seven missing-persons cases in New York, before giving up your high-powered job to move back home to Crescent Cove." He laid a paper on the table, opened to the story. "Here."

She picked it up, glancing nervously over her shoulder for any sign of her boss's glower. There was a picture of her—she recognized it as one that had been used in a piece about her from a New Age magazine. The headline read: Hometown Heroine Back Where She Belongs. The story talked about her success in the big city, quoting other articles at length and crediting her with using her "uncanny skills" to help the police locate missing persons. It added that she was a High Priestess, elder and legal clergy of the Wiccan faith. And that was the only mention of her religion.

She sighed in relief.

"Not as bad as you thought, huh?" Jason asked.

"No. It's not bad at all."

"I'm relieved."

"Me, too."

He met her eyes. He wanted to say something more, but he didn't. She so longed for him to tell her he was feeling the same things she was. She could see the attraction in his eyes every time he looked at her. She could feel it every time he touched her. Why was he holding back?

Could it be that he was liberal enough to understand Witchcraft but still unwilling to get involved with a Witch? She searched his eyes, hoping—waiting.

"I should go," he said. "I just wanted to make sure you saw it. And that you were okay. No one's given you any trouble, have they?"

"No. None at all."

"Good. Call if you need me."

But I do need you, she thought. *I need you right now, to end this aching loneliness. I'm tired of it. Goddess, I can't stand it much longer.*

"Dori?" he asked.

She'd lapsed into staring at him again. "I'll call if I need you," she promised. "Thanks, Jason."

He smiled a little. "See what I told you, Dori? Crescent Cove isn't a bad place at all. Might even be worth sticking around, don't you think?"

She frowned at him, but he left before she could analyze his words or the message that she sensed hiding beneath them.

Chapter Six

She was still mulling over every word Jason had said, trying to read between the lines, beyond the words, when she walked to the parking lot to find that for once, her car didn't require brushing off. No snow today. However, the lack of snow gave her a clear view of the blotch of bright red splattered across her windshield. It looked like paint.

"No." She didn't want this.

"Now, that's a real shame," a voice said.

Turning, Dori saw the old woman from that strange little candle shop, standing on the sidewalk, staring at the car and shaking her head. She wore a cloak-style coat, with fur that lined its edges and its hood, and had a crooked walking stick in one hand.

"Still," she said, "I suppose it's also a good sign."

"In what way?" Dori asked. Her words sounded clipped. She was angry, but she reminded herself she was not angry at Helen from Burning Bright, but at the idiot who had done this. And at Jason for exposing her secret and at this town in general.

"Well, when we met the other night I had the distinct impression you'd lost your faith."

"So?"

"So you must have found it again. True faith—of any sort— tends to bring tests, trials. And this seems like one to me."

Dori narrowed her eyes on the old woman. "My life has been nothing but a series of tests and trials for the past year," she grumbled.

"Really? And have you passed them?"

She blinked, because the words had hit her right between the eyes. How had she responded to the tests of the past year? By complaining, whining, fighting against her fate and turning her back on her calling, her religion and her Goddess.

"I read about you in the paper today," she said. "Tell me, what's the significance of that star?" As she said it she pointed to the blotch on Dori's vehicle.

Dori frowned and examined the stain again—seeing this time that the way the paint had landed formed a rough shape of an inverted pentagram. "I hadn't even noticed…the five points represent the five elements—Earth, Air, Fire, Water and Spirit," she said. "Spirit is usually on top. We often put a circle around it, to symbolize the elements all being connected, all part of the greater whole."

"I see. And inverted, like it is here? Does that have any significance?"

She sighed. "The Satanists have adopted it, made it so well-known that Wiccans in the U.S. rarely use it anymore. But to us it represents the journey of the Second Degree. For most Wiccans it's a time of…."

The old woman remained there, silver brows raised, waiting for her to finish.

"Tests and trials. Challenges and obstacles."

"Tests and trials? Really?" Helen asked. Though Dori got the feeling she wasn't the least bit surprised. "Well, isn't that interesting?"

Dori sighed. "Don't read anything into it. I got through my Second Degree long, long ago. I'm way beyond it now."

"That's right, isn't it? The newspaper called you an elder." She shrugged. "Then again, I guess the learning and growing never really stop, do they? Why, in any faith the initiations are an endless cycle. Don't you think?"

Dori sent her a swift frown.

"Why don't you run into BK's Grocery and see if she has some nail-polish remover?"

"Nail polish?" Dori looked again at the paint on her windshield, ran a finger over it, and finally bent closer and sniffed, realizing it wasn't paint after all. "It is nail polish, isn't it?" she asked, turning again to the old woman.

But Helen was gone.

Dori walked to BK's, located the nail-polish remover and took it to the front to pay. There was only one register open, which was usual on a weeknight. She waited in line behind a woman she didn't at first recognize, and when she did, she instantly bristled.

The dark-haired woman had started all this by refusing to process Dori's application for a table at the craft fair.

"Hello there, Mrs. Redmond," she said, feeling decidedly evil. Oh, deep down she knew a respectable woman like her probably hadn't vandalized her car. But for the moment, she would do.

The woman snapped her head around and her eyes widened. "Uh…hello."

Mrs. Redmond opened her checkbook to make out the check.

Dori peeked over her shoulder, read her full name. Alice W. Redmond. The woman scribbled quickly and paused at the date space, then shot a look at the brunette behind the register, whose name tag read Katie. "What's the date?"

"Twenty-first," Katie replied. She shifted her glance between the two of them with confused amusement. And no wonder. Alice Redmond was in such a hurry to get out of the store you'd have thought she was afraid Dori was going to pull out a wand and transform her into a toad at any moment.

Katie sent Dori a wink. "Happy Solstice."

The Winter Solstice. She hadn't even realized it was tonight. "Thanks. You know, I'd almost decided to give up practicing Witchcraft. I have Alice here to thank for changing my mind."

"Really?" Katie appeared stunned.

Dori said, "Nah."

Katie laughed. Alice Redmond tore her check out of the book and slapped it down on the counter. The cashier was still grinning when she dropped it into the register and handed back a receipt. Alice snatched up her bags and walked out of the store without another word.

Dori set her bottles of nail-polish remover on the counter and pulled a wad of tips from her handbag.

"What's this about?" the woman asked, holding up a bottle.

"Someone decided my car would be nicer with a splash of blood-red nail polish."

Katie went still, all traces of humor evaporating. "Because of the article?"

"I can only assume so."

"Well, I'll be…that's not like Crescent Cove, Dori. Not at all." She shook her head. "I wish I'd known sooner that you were into…that Witch stuff."

"Why?"

"Well, my daughter's been poking around it. She's got a couple of books in her room, has a little stand set up with candles and such." She shrugged. "I'd like to talk to her about it, but I don't have a clue, you know? And she's at that touchy age."

"Sixteen?"

"Almost." She accepted Dori's cash and started counting out change.

"Do you get a lunch break here?" Dori asked.

"Sure, half hour right at noon."

"Why don't you come over to the diner tomorrow. I'll take my break at the same time and you can pick my brain all you want."

"Really? That would be great, Dori." Then she smiled. "You're just what you've always seemed like, aren't you?"

"What's that?"

"An ordinary person. And a nice one, too." She dropped the bottles into a bag and handed it to Dori. "You have a nice night, Dori."

"You, too, Katie."

Sighing, Dori went outside. She took a deep breath of the crisp cold air and gazed up at the darkening sky. Solstice Night.

The timing was no accident, was it? How many times had she noticed how she never had any darkness to work through over the winter months? Well, this year, she did. And it was time to get to work doing it. It was time for her to come back home—to stop fighting and start accepting. To stop working for change and start trying to see the lesson in what was.

She walked to her car, and spent the next half hour wiping away the nail polish. It washed off more easily than she would have expected. Then she went home and began packing a picnic basket full of ritual supplies. Tonight she would observe the solstice outside, at midnight, under the stars. No matter how cold it might get, she was determined to do this up right.

Tonight she intended to bid her darkness farewell, and welcome the return of the light, no matter what it might bring.

MIDNIGHT. Who the hell could be calling at midnight?

Jason rolled over in bed and reached blindly for the phone. Vaguely he heard the moan of the wind. Not too promising, that sound. Familiar, though. They'd already had the first killer storm of the season—just a couple of weeks ago. It was too soon for another.

Right. And he'd lived here long enough to know better. That wind might be a passing front, but he doubted it. It sounded like it meant business.

He pulled the telephone to his ear. "Yeah?"

"Jason, thank God. My son is gone. I'm afraid he's—"

"Hold on, slow down." He reached out and snapped on the light. "Who is this?"

"Alice Redmond! It's Kevin—he sneaked out with those boys."

A chill rippled through his core and he heard the wind all over again. "Do you think they've gone out on the lake again, Alice?"

"I do-on't kno-ow." The words emerged as sobs.

Then a man must have taken the phone from her hands, because his voice came on the line. "Chief? It's Paul Redmond."

"I'm here."

The voice grew muffled. "Go finish getting dressed, hon," he said. There was a pause before he came back on the line.

"All right. Chief, the boy has been out on that lake at least twice before. I lectured him, I grounded him, but if he sneaked out tonight, I can't imagine another reason for it. Seems to me it's the new big thrill for him and his friends."

"I'm on it, Paul. Listen, meet me at the rec center, down on the shore. We'll coordinate from there. I'll call Phil…get him to open it up."

"All right. I've already driven all over town, Jason. I'm worried."

"We'll find him," Jason said, and even as he hung up the phone, he thought of one person. He thought of Dori.

Not just because she had a knack for finding missing people, either. But because…hell, this was the biggest crisis he'd faced as police chief. And he wanted her by his side, no matter how little sense that might make.

He punched in her number, then cradled the phone between his head and shoulder while pulling on his clothes.

But Dori's phone rang and rang. He frowned, worried about her now, as well. Where the hell could she be at midnight with a storm brewing?

Chapter Seven

Dori had chosen just the right spot. A spot where the rocks formed a natural, three-sided barrier, halfway between her uncle's place and the rec center farther down the beach. She knew this spot. Knew it well.

It was where she and Jason had shared that special night so long ago. And maybe that was part of the reason she'd chosen it tonight.

She'd set up her altar—a large flat-topped boulder—with care, but she hadn't got overly fancy. This wasn't about props. She didn't need incense to represent Air, because she had the wind. It blew sharp and cold, but she'd bundled up. It would be fine. She didn't need a cup to hold Water, because she had the lake right in front of her, choppy with whitecaps. She didn't need salt to represent Earth, because she was surrounded by the boulders and rocks that were Earth itself. She didn't need a representation of the Goddess, because the moon, a waxing, lopsided gibbous moon, was up and bright in the sky, despite the dark clouds around it, gathering ever closer.

Fire—all she needed was Fire. And she had brought her special candle. The one the Crone-like Helen had given her, the one she'd said was imbued with a little magic.

Dori piled a few stones around the base of the candle-holder to keep any wind from tipping it over. She lit the candle, and the glass globe kept it from blowing out. Then she sat quietly to meditate before it. She thought about this past year, all the things she had lost. And she thought about the things Helen had said to her. The inverted pentacle glowed before her mind's eye. Spirit at the bottom, moving through the Underworld. She saw herself, making her way through a dark, shadowy place. She heard the old tales she had so often recited to rapt audiences standing in sacred circles—the tale of the Goddess's descent into the Underworld, and how She was stopped at each of the seven gates and made to surrender one of Her prized possessions at each one. Her jewels, Her robes, Her crown—until there was nothing left.

And for the first time, Dori realized that was exactly what her own journey had been like. She had lost everything she thought was of value. Until she was left with—with just what Inanna had been left with in the legend. She was left with nothing but Her own true self. And that was all She had needed to emerge, triumphant, from the darkness.

For a long time, Dori sat there on the ground and worked through all those things in her mind.

The wind gusted harder. Dori opened her eyes. Her magic candle had blown out, despite the protective glass. A deeper darkness had settled over the night. The black clouds that had been threatening blotted out the moon. In fact, the only light seemed to be coming from the rec center farther along the beach. The wind swept in from the lake, hitting her square in the face. "Damn, I so wanted to continue that meditation," she muttered. "Maybe find out who my own true self really is."

Headlights caught her attention, bouncing in her direction from the rec center. What was going on over there? There were several cars visible in the light that spilled from the building's windows. Some of them were police cars.

She tucked her special candle and her lighter into her bag, left an offering of birdseed, then stepped out of her shelter of rocks, hugging her coat more tightly around her, and hurried toward the center. The approaching vehicle's headlights hit her, blinded her, and then the vehicle pulled up beside her.

The passenger door opened, and when it did, the interior

light came on and she saw Jason behind the wheel. "Get in," he called. "We have a situation."

She got into the car without pause and yanked the door shut. Jason immediately turned the car around and took it bouncing back over the rocky beach. "What's going on?" she asked.

"Those damn kids have vanished again. There's a boat missing from the launch down the beach, and a hell of a storm is rolling in."

She closed her eyes. "Oh, no."

"I was on my way to get you. Been trying to call, but—"

"I was outside."

He peered at her as if she were insane.

"It's the solstice," she said.

His face cleared. "You went to our cove, didn't you?"

She nodded.

"Oh, Dori there's so much..." Then he stopped himself and gave his head a shake. "But it has to wait. The boys first. And if it being solstice means it's a good night for calling down magic, put in for some, would you?"

He stopped outside the rec center, a very large, perfectly square, metal building the town used for bingo, auctions, town dances and anything else that came up. It was probably where they would hold their precious Holiday Craft Fair.

Right now, it held people. The entire police force—which consisted of about six cops—and half the town. Maybe more than half. Up close she could see dozens of vehicles parked around the building. They'd been out of her view before as the parking lot was dark and on the far side of the building.

"What are all these people doing?"

"Praying, mostly," he said. "That storm's gonna hit and hit hard, Dori." He started to get out of the car.

She stopped him with a hand to his arm. "Jason...why did you come for me?"

"The first thing I thought of was to call you." He searched her eyes. "Hell, the first thing I think of when I wake up is you these days. And the last thing before I go to sleep."

"Jason—"

"Don't," he said. "Let's not do this. Not now, Dori. I need you to help me with this. Help me find those boys."

She nodded, opened her door and got out of the car. They went into the rec center together, and Dori took in the scene with a swift glance. Women huddled with their husbands, people weeping, people pacing. Cops and others hunched over a table spread with maps and charts. One was talking on a cell phone; another manned a portable radio.

"We have the state police out in boats," Jason explained. "It's too windy for helicopters." He glanced at his officer on the radio. "Anything yet?"

"No sign."

A huge gust hit, and suddenly, the room full of people was pitched into total darkness. One woman cried out.

"Stay calm," Jason called. "If anyone brought a light, get it out now."

Dori thought of the candle in her bag. If ever she had needed its magic, she thought, she needed it now. She took it out, flicked her lighter, touched it to the wick.

Its golden light gleamed.

"You!" a woman said.

One by one other lights came on. Someone lit a gas lantern, which spilled a lot more light on things. Someone else offered to go get a generator.

But Dori was focused on Alice Redmond making a beeline for her. She was about to roll her eyes and tell the woman that this was not the time, but then she noticed the redness of the woman's cheeks and the hollow emptiness in her eyes. She'd seen a look like that before.

"Oh, my Goddess," Dori whispered. "One of the missing boys is yours, isn't he?"

The woman stopped moving when she couldn't get any closer without mowing Dori down. She stood nearly nose to nose with her, only the dancing light of the candle in between them. "Kevin. He's seventeen."

"I'm so sorry, Alice. I mean it."

"Do you?"

Others were starting to turn toward the two of them now. More lanterns were lit, more candles, and several flashlights. Alice's voice was agitated and overly loud.

"Of course I mean it," Dori said. "I wouldn't wish this on anyone."

"Then help him."

Dori blinked. The room went dead silent.

A man who was probably her husband laid a hand on her arm.

"You've done it before," she went on, not even acknowledging her husband's touch. "If you can really do what they say you can do, then do it. Help me find my son. I just want him back. Please…"

The woman was sinking to the floor at Dori's feet, weeping, and her husband caught her in his arms. "Of course I'll do whatever I can," she said, bending down, helping the man bring his wife to her feet again. She handed her precious candle to the nearest person and then smoothed her hands over the woman's back. "I promise, Alice, I'll try my hardest."

She didn't know if the poor woman was listening or not. She didn't care. She turned and found Jason without having to search for him. She said, "I need to get out on the lake. I need some men to help me launch my uncle's boat."

"Dammit, Dori, you can't go out there," Jason said. "Work from here. Wave a pendulum over the charts and tell us where to send the state patrol boats. But don't go out on the lake."

She moved closer to him, clasped his hands in hers. "I think I have to. Don't you get it, Jason? Maybe this is why I had to come back here. To save this kid. And even if it's not, I'm going to try, no matter how much time you waste arguing with me."

He swallowed hard, holding her eyes. "Then I'm damn well going with you."

HE COULD NOT BELIEVE he had let her come out on the boat in this weather. The waves battered the small craft mercilessly, and he was at the controls, following her directions. The boat

had no cabin. A large glass windshield was all that stood between them and the biting wind.

"Where did you say they started from?" she asked. She was
sitting in a vinyl seat beside him.

"The boat launch, a mile down the beach."

"Then go west."

"That's the opposite direction!"

"There's a strong current. It would have pulled them west.
Especially if they've been out here any length of time."

He searched her face. Pale cheeks in the glow of the panel
lights. Wide, intense eyes.

"Trust me, Jason."

"I do." He headed the boat in the direction she told him.
"But I have to ask, what are you basing this on?" he asked.
"Instinct or…"

"Experience."

"With missing kids?"

"No. With the lake. I know every inch of it, Jason. I've
spent every summer out here since I was twelve, right at
Uncle Gerald's side. Studying his maps, charts, the currents,
all the topography of the lake bottom. He took this Champ
stuff seriously. And he taught me everything he knew."

Jason nodded slowly. "You're right. Hell, you're probably
more familiar with the lake than anyone in town." He stared
at her face. "But what about…the other?"

She nodded. "I'm open. I'm just…not getting anything yet."

"So you just…wait?"

"You keep us afloat, Jason. I'll worry about the spooky
stuff, all right?"

He seemed completely baffled. "I can't help in some way?
Like at your place the other night?"

She pursed her lips, sent him a sad smile. "It's all right,
Jason. I realize it probably freaked you out a little—that night,
I mean. All the Witchcraft stuff."

He tipped his head to one side.

"Look, it's all right. Some people aren't comfortable with
Witchcraft, and that's fine. But I can't give it up, Jason. I think

I had to go through this past year of trying to before I realized that. It's who I am." She reached to the wheel, putting her hand over his on it, and moved it slightly.

"I kind of figured that out before you did, remember? Wasn't I the one who tried to tell you that very thing?"

"Yeah, you did at that." She smiled slightly. The wind was whipping strands of hair that had escaped her knit hat. "That was pretty cool of you, especially given your feelings about it all."

"What feelings? What are you talking about?"

She shrugged, averting her eyes, scanning the pitch-dark waters again. Then her eyes went stone-cold serious. "This way," she said. She lifted a hand and pointed.

He steered the boat where she instructed. "Well?" he prompted. "Dori, don't tell me you suspect I have a problem with your witchiness?"

"Are you saying you don't?"

"I don't. Tell me where you got the idea that I did."

She bit her lips, then shrugged and blurted it. "You haven't asked me out again since you found out."

"Ah, hell, Dori." He faced her, gripped her shoulder with one hand to keep her attention. "I haven't asked you out again because you told me you were as determined as ever to leave Crescent Cove. And because I couldn't take your walking out on me again."

She stared at him. "Really? That's why?"

"It almost killed me last time. You've got no idea how hard it hit me, Dori. No idea."

She blinked, and he thought there might have been tears pooling in her eyes. But all of a sudden, they widened, and she swung her head around. "They're close!" she shouted. "This way!" She grabbed up the spotlight and turned it slowly over the water, shouting the boys' names over and over again.

The wind came harder, snow blasting them now with such force it stung his face. He got caught up in her certainty, though the logical part of his brain told him this wasn't possible. There was no way she could just know. No way.

And then her light fell on something, and she whispered, "There they are."

It was a little boat, bouncing on the rough waters. And it was capsized.

Chapter Eight

The boys were in the water, clinging to the boat, cold and exhausted and weak. "Over here, help us," was all Dori heard. There were three of them. Dori clutched Jason's arm as he steered the boat closer. "How many were missing?"

"Three. It's all right, Dori. They're all there."

She felt the tension rush out of her, and would have sagged in her seat, except that he needed her. Those boys needed her. Jason eased the boat alongside the capsized, smaller craft, and before he even came to a stop, Dori was leaning over the side, reaching for them.

"Take Kev first," said the boy nearest her outstretched arms. He pulled his limp, soaking wet friend nearer, struggling to keep a grip on him at the same time. "He can't hold on anymore. I've b-been keeping his head above water for the p-past half hour."

Kev. This was Kevin, she thought, as she pulled the boy's soaking wet, icy cold upper body into the boat. Jason was beside her then, helping her. They got the boy into the boat, but he didn't open his eyes.

Dori dragged him to the port side, to provide a counterbalance to Jason as he hauled the other two boys aboard. Kevin was freezing cold and drenched, but he was breathing and had a pulse. Poor thing must be damn near frozen.

"We have to get him warm, Jason."

"We have to get back to shore first." He helped the other

two boys onto the bench-type seat. Kevin was on the floor in front of them.

Dori leaned over the boy, tucking an emergency blanket around him.

"I can't believe you managed that, Dori. I can't…you're something else."

"Yeah. The question is, what?" She'd done all she could. She was shivering, her fingers numb with cold as she got back into her seat. Jason had put the boat back into motion now, was speeding along, into horizontal snow and a wind that blew the small boat sideways with at least as much velocity as its small engine drove it forward. They continued that way for more than thirty minutes, plenty of time for them to have gotten back to where they'd started. But there was no shoreline in sight. Then again, it could have been twenty yards away and they wouldn't have seen it in this blizzard.

"Jason?"

"Yes?"

"Where are we?"

He looked at her, licked his lips. "I don't know. I do know we're headed east, and I believe that wind is blowing us toward shore. We'll find it."

She leaned closer to him. "Will we find it before that boy goes into shock?"

"I don't know." He stared into her eyes. "But if you have any more tricks up your sleeve, baby, now would be a good time to pull them out. Can't you conjure up or something? Isn't that what Witches do?"

"I haven't been much of a Witch for a year now. And when I tried, my casting and conjuring didn't amount to much." She drew a breath. "Then again, maybe I wasn't working for anything I really needed. I thought I was at the time. But with hindsight…"

He frowned at her. "Dori?"

"Stop the boat."

He didn't even question her. He just eased back on the throttle. "I can't stop us entirely. The wind…"

"This is fine."

She sat there a moment, grounding into herself, into her body, into the waters beneath them, all the way to the bottom and then into the Earth. She opened her senses, becoming one with the wind that blew around her, even with the frigid, piercing snow that snapped the skin right off her face. One. One. She swore her body temperature dropped. She opened her arms wider, rose slowly from her seat.

"I am the wind," she whispered. And she felt it. The wind moving through her, within her, her body, her mind. And she was the wind. "I am calming. I'm slowing. I'm easing."

It was working. She felt it.

"I am the snow," she said. "And I am fading, slowing, stopping. I am the lake and I am calming, calming, calming. I am the Goddess, and all things are within me. By my power, I still the wind, and the water, and the snow."

She opened her eyes slowly, brought her hands down to her sides with deliberation and intensity. "So mote it be!"

For a moment, just a moment, nothing happened. But she stood there, still, holding up a hand to the others for silence, her eyes straining in the darkness. And then, so gradually it might have been all in her mind, the winds began to die down. And then a little more, and a little more.

"Holy cow," one of the boys muttered.

The snow fell, soft puffs instead of a blinding blizzard and the water lay calm. And still she stood, scanning the horizon. But it was Jason who pointed and said, "Look! What is that?"

A single tiny flare of light caught her eye, and she didn't know how she knew it or why she knew it, but she knew without any doubt that it was the light of that magic candle. Her special solstice candle.

In an instant, it changed. It became another light and another, until it seemed a thousand stars twinkled in the distance. But they were not stars. They were candles, and lanterns, and flashlights, and lighters and anything else the people of Crescent Cove could find that would give off light. They were guiding them back, showing them the way home.

Jason clutched her hand, pulled her until she sat down, and guided the boat in the direction of the lights. As soon as she sat, her concentration broke. The wind picked up, blasting her, and the snow whipped again. But it didn't matter. They had found their way.

"At the darkest moment of the darkest night," she whispered, "that's the very instant when the light is reborn."

She felt Jason's eyes on her, felt something in them, but couldn't quite tell what it was. And then they were at the dock, and men came running out to grip the sides of the boat, tug it farther in and tie it off. Jason handed the still-unconscious Kevin off to one of them. Others had helped his two companions out. Then Jason helped Dori out, as well, and climbed onto the dock.

"You're nearly frozen yourself," he told her.

"I could use some dry clothes," she admitted. She watched the boys being taken to the ambulances that waited on the shore, amid what had to be a hundred people, all holding lights and candles.

Someone started to sing "Silent Night." Dori thought it fitting, whether one was celebrating the birth of the son, or the rebirth of the sun, or the reuniting of these mothers and their sons. One by one, others joined in the song. Dori's eyes filled with hot tears that she imagined were probably freezing on her cheeks even as they fell. Jason's arm came around her, and he helped her away from the dock, toward his car.

As they moved through the crowd, people touched them, patting their shoulders, arms. Voices broke in their singing to thank them.

They stopped near the ambulance where the men had taken Kevin. He was already inside, bundled in blankets, and his mother was about to get in with him, when she paused and met Dori's eyes. She didn't say anything, just stared at her for a long moment. Then a sob broke free as if ripped from her lungs, and she flung her arms around Dori's neck. It was a brief, fierce embrace. The woman turned away just as quickly and climbed into the back of the ambulance. The doors closed, and the vehicle trundled away.

A hand fell on Dori's shoulder. The husband. Dori had already forgotten his name. He smiled at her. "He's going to be all right," he said. "Thanks to you. Both of you," he added. He reached out to clasp her hand, then Jason's. Then he hurried off to his vehicle, a pickup truck, and took off to follow the ambulance.

Jason asked one of his men to lock up the rec center and another to let the state police know the boys had been found. Then he led Dori to his car and put her inside. "Your place or mine?" he asked.

She stared at him blankly.

"For dry clothes, some heat and maybe something hot to drink," he clarified. "And then a talk I think is long overdue."

"My place is closer. And I'm sure there's something of Uncle Gerald's you could put on. Not to mention, I have cocoa."

"No power."

"Gas range. And I always have p-plenty of candles. Hell, I'm starting to shiver."

"Yeah, me, too." He put the car into gear and drove.

Chapter Nine

She heeled off her hiking shoes as soon as she got through the front door, peeled off her coat and ran in damp socks into the living room while Jason was still shucking his frozen outerwear. The fire had burned low. Glowing coals gleamed from the hearth, and were the only light in the room.

Dori removed the fire screen, set it aside and knelt to take logs from the nearby stack and toss them onto the coals. Tongues of flame licked up around them, and the room grew brighter. She replaced the screen as Jason's footsteps came closer.

"Get warm by the fire," she said. "I'll go find you some dry clothes."

"Change first," he said. "Here." Something clicked and a light appeared. "Take my flashlight with you."

"Thanks. There are some candles on the mantel. Matches, too."

"Got it."

Dori took the light and headed up the stairs to the loft bedroom, still shivering. She opened dresser drawers, pulled out items, happy to have the flashlight to help her find a warm pullover, plaid flannel pajama pants and, best of all, a pair of thick, cushy socks. She set the light on her dresser, than sat down on her bed to remove her frozen socks. The bottoms of her jeans were stiff and icy. She stripped everything off and put on the comfortable clothes. Then she went to the closet, where she'd packed away the clothing Uncle Gerald had left behind. Suits hung in a fat garment bag, but the more practical items were packed in boxes. She found sweatpants, a sweatshirt, put them on the bed and then found her way back down the stairs with help from the flashlight.

She'd only been gone a few minutes, but Jason was efficient. He'd lit every candle he could find. She heard him rattling around in the kitchen. "Jason?"

He appeared in the doorway, lit by the glow of the ancient hurricane lamp that had hung from a nail beside the front door for as long as she could remember. "Sit by the fire. I've got the water heating."

She went to him and took the lamp from his hands, replacing it with the flashlight. "I'll finish the cocoa. Go on upstairs and change. I left some clothes on the bed for you."

He was about to argue, so she held up a finger. "Go on."

Smiling, he obeyed. By the time he came back into the living room, she had two mugs of hot cocoa sitting on the coffee table, and she'd pushed a rocker and an overstuffed chair up closer to the heat. She was sitting in the rocker, a blanket from the back of the sofa draped around her shoulders.

"I smell chocolate." He flicked off the flashlight and set a bundle of clothes on the floor near the fire before sitting down. "Getting warm yet?"

"My feet have thawed out. Now they hurt. You?"

He lifted his cup of cocoa from the table and stretched his feet out so they were closer to the fire. "Getting there." He sipped his cocoa. "So."

"So," she said.

He drew a breath. "So you really thought I stopped asking you out because you're a Witch?"

She shrugged. "Yeah. I really did. It wasn't such an illogical conclusion, was it? You asked me several times and then you stopped."

"I stopped right after you shot me down the first time. And then we had that talk the other day. The one where you told me you still planned to leave here as soon as you could."

She tipped her head to one side. "I never made any secret about that. I always planned for my stay here to be a temporary one."

He shrugged. "Maybe I was a little too dense to get that. Or maybe I was hoping you'd change your mind. But when you put it to me the way you did…well, I realized I was deluded."

"Maybe I was the one who was deluded."

He stared at her in the light of the fire. "Meaning?"

"Meaning, every résumé I've sent out has resulted in a response of 'Thanks, but no, thanks.'" She shrugged. "Maybe I'm not supposed to go back to Manhattan."

"But you still want to."

She frowned at him. "I thought I did. All this time, I thought that was all I wanted. My old life back. Now I…now I don't know what I want."

He sipped his cocoa again, didn't say anything for a long time. The fire painted his face in shadows and light. He seemed brooding, deep, and clearly, hours had gone by since his morning shave. She caught herself wanting to run her palms over his stubbly cheeks.

"I owe you an apology. A long overdue one."

He looked up at her, met her eyes. "For what?"

"For leaving you the way I did. With just a letter."

He shrugged. "It wouldn't have mattered how you left me, Dori. It was the leaving that did me in."

"I'm sorry."

"Hell, it's water under the bridge. It's not your fault. I felt something you didn't. It happens."

"If I had known—"

"You'd have what? Stayed? No, Dori. I don't think that would have happened, and I'm not sure it even should have happened. You needed to get out of here, test your wings. It changed you."

"Did it?"

He nodded. "You figured out who you were. You have something now that you didn't have before. I've been trying to figure out what it was since the first day I saw you back in town, and now I think I've nailed it."

"Really? What is it?"

"I don't know if it has a name. It's like you always had this wellspring of…something deep down. But going away gave you the chance to find it, to tap into it, to bring it all bubbling up to the surface. You glow now. An inner light. A core of power. Maybe…maybe it's that you found your magic."

"I thought I had," she said. "And then I thought it was gone again, when I lost everything and had to come back here. Only—it wasn't really. I turned my back on it, not the other way around. It came so clear to me out there on the lake tonight."

"Did it?"

"Yeah. I've been lost. I've been floundering around in the darkness, wondering where the light went. But it's here, it's been here all along, just waiting for me to see it. It burns just the same, whether I'm here or in Manhattan. I'm the keeper of my own flame. No one has the power to put it out but me. Not a job, not prestige, not a huge income or a Mercedes or a penthouse apartment. Where I live or what I do for a living has nothing to do with who I am."

He smiled at her. "That's great, Dori. I'm glad for you."

"But?" She waited, draining her cocoa, then putting her cup on the floor.

He shrugged. "But nothing."

"Come on, Jason, don't hold back. You've been pretty instrumental in my reaching a lot of the conclusions I have. Don't stop now."

He pursed his lips in thought, then finally nodded. "Okay. I'll give it to you straight." He set his cup down, got out of his chair and took her hands to pull her to her feet.

For a moment he simply looked at her, really looked, deeply into her eyes. Then he cupped her head in his hands, and he kissed her. Dori's eyes fell closed as his lips covered hers. His fingers spread through her hair, and one hand slid lower, to the small of her back and eased her closer, and still closer, until her body was pressed to his. His hand stroked her hair, a sensual massage as his lips moved over hers. Gentle suction, constant motion. His body molded to hers a little harder, his hand at her back drawing her tighter. Fingers splayed at the back of her head as the kiss deepened. He played her the way a master played a violin. He made her body sing. He always had.

Dori gave in to the music, sliding her arms around his waist, parting her lips to let him in. She wasn't cold anymore.

They kissed, standing near the fire, for a long time. And when he finally lifted his head, his eyes glittering as they stared into hers, he said, "I want you to stay."

She blinked at him. "But…Jason, this is…"

"What? So sudden? So new? It's not, you know. I'm just picking up where we left off ten years ago, Dori." He let his arms fall to his sides from around her. She felt lonely without them. "I didn't want to do this, not until I was sure you'd decided to stay. I didn't want to lay my heart out there on the platter again, just waiting for a cleaver to whack it in two. But maybe…maybe you just need a reason to make that decision. Or maybe not. Maybe I'm dead wrong here. It could be that this incredible thing I feel between us is all in my head. God knows I thought it must have been when you walked away the last time. But then…you came back. And I know it wasn't for me, but I can't help wondering if…it was fate that brought you back here. Back to me."

The lights flicked on, off, then on again. They stayed on this time. He smiled at her. "Guess that would be the return of the light you were talking about in the boat, huh?"

"Not even close," she said, but she knew he was only joking, trying to lighten up what had become an intense and heavy moment. He wanted an answer from her, a decision. A commitment.

A repetitive beeping sound distracted her and she couldn't stop the phrase *saved by the bell* from whispering through her thoughts. Frowning, she spotted the answering machine, its light flashing insistently.

"Talk about timing," Jason muttered. Then he sighed again. "Maybe we needed a break anyway. Go ahead, get your messages. I'll put out all these candles before we burn the place down."

"Thanks, Jason."

He wandered into the kitchen with their cocoa cups, blowing out candles on the way. Dori went to the machine and poked the Play button.

"Hi, Doreen. This is your old boss, Marie Brown, from Mason-Walcott. We've acquired another publishing company and we'd like to offer you a position—as publisher. You'd be making significantly more than you were the last time you worked for us, but we have to hear from you soon. Call me and we'll discuss the details."

Dori stood there staring at the machine as Marie's voice recited her telephone number. "Wow," Jason said.

She jumped, because she'd been so distracted she hadn't heard him come up behind her, and turned to face him. He had two fresh mugs of cocoa in his hands, and a sad look in his eyes. "This is what you've been waiting for, isn't it? The job offer of your dreams?"

She nodded slowly.

"So you're going to take it?"

"I don't—Jason, I don't—"

He shook his head and bent to set the mugs down. "Don't. It's okay. I get it." He walked past her to scoop up his pile of clothes from the floor.

"No, you *don't* get it. Goddess, one minute you're telling me all these things I never knew, and the next minute I get what I thought I always wanted handed to me. My mind is still spinning. Can't you even give me time to sort this out?"

He looked at her, and the emotion in his eyes was so powerful it made her throat close up. He looked heartbroken. As if he already knew what her decision would be. But he didn't say that. Instead, he gave her a sad smile, came to her, touched her face. "Sure I can, Dori." Leaning closer, he kissed her cheek. "I'm gonna clear out of here, let you sleep on all of this. Okay?"

She swallowed hard. "Okay."

Walking with him to the door, Dori found herself fighting the ridiculous impulse to throw her arms around him and beg him to stay. But she couldn't do that to him. Not until she sorted things out.

He stomped into his boots, pulled on his coat, opened the door.

"Good night, Jason."

"Goodbye, Dori."

Then he was gone.

Chapter Ten

Dori didn't go to sleep. She turned off the lights and sat in front of the fire, staring into the flames and searching them for help.

What had she lost by leaving the city? Money, yes, she'd lost a lot of that. Friends? Well, maybe not. Friends weren't friends if they vanished so easily. She'd sold her precious crystal ball. But the Witches of old hadn't needed four-hundred-dollar gazing balls to see into the future. They hadn't needed much at all. A bowl of water. A dark mirror. A leaping flame.

She relaxed her mind, let her vision blur, her body go slack. One by one, she opened her chakra centers, felt them fill with energy. She focused her thoughts on her life, her future; saw herself picking up the phone and returning Marie's call; heard herself accepting the offer; and let herself sink into the future.

The images came floating like bits of a dream, one following another. A beautiful apartment. A new Mercedes. Respect and admiration. The Wiccan community gathering around her once again. It all seemed lovely. Except that in each of those flashes, she saw herself alone. She saw the longing in her eyes, the loneliness. The same heartsick loneliness she'd been feeling since she'd come back here—no, for even longer than that. She felt herself wishing she were somewhere else. With someone else.

Drawing a breath, she closed her mind to the visions,

cleared them away and began again. This time she started by clearly visualizing herself phoning Marie and refusing the offer. It was a difficult visualization to manage—saying no to something for which she had been waiting an entire year. But then she relaxed again, and again the images came to her. Stubbornly, slowly. But they came.

She saw herself on the boat in the summer, taking tourists around the lake, telling them all Uncle Gerald's old Champ stories. Smiling. She saw herself expanding the business, adding an inn, maybe a restaurant, a bigger gift shop. And smiling. And in every picture that came, Jason was with her.

She saw him sitting across a candlelit table from her, at Sister Krissie's Bar and Grill, the best restaurant in Crescent Cove, holding her hand. And she nearly gasped at the matching gold bands they wore. She saw him get up and come around the table, lowering his hand to rest it on her belly—a belly that was huge and round and filled with new life.

Dori gasped and her body went rigid. The visions faded.

She tried to ground and center, but couldn't quite make it work. But she did know one thing. There had been no sense of loneliness in that second vision. No sadness in her eyes. There had been bliss, pure joyful bliss.

She reached for the phone, snatched it up and dialed Jason's number.

His voice, when he answered, wasn't sleepy. Maybe he'd been lying awake, too? He didn't say, "Hello." He said, "Dori?"

"Come back, Jason. Please, come back to me."

There was the briefest pause. Then he said, "I'm on my way."

Fifteen minutes later his headlights bounced into the driveway. She was waiting for him, outside, bundled, a hood pulled up around her head. She took his hand when he got out, ignored the questions in his eyes and tugged him toward the lake.

The storm had eased. The wind still blew, but the sky was clearing. Stars peeked from between the clouds now. Standing there on the shore, she faced him, clasping both his hands in hers. "I have something to say."

He nodded, and she could see in his eyes that he was expecting her to break his heart again. "I'll try not to interrupt."

"All right. Here it is. All this time, I thought I was being punished for something. Or that I'd been laid so low in order to learn some kind of a lesson. I turned my back on my own beliefs." She shook her head slowly. "But the whole time, all that was really happening was that the clutter was being cleared out of my life, so I could find my heart's desire. Everything I had—those were just things—just obstacles standing between me and the life I was really meant to lead. Once they were gone, I could finally find my way through my own darkness, to a gift more precious than anything I ever had or ever will. I found my way back to where I belong. To the light. To Crescent Cove. And to you, Jason."

His eyes filled with wonder and dampness. "You're staying?"

"I'm staying."

"But…the job offer…"

"I had a better offer. The one where you asked me to stay. And marry you. And bear your children."

He stared so intensely at her she thought he must be able to see straight through her, and into her heart. "I didn't ask you those things…not yet."

"But you will, won't you, Jason?"

He swallowed hard. "Is that what you want? Are you sure, Dori, that you won't change your mind and want to go?"

"How could I go?" she asked with a smile. "It's taken me a while to figure it out, Jason, but I'm in love with you. Madly, deeply, completely in love with you. I think I have been for a long, long time."

He gathered her into his arms and kissed her as if there were no tomorrow. When he came up for air, he said, "Do you know how long I've been waiting for you to say those words to me, Dori?"

"Too long. I'm sorry I made you wait."

"I'd have waited forever." He kissed her again, deeply, tenderly, and she knew down deep in her soul that she had made the right decision. She was home.

When Jason lifted his head, they both turned to see the sun rising slowly over Lake Champlain. "And this is what you meant by 'the return of the light.'"

"This is what I meant," she whispered. And looking at the sky, she added, "Thank you."

ONE FOR EACH NIGHT
Judith Arnold

In memory of my grandma

Dear Reader,

My grandmother used to serve marshmallow-and-apricot treats at all her parties. I never ate them—I don't like apricots—but most of her guests happily devoured them. And since my grandmother was one of my inspirations, both in life and in the writing of *One for Each Night*, I had to include her marshmallow-and-apricot treats in the story.

Like Alana's grandmother in *One for Each Night*, my grandmother adored entertaining. She'd grab any excuse for a party, invite as many people as she could squeeze into her apartment, prepare her special foods and have a blast. And like both Alana's and Jeff's grandmothers, when my grandmother made potato latkes, she always wound up with bandages on her hands from having scraped her knuckles on the grater—and she always joked that a little blood added flavor to the latkes.

Writing *One for Each Night* was a great pleasure for me, not only because it allowed me to bring my grandmother back to life, but also because it offered me the chance to work with two dear friends and wonderful authors, Maggie Shayne and Anne Stuart. May the time you spend in our little town of Crescent Cove, Vermont, be joyful, and may your holidays be filled with love.

Judith Arnold

Chapter One

Alana had potatoes. She had onions, dreidels, a brisket of beef, blue-and-white paper plates and matching napkins, gold-foil-wrapped chocolate coins, marshmallows, dried apricots and toothpicks. All she needed was candles.

And she needed them desperately. Without candles, what was the point?

She'd been thrilled to find Hanukkah candles for sale at the stationery store across from the post office. Just a few boxes, but she supposed Hanukkah candles weren't in huge demand in Crescent Cove, Vermont. The town lacked a synagogue. That didn't bother her—she wasn't particularly religious—but Hanukkah without candles burning in a menorah was beyond pointless. It was unthinkable.

The problem was, the candles she'd bought at the stationery store didn't fit her menorah. It was an antique, carried across the ocean from the tiny Polish village where Alana's great-grandparents had grown up. They'd given it to Alana's grandmother, and when she'd died last spring, Alana had inherited it. Clearly, it had not been constructed with standard-size twenty-first-century Hanukkah candles in mind.

She should have had her mother buy candles down in Philadelphia and mail them to her. Or she should have ordered some candles on the Internet. Of course, candles purchased long-distance might not fit, either. Only by trying them in the menorah would Alana know she'd gotten the right size. If necessary, she would schlep up to Burlington—surely that city was big enough to have stores that sold candles in a variety of sizes. Before she made that trek, though, she would try Burning Bright.

She must have passed the strange little candle shop on the corner of Hope and Evergreen a dozen times since joining the staff of the *Crescent Cove Chronicle* and moving to Crescent Cove last summer, but she'd never gone inside. She wasn't the sort to soak in a tub surrounded by hundreds of flickering scented candles, or to dine formally with tapers in elegant silver candelabra illuminating the table. She'd celebrated her thirtieth birthday last October as quietly as possible—no cake covered with a multitude of candles, thank you very much. Until now, she'd had no reason to shop at Burning Bright.

It didn't look like the kind of store that would sell Hanukkah candles. The door was narrow, the windows cluttered with fashion candles, molded candles, candles encrusted with sand and wrapped in ribbons. But she had nothing to lose by taking a peek inside.

Pushing open the door, she was assailed by a perfume of cinnamon, flowery potpourri and wax. Candles of every size, shape and color crowded the teeming shelves. Decorative candles, utility candles, candles carved and dyed to resemble cats, cows and clowns, fat ceramic bowls filled with wax and multiple wicks—everywhere Alana looked, she saw candles.

"*Bubbela.* You seem a *bissell* confused."

Flinching, Alana clutched her tote and peered around one of the shelves to see who had addressed her. The voice had sounded uncannily like her grandmother's. Its owner, approaching from the cashier's counter, resembled her grandmother, too, short and plump, her unkempt hair curly and white. The woman had a round face and oversize glasses shaped like TV screens, and her smile…it was so reminiscent of Grandma's, Alana felt dizzy.

"*Nu?* I startled you?"

"A little," Alana managed to whisper. People didn't talk like that here in small-town Vermont. People said "well" and "little" and "sweetheart," not *nu* and *bissell* and *bubbela* in voices that still carried a trace of their Old World roots. This woman, in her no-nonsense brown dress and white cardigan, simply didn't belong.

"So." The woman clapped her hands. The joints of her fingers bulged with arthritic swelling, reminding Alana again of her grandmother. "What can I get for you?"

"I need candles," Alana said.

The woman laughed. "So you came to a candle store. You're a very smart girl. Tell me, what kind of candles?"

Alana hesitated, then smiled. If anyone would know what she was searching for, this woman would. "They're for my grandmother's menorah. It's an antique, and I can't find anything that fits."

"For a special menorah you need a special candle." The old woman scuttled past shelves of candles wreathed in plastic vines, candles nestled within puffs of gingham, candles standing in colonial-style pewter holders. Before Alana could collect herself enough to follow her, the woman was back, brandishing a plain white candle. "Here, *bubbela*, this is the candle you need."

Alana suppressed a laugh. Despite the woman's use of Yiddish words, she was no more knowledgeable about menorahs than the clerk at BK's Grocery, who'd urged Alana to buy a box of special birthday-cake candles, instead. "These are hilarious," he'd told her. "If you blow them out, they reignite! Drives folks crazy."

"I need more than one candle," she explained to the candle-shop proprietor. "I have to light candles every night for eight days. One candle the first night, then two candles the next night, plus the *shamas* candle, which is used to light the other candles every night—"

"No, listen, *bubby*. This is all you need." She pressed the white candle into Alana's hand. "This one will light every night."

"But the candles have to burn all the way down. They have to burn themselves out each night, and the next night you use new candles."

The woman shook her head. "Trust me. This is the one you need. It'll burn down, it'll burn out, and then the next day everything will be fine."

Alana considered explaining once more the way a menorah worked, then thought better of it. She couldn't bear to tell this sweet, helpful woman who reminded her so keenly of her grandmother that one candle would never be sufficient, and that this particular candle probably wouldn't fit in the menorah anyway. She'd buy the white candle to make the woman happy and then drive up to Burlington to get the proper candles to fill her menorah.

"All right," she said, closing her fingers around the candle the woman had given her. "Thank you. How much do I owe you?"

"Owe, schmowe. Take it."

"I couldn't."

"Of course you could. Use it in good health." With that, the shopkeeper nudged Alana toward the door. For someone fairly elderly, she was surprisingly strong. Alana felt the pressure of her palm against her shoulder even after she was outside.

One thing she'd learned since moving to Crescent Cove was that eccentric Yankees were not mythical. They really existed. They usually didn't talk as if they'd been conceived in a shtetl, born in steerage, raised in Brooklyn and driven to the Borscht Belt for vacations, but the proprietor of Burning Bright was obviously one of the odder ones.

A soft snow swirled in the air as Alana hurried down the sidewalk to her car. Once inside, she started the engine, cranked up the windshield defroster and paused.

Tucked inside her tote bag was the menorah, wrapped in a flannel cloth. Alana had brought it with her to size candles. Although she knew damn well that a single white candle would be totally useless, she couldn't drive back to work without first checking to see if the candle fit.

She eased the menorah out of her tote and unfolded the fabric. Viewing it brought tears to her eyes. She missed her grandmother terribly, and she would miss her grandmother's annual Hanukkah open house. She must have been crazy to think that carrying on her grandmother's special tradition and hosting her own open house in Crescent Cove would somehow make her feel better.

The menorah was bright yellow brass—Alana had polished it the way her grandmother always did, readying it for the holiday—with a solid elliptical base and eight gracefully arching arms, each tipped with a round cup to hold a candle. The *shamas* holder extended straight up the center, its stem adorned with a Star of David. The menorah was a classic design, simple and beautiful.

Alana attempted to stick the white candle into the first cup on the right. It didn't fit. "Figures," she snorted. That old lady knew *bupkis*—and if Alana had said that to her, she'd probably have understood what Alana meant.

Sighing, she rewrapped the menorah in its protective flannel and slid it back into her tote, along with the candle. At least her visit to Burning Bright hadn't cost her anything, she thought as she clicked on her wipers, shifted into gear and wiggled her car out of its tight parking space.

She reached the *Chronicle*'s employee lot in just a few minutes. The only empty spot was the one next to a huge mound of snow left by the snowplow after the last storm. Crescent Cove got an awful lot of snow, she'd learned. After a few autumn weeks of flurries and squalls, the first blizzard had hit in early November and the ground had never been totally clear of the white stuff since then. Down in Bridgeport, Connecticut, where she'd lived before moving to Vermont, white Christmases were a rarity. Here, she assumed nonwhite Christmases were unheard-of.

Not that she was complaining. She'd been happy to trade her ugly situation at the *Bridgeport Journal* for the rugged winters of northern New England.

She entered the *Chronicle* building, a squat granite structure two stories high. The actual production of the *Crescent Cove Chronicle* took place in a larger facility on the outskirts of town, but this building housed the editorial, sales and advertising departments.

Welcoming the warmth inside the building, Alana peeled off her gloves and unzipped her parka. The spiffy leather jacket that had gotten her through her winters down in Connecticut offered little defense against a Vermont December. She'd learned to dress like a native—in a waterproof insulated parka, fleece hat and scarf, lined gloves and utilitarian boots with skidproof soles. Fortunately, her boss, Chet Holroyd, didn't care much about professional apparel. In this weather, wearing a skirt would probably have given Alana frostbitten knees.

Once she'd thawed out a bit, she abandoned the vestibule for the newsroom. Several desks occupied the center of the room, and glass-enclosed offices and a conference room ran along the perimeter. Chet was in the largest office, and he wasn't alone.

"Who's that with Chet?" Alana asked Patsy, whose desk faced hers. Patsy covered the *Chronicle*'s arts beat. Alana had been pleasantly surprised to discover that Crescent Cove had enough arts activity to warrant a full-time reporter.

Patsy glanced up from her computer, eyed Chet's office and shrugged. "He got here ten minutes ago. They've been going at it ever since."

Alana lowered her tote to her desk, draped her jacket and scarf over the back of her chair and fluffed out her hair, which had gotten flattened by her hat—all the while observing the encounter taking place in Chet's office. Chet was seated at his desk, his feet propped up on it and his hands folded over his middle-age paunch. Alana had learned that his tousled hair and benign smile disguised a sharp, stubborn mind. He was firm, he was demanding, and his temper was known to spike when his agenda was tampered with. Whoever his visitor was, Alana doubted the poor guy had a chance.

He didn't look like a poor guy, though. He had his back to Alana, so she could see only thick dark hair, broad shoulders and an obviously expensive gray coat. Cashmere, she guessed from this distance. Whoever he was, he probably wasn't from "these parts," as the locals would put it.

Because the glass wall was soundproof, she couldn't hear

what the men were saying. But she could read Chet's face pretty well. He seemed calm enough, but his eyes were as hard as the bedrock beneath the building, and his mouth was set in a stern line. Alana wouldn't want to be a part of that conversation, for sure.

Abruptly, the visitor turned toward the glass, and Alana's breath caught in her throat. He was gorgeous. His hair was straight and just spiky enough to add a whiff of danger to his elegant grooming, and his eyes were the color of the sky outside. He had a long nose and a strong chin, and…God, those eyes were riveting. She wanted to grab Patsy's shoulder and beg her to reveal the man's identity—except that Patsy obviously didn't know who he was, and just as obviously didn't care.

She must be blind, Alana thought. How could she not find the stranger utterly mesmerizing?

He stared at Alana through the glass. Did he know who she was? Why would he? She'd never seen him before. If they'd ever met, she wouldn't have forgotten him.

Trying to ignore his gaze, she turned back to her desk, lowered herself into her chair and hit a key of her computer to kill the screen saver. The monitor filled with her notes from a recent interview with a disgruntled member of the zoning board. The board member didn't favor any more vacation homes along the lake, and she was counting on Alana and the *Chronicle* to make sure everyone in town was apprised of her position.

The phone at her elbow rang. She lifted the receiver. "Alana Ross speaking."

"Please come into my office," Chet said without preamble.

So Alana was going to be a part of Chet's conversation with the stranger after all. She was going to meet Mr. Gorgeous in his pricey threads. Not a problem, she assured herself. Back in Bridgeport, she'd interviewed the governor plenty of times, as well as business titans, labor leaders, senators and the occasional presidential candidate passing through the city. Surely she could handle a handsome outsider in Crescent Cove.

"I'm on my way," she said before lowering the phone. She straightened her V-neck sweater over her sturdy brushed-denim slacks, scowled at her clunky boots and scolded herself for caring what she looked like. She didn't have to impress this man. Whoever he was, he'd apparently been giving Chet a hard time, and Alana was nothing if not loyal to Chet.

She crossed the room, opened the door and stepped inside Chet's office. Chet kept his seat and the man remained standing, eyeing her with the sort of contempt most people reserved for termites. She leveled her chin at him—not easy to do, given that he stood at least six inches taller than her—and met his gaze unflinchingly. Damn him for being such a hunk.

"Alana, this is Jeffrey Barrett," Chet introduced them. "Mr. Barrett, this is Alana Ross."

She remembered her manners enough to extend her right hand. His grip was firm but not crushing, even though he continued to study her as though she were a bug. "How do you do?" she said in a calm, artificially pleasant voice.

A pat question, not demanding an answer, but he supplied one anyway. "I guess that depends on how we resolve this problem."

She slid her hand from his and flexed the fingers, wishing her circulation would return. Glancing at Chet, she asked, "What problem would that be?"

"Mr. Barrett is an attorney up from Boston," Chet informed her, his avuncular smile belied by the steel in his voice. "He's upset about your article on the investigation into the school department's finances."

Alana remembered the article well, since it was an ongoing story and she'd been pursuing it for quite some time. Seventy-five thousand dollars had mysteriously vanished from the school budget. In a town the size of Crescent Cove, seventy-five thousand dollars was nothing to sneeze at.

In a town the size of Boston, seventy-five thousand dollars amounted to barely a sniffle. "Why would that story interest you enough to travel all the way here?" she asked Barrett.

"The article implies that Robert Willis is responsible for the money's disappearance."

"It more than implies that," Alana agreed, her gaze still locked with Barrett's. He was obviously trying to intimidate her with his sheer presence—his height, his solidity, his uncompromising stare. She lacked his height and solidity, but she could compete in the staring contest. And she could arm herself with her confidence. "Robert Willis is the superintendent of schools. When a budget discrepancy as large as this one turns up, who else would be responsible?"

Barrett appeared annoyed. "You see the problem?" he said, apparently addressing Chet, although he still faced Alana. "You media types besmirch the reputation of a good man, even though you have no evidence."

Robert Willis was neither a good man nor a bad man, as far as Alana was concerned. He was simply the superintendent of Crescent Cove's schools. And money had disappeared on his watch. "I didn't besmirch anyone's reputation," Alana said, struggling not to grin at Barrett's stuffy phrasing. "I wrote an article, and I stand behind every word of it."

"You wrote an article," Barrett echoed. He lifted a fax of a clipping from Chet's desk. Alana recognized it; it had appeared on the front page of the *Chronicle* on Wednesday. "'As superintendent of the school system,'" Barrett read, "'Robert Willis oversees the entire district's budget. All expenditures, major and minor, pass through his office, and he is accountable to the town for his decisions and actions. Yet he has refused so far to explain where this money has gone or how it has been used. After issuing a written statement claiming there were no anomalies in the budget, Willis declined to answer further questions.'" Barrett lowered the article and directed his gaze back to Alana.

She returned his stare. "As I said, I stand by every word."

"Even though you have no proof that Robert Willis did anything wrong?"

"I never said he did anything wrong," she reminded Barrett. "I said he was the superintendent of schools, he was in charge of the budget, he was accountable to the town, money was missing and he refused to speak to me. All of which is true."

"And you don't see how that tarnishes his name?"

"If he didn't want his name tarnished, he could have talked to me. He could have explained the discrepancy in the budget. He could have even said he had no idea where the money went, but he was looking into it. He did none of those things."

"Do you understand libel law?"

Barrett was pulling out the big guns now. Alana squared her shoulders beneath her bulky sweater. "Yes, I understand libel law. For one thing, Mr. Barrett, Robert Willis is a public official, which raises the legal threshold for libel way high. For another, I wrote nothing libelous in that article. And I'll tell you this," she added angrily. "If Robert Willis is paying you Boston-lawyer rates and you're telling him he's got a libel case against me, you're giving him lousy legal advice."

"Alana," Chet interceded.

"Well, he is," she said, rotating to face her boss.

"I'm not looking to sue anyone," Barrett said.

Alana refused to turn back to him, and she stifled the urge to argue. Chet clearly believed she was close to losing control. So she pressed her lips together and stared at the fax of the article from Wednesday's paper, which Barrett had set back down on Chet's desk.

"You could certainly write," Barrett continued, "that Robert Willis hasn't been accused of anything or implicated in any investigation. You could clear his name, so he can walk around the streets of this town without having to wear a paper bag over his head."

Alana could, but why should she? Robert Willis hadn't been cleared. The investigation was continuing. And whether he'd personally pocketed the missing seventy-five grand or simply been asleep at the wheel when the money had disappeared, he had to accept responsibility for the shortfall.

"Look," she said, eyeing Chet to make sure he'd back her up. "I'm going to continue to report on this story. If your client wants to talk to me, great. I'd love for us to print his explanation for how the money disappeared. But if he doesn't want to talk to me, I'll report the story without his statement.

If the police discover someone stole the money, I'll report it. If an audit locates the missing funds, I'll report that. I'm not going to base my articles on some big-city attorney's veiled threats."

"I haven't threatened—"

"If that's all, Chet," she went on with what she considered consummate poise, "I've got to finish that piece on the lakefront zoning."

"Mr. Barrett wants to go through our archives to see what other articles we've published on Bob Willis," Chet told her. "I said we'd have no problem with that."

Alana suspected Barrett wanted to go through the newspaper's archives to read other articles by her, no doubt searching for examples of what he considered bad reporting. Well, that hope would be dashed. Let him spend the whole weekend reviewing every article Alana had written since she'd joined the *Chronicle* staff last June—and every article she'd written for the *Bridgeport News* before then. He wouldn't find anything but solid writing and unimpeachable ethics. And he could send Robert Willis an exorbitant bill for his wasted time.

"Be my guest," she said coolly, shooting Barrett a final glower as she shoved open the door.

For some reason, he was smiling as he nodded a farewell.

THREE HOURS LATER, Jeff was seeing double. Trying to read all that tiny print crammed onto a low-grade computer screen in the basement of the *Chronicle* building was enough to give a stronger man a migraine. And all he'd learned from his efforts was that Alana Ross was a tenacious reporter with a solid grasp of grammar.

He didn't have a migraine, but he pulled two ibuprofen tablets from the travel bottle in his pocket and downed them dry. Then he clicked off the machine. *Aunt Marge,* he thought, *I'm doing this for you. You sure as hell better appreciate it.*

Of course, he was doing it for Uncle Bob, too—but Aunt Marge had been the one who'd phoned Jeff and begged him to come up to Crescent Cove. Uncle Bob had blown off the article in the *Chronicle,* insisting it was much ado about nothing. "Just a bored reporter with dreams of winning a Pulitzer," he'd said, dismissing the piece.

But Aunt Marge had seen it as an attack on her husband, and she'd asked Jeff to come to Crescent Cove. The class-action age-discrimination case Jeff had been working on for the past six months had unexpectedly reached a settlement yesterday, so he'd taken the day off and driven up to the picturesque Vermont town on the shore of Lake Champlain. He wasn't sure what he could do to salvage Uncle Bob's reputation—Alana Ross and her editor were right in claiming no libel had occurred—but if he could throw his weight around a little and give everyone a good scare, they might keep Uncle Bob's name out of subsequent reports on the school's budget problems.

Jeff pinched the bridge of his nose and shut his eyes, waiting for the pills to kick in. Alana Ross's image floated across the blank screen of his mind and he let out a long breath. He'd expected the author of the article to be strong-willed and verbally nimble, but he hadn't expected her to have such soulful brown eyes, or long, rippling hair the color of maple syrup. Her chin was too pointy, her cheeks too angular, her face too narrow, but put them all together and add a pair of snug-fitting black jeans, and a man noticed.

She'd noticed him, too, if not exactly the way he'd noticed her. He'd scored pretty damn high on her enemies list. It wasn't as if he was trying to deprive her of her First Amendment rights, for God's sake. She hadn't had to regard him as if he were scum.

But he was a lawyer. He was used to people regarding him that way.

His headache faded. He opened his eyes, stretched and smoothed out the tie he'd loosened as soon as the newspaper's archivist, a skinny young man with geeky eyeglasses and a hole in the elbow of his crew-neck sweater, had led him to this basement computer and booted up the newspaper's archives for the past six months. The archivist was banging away at a much newer computer with a nineteen-inch flat-screen monitor—no eye strain for him—and Jeff called a quick thanks as he shoved himself to his feet and donned his coat. He climbed the stairs and peered through the glass doors at the far side of the vestibule. Night had fallen—and plenty of snow had fallen, too, in the hours he'd been perusing the archives in the basement.

The snow didn't concern him. He hadn't been planning to drive back to Boston tonight anyway. Aunt Marge had already made up the spare room for him.

A glance at the well-lit newsroom revealed a few people at their desks, tapping away at their computers. Alana Ross had already left. Chasing down a hot lead? he wondered. Hell, the missing school-budget money was probably the hottest story this cute little town had ever seen.

He buttoned his coat, turned up the collar and exited the building. The icy air sent a shiver through his body. As chilly as Boston could get in December, Crescent Cove was much colder.

Hunching against the biting wind, he strode around the building to the adjacent parking lot. He dug his hand into his coat pocket and pressed the button on his key. The headlights flashed on his BMW.

Three steps from his car, he heard the ghastly, familiar whine of tires spinning on ice. Scanning the lot, he saw the glowing red taillights of the car in trouble: a nondescript compact sedan parked right next to a mountainous pile of snow at the far end of the lot. The tires whined again as the driver pressed the gas and went nowhere. The car's headlights glared against the wall of the building.

Jeff crossed the lot, doing his best to avoid the patches of ice. He'd worn a pair of dress loafers, not the best shoes for a night like this.

The stuck car revved again, backed up an inch, then forward, then back again. No progress. He reached the car and tapped on the driver's side window.

Alana Ross gazed at him. All bundled up in a hat, a scarf and a parka, she looked warm—and exasperated. She rolled down the window. "I take it you don't have four-wheel drive," he said.

Her scowl intensified. She was cute when she frowned, but he didn't think she'd appreciate his saying so. "This is the first time I've ever gotten stuck. I knew this parking space would mean trouble, but it was the only one available when I returned from lunch."

Because he'd taken the only other open spot, just a few minutes before she'd arrived. He didn't think she'd appreciate hearing that, either. "Do you have anything to stuff under the tires?"

"Like what?"

"A copy of last Friday's *Chronicle* would work."

She permitted herself a reluctant smile. "Your tie might work just as well," she said.

He smiled back. "I'll give you a push," he offered, "but only if you promise not to roll forward and pin me to the wall."

"I won't."

"All right." He moved around to the front of the car, braced one foot against the wall, gripped the front bumper with his hands and signaled her with a nod. She touched the gas pedal—very gently, he noted with some relief. He pushed. She gave the engine a little more gas. The tires spit slush at his shins. The soles of his shoes slipped against the ice. He pushed some more.

The car fought him, but he won. Slowly, shimmying and spraying snow in all directions, the vehicle eased out of the spot.

He straightened up, wiped his gloves off against each other and circled around to her open window. "Oh, God," she groaned, surveying him. "You're all wet."

"It's just snow."

"And slush and…oh, your shoes."

He glanced at his shoes. They were soaked, his socks damp, his toes beginning to go numb. He should shut himself inside his own warm car and crank up the heat, but Alana

seemed so worried, her eyes swimming with guilt and grati-
tude. Her plaintive expression was worth sacrificing a toe or
two to frostbite.

"If you follow me back to my house, I'll give you a towel.
And a drink. It's the least I owe you."

He could get a towel and a drink from Aunt Marge, too.
But he'd much rather follow Alana home. "I'll be right behind
you," he said, then headed back to his car, trying not to grin.

Chapter Two

Jeffrey Barrett offered to lug two bags of supplies from the trunk of Alana's car into her house. She'd bought her brisket yesterday on her way home from work so she could put it right into the freezer—although on a snowy evening, the interior of her trunk was probably just as cold. Before she'd gone to Burning Bright that afternoon, she'd spent most of her lunch break combing the aisles of BK's Grocery in search of other necessities for the Hanukkah open house. Barrett thoughtfully carried the bags containing the potatoes, the heaviest of the bunch—and this after having sacrificed his shoes to the effort of pushing her car off the ice in the parking lot. He deserved a few points.

But he wanted her to tone down her reporting on Robert Willis and the missing school-budget money, so he lost all the points he might have earned with his good deeds.

She hit the light switch with her elbow before leading him into the kitchen. Nellie let out a raucous bark and scampered across the floor, her paws skidding on the smooth linoleum. She swept right past Alana and zeroed in on Barrett, nearly tripping him in her eagerness to sniff him.

"Whoa," he said, setting the bags on the table and then hunkering down to scratch Nellie behind her floppy ears. Nellie was a slutty mutt—she fell in love with anyone who rubbed her in the right places—and Alana didn't take her instant infatuation with Barrett as proof of his sterling character. The fact that he was acting friendly toward Nellie didn't mean anything, either. Even despots and sadists liked dogs.

Not that Barrett was a despot or a sadist. He was a lawyer trying to shut her up in the middle of a big story, that was all. A fat-cat attorney from Boston throwing his weight around.

"Come on, Nellie," she scolded after putting her grocery bags on the counter. "Outside." She opened the door from the kitchen to the back porch and into the tiny fenced-in yard. As soon as Nellie heard the squeak of the door hinges, she abandoned Barrett and raced outside, eager to empty her bladder and romp around in the snow after a long day indoors.

Barrett straightened up and removed his coat, which glistened with drops of water where snowflakes had landed and melted. "I hope she's not supposed to be a guard dog," he said.

Alana laughed, and resented his sense of humor. "A robber could walk away with everything I own, as long as he scratched her behind her ears," she admitted. Not that she had much worth stealing. The only valuable jewelry she owned was the stuff she wore every day: her watch, her gold hoop earrings, the opal birthstone ring adorning her right hand. Her laptop, printer, stereo and TV might tempt a robber, but they were insured and easily replaceable. Nellie was the only thing in her house she'd grieve losing.

Barrett draped his coat over a chair. His hair glistened with melting snow, too. She recalled why she'd invited him back to her house—because he'd sacrificed his shoes to rescue her car from its slippery space. "Let me get some towels so you can dry off," she said.

Before he could respond, she headed down the hall to the linen closet. She grabbed an old towel for Nellie and two newer towels for Barrett. Back in to the kitchen, she found him rubbing a paper towel over his hair. "I don't think I need those," he said, eyeing the towels in her hand.

"Of course you do." She handed him the two nicer towels and hooked the old one over the knob of the back door. "While you're at it, give me your shoes and socks."

What he gave her was a sharp, dubious look.

"They're soaked. You'll make yourself sick if you keep them on." She extended her hand expectantly.

He continued to stare at her. "What are you going to do with them?"

"I'll throw your socks in the dryer for ten minutes, and I'll blast your shoes with a hair dryer." She kept her hand out, waiting.

He seemed to weigh his options before dropping into a chair. "I really don't think this is necessary," he muttered, although when he yanked off his shoes, splashes of water and slush scattered across the floor. Alana took his soggy shoes and socks and hurried back down the hall, first to the laundry alcove to stick his argyle socks into the clothes dryer and then to the bathroom, where she propped the nozzle of her old hair dryer into one of his shoes and turned the hairdryer on. Patsy recommended drying shoes in the microwave, but Alana had found that a hair dryer worked better. When she'd bought a new blow dryer last fall, she'd saved the old one for just this sort of situation.

Back in the kitchen, she found Barrett still seated, one leg crossed over the other knee as he dried his feet with one of the cloth towels. Men's feet were ugly, but Barrett's were no worse than most—and of course the rest of him was so far above average that his knobby toes and bony insteps hardly mattered. He did appear oddly vulnerable, though, without his shoes on. She liked thinking of him as vulnerable.

She walked past him to the bags she'd left on the counter and started emptying them. "Let me just put these groceries away, and then I'll get you that drink I promised," she said as she unpacked the onions and apricots.

He slung the towel over the back of a chair and rose. Even without shoes on, he was much too tall. Maybe inviting him here had been a major mistake. Just because he was an allegedly reputable attorney who knew the right way to scratch a dog's ears didn't mean he was sane or safe.

She'd been living in Crescent Cove too long, she realized. Back in Bridgeport—or in Philadelphia, where she'd grown up, or Manhattan, where she'd gone to college—she would never have brought a strange man into her house. Especially one as dangerously handsome as Barrett.

She had her cell phone in her pocket. If he tried anything, she'd bolt and call the cops.

Barrett lifted the second towel and ran it over his hair. In the amber light from the fixture above the table, she noticed the shadow of beard darkening his jaw. The collar button of his shirt was unfastened, the knot of his tie loosened. He looked somewhere between relaxed and exhausted, except for his alert silver-gray eyes. "Do you have roommates?" he asked.

Her defenses shot up. Was he trying to find out whether they were alone? She lowered the bag of marshmallows she'd been about to stash on a shelf, tucked her hand into her pocket and brushed her thumb against the buttons of her cell phone. "Why do you ask?"

He gestured toward the bags he'd brought inside. "That's a lot of potatoes for one person."

Panic subsiding, she released the cell phone and nodded. "It's for a party," she explained as she resumed unpacking her bags.

"A potato party?"

"They're for latkes," she told him. "It's a traditional Hanukkah dish."

"Ah." He gave up on his hair, leaving it sticking out from his scalp in damp tufts, and bent over to sop some of the moisture from the hems of his trousers. "A Hanukkah party?"

She was amused that he would continue chatting from such an undignified position. Evidently, his ego was healthy enough that he didn't care if he was presenting his butt to the world. A small, taut butt it was, too—and Alana was ashamed of herself for admiring it. "Hanukkah starts next Tuesday at sundown," she said, her voice betraying nothing of her thoughts about his physique. "I'm hosting a party the fifth night of Hanukkah, on Saturday. My grandmother…"

He straightened up, and the sheer beauty of his face caused her breath to catch in her throat. The hell with his physique.

His eyes alone were enough to light a fire inside her. His eyes and his lips, and—

"Your grandmother what?" he said, breaking into her thoughts as he dropped the second towel next to the first on the chair.

She snapped out of her daze. "My grandmother hosted an open house on the weekend that fell during Hanukkah. There's always a Saturday night—unless Hanukkah starts on a Saturday. Then there are two, because the holiday lasts eight days."

He nodded, the strained patience in his expression indicating that she wasn't telling him anything he didn't already know.

"Anyway, my grandmother died last spring, and I thought I'd try hosting an open house like the ones she used to host. In her memory, I guess." She spoke quickly, certain that he couldn't possibly be interested in all this.

"And your grandmother served marshmallows for Hanukkah?"

All right, maybe he *could* be interested. "She'd take a marshmallow, sandwich it between two dried apricots and hold the thing together with a toothpick."

"That sounds disgusting."

She considered defending the odd treat, then decided to save her strength for what mattered: the *Chronicle*'s investigation into the missing school-budget money. "It's very tasty," she said. "I'll go check on your shoes."

She hurried down the hall to the bathroom, taking deep, steady breaths and reminding herself that Jeffrey Barrett was her adversary, in town to silence her. His cute butt and his devastating eyes were irrelevant, as was his help in the parking lot earlier. He was trouble, and she'd better not forget it.

She pulled the hair dryer out of his left loafer, tucked it into his right loafer, turned it back on and inhaled another deep breath. If he thought her grandmother's recipes were disgusting, screw him. He wasn't invited to the party.

She stopped in the laundry alcove, removed his toasty socks from the dryer and carried them to the kitchen. "Here," she said, tossing them to him en route to the coffeemaker.

"Your shoes will be ready soon." She busied herself stuffing a filter into the basket and scooping in ground coffee beans, then hesitated. "Would you prefer coffee or tea? Or cocoa?"

He appeared briefly startled, then a smile traced his lips. "Coffee's fine."

His smile disconcerted her. "What's so funny?"

He sat down to put on his socks. "When a woman asks a man if he wants to come to her house for a drink, she usually doesn't mean coffee."

"I usually do," she retorted. She finished preparing the coffee and switched on the machine, then crossed to the back door and opened it. Nellie bounded into the warm room. With deft timing, Alana flung the old towel over her and squatted to dry the snow from her tawny fur. As soon as Alana released her, she trotted over to her water dish and drank, slurping loudly.

"What did you say her name was again?" Barrett asked.

Alana glanced at him. With his socks on, he looked less vulnerable. Unfortunately. "Nellie. She's named after Nellie Bly, the crusading reporter back at the turn of the twentieth century."

Barrett watched Nellie lap up her water, her tail slashing through the air. "Oh, yeah. She's got crusading reporter written all over her."

Again, in spite of herself, Alana laughed. She used the time it took to scoop some kibble into Nellie's food dish to erase her smile. The coffeemaker beeped and she fetched two mugs from a shelf. "Milk or sugar?" she asked, all traces of amusement vanquished.

"Straight up, thanks."

Alana filled the two mugs and brought them to the table. She sat across from Barrett and tried not to let his steady gaze or the sturdy line of his jaw distract her. He was in Crescent Cove to give her a hard time, she reminded herself. "Speaking of crusading reporters," she said, "I assume your afternoon of research proved that I'm a fair and honest journalist. I'm not out to destroy anyone's reputation. I *am* out to report the facts, and I intend to continue doing that. It's my job."

"How did you wind up here? The *Crescent Cove Chronicle* is a step down from the *Bridgeport News.*"

She sat up straighter. He hadn't learned about her previous job by reviewing the *Chronicle* archives. He must have done research on her before coming to town. Sheesh. How many hours was he going to bill Robert Willis for? And why? Alana hadn't accused Willis of anything other than being responsible for the missing money.

She could only hope Barrett's research hadn't uncovered the whole unpleasant story about her departure from the *News.* "Chet Holroyd offered me an opportunity to do more than just report," she said, which was true. "Since joining the *Chronicle* staff, I've done some text editing and written a couple of unsigned editorials. I've consulted on layout and design and helped select photos. Because it's a smaller paper, I get to do more." She sipped her coffee. "Crescent Cove is much prettier than Bridgeport, too."

"Much snowier," he muttered. "But thanks to you, my feet are warm and dry."

She sipped some coffee and waited for him to continue speaking. She'd already told him more than he ought to know about her.

"How will you feel," he asked, "if you discover that the missing money has nothing to do with Robert Willis?"

"Relieved," she admitted. "I'm hoping it's a bookkeeping error. Right now the town auditor is going through the records. Maybe that's what she'll find."

"You won't feel guilty for having smeared a good man?"

"I didn't smear Robert Willis."

"This is a small town," he said unnecessarily. "Everyone knows everyone. And they all read the *Chronicle.*"

"And they want to learn what happened to their tax money. As a reporter, it's my job to find out for them."

He let out a long breath. "All right. It's late. We can talk about this more tomorrow."

Tomorrow? He was planning to work through the weekend on this nonsense? "I'll be out of town tomorrow," she told him.

"You're traveling in this storm?"

"It's supposed to stop by morning. The roads will be plowed."

"You're driving somewhere? Can your car handle it? You don't have four-wheel drive, do you?"

"I don't need it, most of the time."

"Where are you going?"

If she didn't answer, he'd assume she was hiding something. "Burlington," she told him. "I've got to buy candles."

"For your party?"

She nodded.

"They don't sell candles in Crescent Cove?"

Once again, his interest surprised her. She glanced at Nellie, who was happily devouring her kibble, and drank some coffee. "I can't find candles here that fit my grandmother's menorah. I inherited it when she died. It's an antique. I guess they had different-sized candles back then."

"An antique?"

She stood to refill their cups, then decided to show him the menorah, since he seemed to care and she loved to look at it herself. She exhumed it from the depths of her tote bag, unwrapped it and placed it at the center of the kitchen table.

He leaned back and admired it. "Wow. That's really nice."

"I bought some Hanukkah candles in town, but they were too narrow. And then this lady…" She reached back into her tote and removed the candle the woman at Burning Bright had given her. "The saleslady at a candle store told me this candle would work, but it didn't fit, either."

Barrett lifted the candle, studied it as intensely as he'd studied the menorah and then propped the candle into the *shamas* holder, the top candle separate from the other eight. "It fits fine."

To Alana's amazement, it did. Apparently, the *shamas* holder was a different size from the other eight holders, since the candle hadn't fit those when Alana had tried it out in the car. "I'll be damned," she murmured, shaking her head. "I've got one candle that works. I still need a whole bunch more."

"Let me see the ones you bought."

Wonderful. Barrett had gotten the white candle into the *shamas* holder, and now he thought he could work miracles. Humoring him, she handed him the box she'd bought earlier that week at the stationery store. He opened it, pulled out one candle and stuck it into the first holder on the right. It fit.

"How'd you do that?" she asked, annoyed that he'd gotten the candle to work when she hadn't, but also thrilled to think she wouldn't have to drive all the way to Burlington this weekend to buy candles. She pulled the candle out of the left holder and reinserted it. It nestled perfectly in its cup. "It's not like I didn't try to get these candles to work a dozen times."

"You obviously don't have the right touch," Barrett teased.

She glanced sharply at him and saw him smiling. His smile was much too sexy, only adding to her indignation that he'd succeeded where she'd failed in getting the candles to fit. The menorah had been her grandmother's, after all. She should have been able to manage the candles better than some silver-eyed stranger.

"Well," she said, tamping down her annoyance. "Thank you."

"I know my way around menorahs," he told her. "I've lit a few in my day."

She stared at him, surprised. Given his *Mayflower*-sounding last name, she never would have guessed. "Are you Jewish?"

"My mother was," he said. "I guess she still is, although she isn't observant. My dad was raised Presbyterian, so when they married they joined the Unitarian Church. There were lots of us half-and-half kids in that church. It's a good faith, very accepting, embracing all paths. One of those paths included my grandmother and her menorah. And her candles always fit."

"So do mine, apparently." *Thanks to you,* she almost added.

"Does this mean I can come to your party?"

"It's a week from tomorrow. You won't still be in town then, will you?"

His smile increased. "Publish an article clearing Robert Willis's name and I'll be gone," he promised.

Tempting though his offer was, her journalistic ethics weren't for sale. "The *Chronicle* will clear his name once we have evidence that he isn't guilty of theft or mismanagement."

"Such lofty principles." He drained his mug, set it on the table and stood. Nellie peered up from her bowl, clearly enthralled by the very big person in the kitchen. He slid his arms through the sleeves of his coat and winked at the dog before turning back to Alana. "So what time is your party? Just in case I'm still in town."

"If you're still in town, I'll be sure to let you know," Alana answered, thinking that as honest as she was in her work, she'd just told a whopper. If Jeffrey Barrett was still in town by next weekend, she would most certainly not let him know. He'd never be welcome at her party, even if he did have a way with candles.

Chapter Three

"Jason Farrar? Yeah, he's here." The hostess at Mort's Diner, an old woman dressed in purple, with a long silvery braid trailing down her back, cupped her hand against her brow as if searching for a pirate ship on the horizon rather than a customer at a table. "There he is, in the fifth booth." She pointed out one of the booths lining the front wall. The man she'd indicated had his back to the entry.

A clerk at the police station had told Jeff he could find Police Chief Farrar at Mort's. Jeff hadn't realized he needed to talk to the chief of police. All he'd asked was whether the police had launched a criminal investigation into the missing school-budget money. Aunt Marge had insisted they hadn't, although she'd added that every time the doorbell rang she flinched, expecting to find an officer on her front steps.

Evidently, the clerk felt Jeff ought to discuss Uncle Bob's situation with the police chief. Jeff tried not to read too much into that.

After thanking the hostess, he started down the narrow aisle toward the booth where Chief Farrar was seated. Farrar shifted and Jeff saw the woman facing him across the table, a heavy porcelain mug halfway to her lips. She saw Jeff, too; her eyes widened and she lowered her mug without drinking.

He hadn't imagined his attraction to Alana Ross; he felt it just as keenly this morning as he had yesterday. He couldn't pinpoint exactly what it was about her that drew him in. Sure, her eyes were pretty. So was her hair, long and brown with sweet golden highlights. So were her delicate lips and her perfectly proportioned body. But hell, Boston was full of pretty women. Jeff didn't have to travel all the way to the shores of Lake Champlain to find one.

He couldn't say her personality was warm and welcoming. Granted, she'd offered him a drink last night—coffee, nothing exciting, and that was only because he'd been a Good Samaritan, risking the destruction of his loafers for her in the parking lot. Her invitation hadn't been personal.

On the other hand, she'd insisted on drying his shoes and socks, which struck him as extremely personal. Sometimes, when things were going well, a woman might ask him to remove his clothes. But he couldn't recall any woman besides Alana who had ever specifically asked him to remove his shoes and socks.

He liked that about her. He liked her dog. He liked her confidence. He appreciated a woman who knew what she was fighting for and then gave the fight her all.

Even from a distance he could read the series of emotions that passed across her face as her gaze met his: shock followed by a fleeting look of—could it be pleasure?—followed by irritation, resignation and finally begrudging tolerance. Jeff wondered if she realized how expressive her eyes were, how easily they gave her away.

Farrar must have noticed her staring, because he twisted in his seat and watched Jeff's approach. "Jason Farrar?" Jeff asked, extending his right hand. The chief seemed friendly, especially compared with Alana. He was dressed casually, as was Alana, who had on a colorful sweater and jeans. Jeff had also chosen jeans today, as well as the thick-soled work boots he'd tossed into his car before leaving Boston, when he'd heard a weather forecast predicting snow in northern New England. "I'm Jeff Barrett," he introduced himself to the police chief. "I was wondering if you could spare a few minutes sometime today so we could talk about the missing school-budget money."

"Right," the police chief said, as if he'd been expecting Jeff. "Alana and I were just talking about the school funds. Why don't you join us."

"If you're sure you don't mind…" One glance at Alana informed Jeff she *did* mind.

"Not at all," Farrar assured him. "So you're Jeff Barrett. Your aunt Marge talks about you all the time."

"Aunt Marge?" Alana eyed him curiously.

Opting not to answer, Jeff slid onto the seat next to her. The banquette was big enough for two, but not so big he could avoid brushing hips and shoulders with her, a contact that sent a hum of awareness through him. "I don't know what she could be saying about me," he told Farrar. "Maybe she was talking about someone else."

Farrar grinned. "You want to order something? We're about done eating already." He gestured toward his plate, which held some toast crusts and a few remaining forkfuls of omelette. The plate in front of Alana contained only a bran muffin from which she seemed to have taken no more than a bite or two.

"I'll have…" Jeff paused when he spotted a waitress approaching their table, her pad at the ready. "A cup of coffee, please," he said, directing the rest of the sentence to her.

As soon as she was gone, Alana again asked, "Aunt Marge?"

Jeff supposed she'd find out sooner or later that Bob Willis was his uncle. He'd prefer that she find out later, so he ignored her question. "What I'm wondering," he said to Farrar, "is whether Bob will be charged with anything."

"I was just telling Alana, the auditor is still going through the past year's records. We don't charge without evidence of wrongdoing, and so far there's no evidence."

Jeff sent Alana a triumphant grin. "The *Chronicle* article implied there was."

"I didn't say there wasn't," Farrar reminded him. "I just said we haven't found the evidence yet. The auditor is suspicious, though. The money disappeared in small increments, as if someone wanted to escape notice. A bookkeeping error would show up in big chunks—you know, someone misplaced a decimal point and it says ten thousand dollars where it should say a hundred. But when a little money goes missing here, a little there, some from this account and some from that, it usually means an embezzler is trying to cover his tracks."

Alana sat taller in her seat. She broke off a chunk of muffin and popped it into her mouth, managing to chew and smile at the same time.

Of course she was smiling. She thought she had a big crime to report on. Nothing as exciting as what she used to write about in Bridgeport—Jeff had done a Web search last night at Aunt Marge's house and read some articles with Alana's by-line on them from the *Bridgeport News*'s on-line archives. One dealt with rising crime in a public housing project, another with the arrest of a pharmacist for forging painkiller prescriptions and selling them on the street. Those stories were a little juicier than missing school-budget money in Crescent Cove, where the word *embezzler* seemed grossly out of place.

Why had she left Bridgeport? It sure seemed like a step down, career-wise.

"Do you think Dorothy would talk to me?" Alana asked Farrar. Jeff wondered who Dorothy was.

Farrar shrugged. "She'll be in her office today. She's aware we need the audit done as quickly as possible, so she said she'd work through the weekend. Whether she minds being interrupted I can't say."

Dorothy must be the auditor. If Alana was going to talk to her, Jeff would, too. On the off chance that Uncle Bob was ultimately charged, Jeff as his lawyer would be privy to whatever evidence the police had against him—and whatever evidence they had would probably turn up in the audit.

The waitress arrived with a mug of steaming coffee for Jeff. He lifted it at the same moment Alana lifted hers and their elbows bumped. She had on a thick sweater, he hadn't even removed his coat, yet a spark, hot and sharp, passed through all that insulation. Static electricity, probably. Cold, dry air and wool could cause that.

So could a woman like Alana Ross.

Stay focused, he ordered himself. He was in Crescent Cove for one reason only: to save his uncle's ass. Alana was nothing more than a distraction.

Well, she was something more than that. She was the woman who'd written the damn article putting his uncle's ass in jeopardy in the first place.

"I've got to run," Jason said, swallowing the last of his omelette and then wiping his mouth with a napkin from the chrome dispenser beside the tabletop jukebox. "If you want to try Dorothy, you'll probably find her at Town Hall most of the day. And if anything else breaks—" he nodded at Alana "—I'll be in touch." He turned to Jeff. "Give your aunt my regards, okay?"

"Sure. Thanks," Jeff said, shaking the police chief's hand once more as the man slid out of the booth.

The seat across from Alana was now empty. Jeff could move across the table from her. But the chances of their bumping elbows across the table were slim, so he decided to stay where he was.

She twisted in her seat, poking his thigh with her knee, and glowered at him. Even glowering, she looked magnificent. "Is 'Aunt Marge' Marjorie Willis?" It was an accusation more than a question. "Is Robert Willis your uncle?"

"By marriage," Jeff admitted. "Marge Willis is my father's baby sister."

"You didn't think to mention that yesterday."

"What difference would it make? Bob might need a lawyer, and I'm the best one he knows. So here I am."

"He *might* need a lawyer?" Alana harrumphed and twisted forward again, repeating the knee bump.

He smiled, wishing she would bump him some more. "You don't sound too objective," he chided. "As a journalist, shouldn't you keep your opinions out of your reporting?"

"I've never said Robert Willis was guilty."

"You just implied he needs a lawyer."

"I mean, I never said it in the newspaper. The article I wrote was very fair. And as the story continues to unfold I'll write another article, and it'll be fair, too."

"I'm sure it will be." He didn't bother to filter the skepticism from his voice. "Are you going to eat that muffin?"

She nudged the plate toward him. "Help yourself."

He allowed himself another smile. Just like last night, when she'd invited him back to her house for a drink, she seemed occasionally able to forget they were adversaries. Her instinct was to be generous. Not necessarily a useful trait in a journalist, he thought, but a very desirable trait in a friend.

He helped himself to a piece of her muffin. It was bran with bananas rather than raisins, and infinitely tastier than the bowl of oatmeal Aunt Marge had insisted he eat before leaving her house. "So, what happened? Did the *Bridgeport News* fire you?"

Whatever kindness he'd sensed in her evaporated like dew on a hot morning. "No, they didn't fire me," she said curtly.

"You quit?"

"Yes."

"Why?"

"What makes you think that's any of your business?"

"I'm eating your muffin," he said.

For some reason, she accepted his answer as reasonable. "I had no mobility there," she said. "I wanted to do some editing, some news analysis, but that wasn't going to happen at the *News*, so I quit. At the *Chronicle,* I'm encouraged to do everything. It's been a great experience."

"Yeah, but you're in Crescent Cove. The middle of nowhere."

"This is a lovely town," she argued.

"You like living in a town where the biggest story your paper's covered is that seventy-five thousand dollars of the school-board's budget has been misplaced? In Boston, seventy-five thousand dollars gets misplaced in at least three city departments every day. News like that wouldn't even make the comics page."

"Maybe that's why I like Crescent Cove," she pointed out,

sounding less argumentative than philosophical. "There's something nice about a town where this is a big deal. We don't have big-city crime or corruption here. Reports of murders and assaults and fatal accidents don't dominate our front page."

"Can you actually imagine yourself spending the rest of your life here?" he asked.

She helped herself to another bit of muffin. "The rest of my life? That's a long time." She mulled over the idea, then added, "It depends on how my Hanukkah party goes."

Jeff let out a laugh. "If the party is a bust, you're going to move back to Bridgeport?"

"I have no intention of ever moving back to Bridgeport," she muttered, a hint that more than just a lack of professional mobility had driven her from that city. "It's just…I want to feel at home here. And I do. But things like Hanukkah…" She appeared to be thinking aloud. "The Jewish holidays are important to me. I don't know how I'd feel if I was the only person in town they were important to."

"Your party's going to be a big success," he predicted, because she seemed so pensive, all of a sudden. "Of course, it would be an even bigger success if you invited me."

She grinned and shook her head, her spirit recovered. "Yeah, right. Sue me for libel and then come and drink my wine."

"Only if it's good wine. Not that sweet kosher stuff."

She crumpled her napkin and tossed it onto the table. "Why don't you go find out if Aunt Marge has any errands she wants you to run. I've got work to do."

Reluctantly he stood to allow her to escape the booth. Sitting so close to her had been nice. Much too nice. "No errands for Aunt Marge," he said as he pulled his wallet from the hip pocket of his jeans. "I've got work to do, too."

HE WORKED at a polished mahogany table three away from hers in the reference section of the library. Like her, he was flipping through old school budgets. Like her, he had a pad at his elbow, a pen in hand. What was he looking for? Something that might exonerate his uncle?

What Alana was looking for had nothing to do with exonerating Robert Willis. She'd spent nearly an hour in Dorothy's office. Barrett had accompanied her there and she'd been unable to come up with an excuse to bar him from the discussion, since it was about a public matter. Then he'd accompanied her to the town library to examine school budget reports dating back more than a decade. He knew what she did: that Dorothy believed someone had been systematically skimming money from this year's school budget, that she was currently reviewing past budgets to see if the theft had been going on prior to this year and that she had asked Jason Farrar to scare up a bunch of bank statements for her.

Alana glanced at Barrett. His head was bowed over the ledger and a frown line creased his forehead. The ceiling fixture captured the highlights in his hair and his shoulders filled out his sweater much too nicely. What would he look like without that sweater? she wondered. What would it be like to sit as close to him as she had at Mort's, only without layers of clothing separating them?

With a sigh, she lowered her gaze back to her own ledger. She had no good reason to think about Jeff Barrett that way— other than the obvious one, which was that he was the most handsome man to enter her field of vision since she'd settled in Crescent Cove, and arguably for a long time before then. When a man could look as sexy as he did in a bulky sweater and old jeans and poring over school budgets, a woman was entitled to ogle. And fantasize.

The librarian had brought out so many ledgers for them to review that they'd decided to divide them. This meant that if she found any questionable calculations or mysterious deficits, she'd have to share her discovery with him. And if he found any, he'd have to share it with her. She hoped she could trust him. Even if he hid discrepancies from her, hawk-eyed Dorothy Callahan would unearth them eventually, so it wasn't as if he could protect his uncle forever. And discrepancies might actually work in his uncle's favor; some of the ledgers Barrett had dated back to a time before his uncle became the superintendent of schools. If he discovered a pattern of lousy bookkeeping, he could make a convincing case that the school department's comptroller was habitually careless.

So far, Alana had seen nothing worth noting. A couple of errors appeared in the records, with asterisks and corrections penned in. The numbers were beginning to blur before her eyes. To rest them, she shifted her gaze, and it zeroed in on Jeff Barrett again.

Had she noticed yesterday how rugged his jaw line was? She'd been keenly aware of it that morning at Mort's, when she'd had a close-up view of his profile. She'd had to exercise enormous willpower not to reach up and trace the sharp angle of his chin with her fingertips. Thank God she'd had a mug of coffee to occupy her hands.

A muted voice spilled from speakers in the ceiling: "The library will close in fifteen minutes. If you wish to check out material, please do so now."

She glanced at her watch: quarter to five. On weekdays, the library stayed open until eight, but on Saturdays it closed early. Just as well; she was tired of reviewing the records, and she doubted she was going to find anything interesting in them.

Three tables away, Barrett folded his ledger book shut, leaned back in his chair and stretched. His gaze collided with hers and he smiled.

She felt warm. More than warm. She felt the way she had when he'd appropriated her muffin that morning. It had been such an intimate act—just as her drying his socks in her clothes dryer had been an intimate act. She shouldn't have done that, but she couldn't have let his feet freeze, could she?

The way he was smiling at her now, his arms extended above her head and his back arching… It made her contemplate what he would look like when he woke up after a night's sleep. Without any clothes on.

Shrugging off the thought, she closed the book she'd been scrutinizing, pushed back her chair and stood. She turned to lift her parka from the back of her chair and spun around when she heard a muted thump. Barrett stood directly across from her, adding his ledgers to her stack. "Uncover any deep, dark secrets?" he asked in a hushed, library-appropriate voice.

"Not even any shallow, light ones," she said, relieved that her words didn't reveal her thoughts about waking up with him. "How about you?"

"No, but I'm pretty hungry. Is there someplace a step up from that diner where we could get some dinner?"

We. He assumed she would join him. Well, why not? If she went home, she'd spend the evening fussing with the candles for her menorah and trying to figure out her grandmother's recipe for potato latkes. "This isn't Boston," she pointed out, "but you can get a decent meal at Sister Krissie's."

"Great." He hoisted the ledgers into his arms and lugged them to the reference librarian's counter while Alana put on her jacket and ordered her imagination to stick close to home. She could eat dinner with Barrett without getting fixated on his silver eyes and his heart-stopping smile. She could eat, and she could remember that he was a hired gun in town to defend his uncle from a journalist who had the audacity to report the truth.

Dark had fallen while they'd been shut up inside the library, and the night air was raw. His car was parked near hers in the lot behind the building. "Why don't we use my car," he suggested. "I'll drive you back here after dinner."

Hopefully, the pavement under her tires wouldn't be slick with ice when they returned. But if it was, he could push her out of the spot. The parking lot was relatively clear, and he was wearing what appeared to be waterproof work boots, so she wouldn't have to dry his socks afterward.

Sister Krissie's was bustling on a Saturday night; in Crescent Cove five o'clock was considered a fashionable hour to dine. Fortunately, the hostess found a small table in a back corner for them, and within a few minutes they'd ordered: steak and a beer for Barrett, grilled salmon and a glass of Chardonnay for Alana. The waitress brought them their drinks and a basket of warm bread, removed their menus and vanished.

"So," he said, "do you think your buddy Jason Farrar is going to arrest my uncle?"

Talking about Robert Willis was safer than pondering Barrett's bedroom eyes. "Jason knows his job," she assured him. "If he arrests Willis, it'll be because he's got the evidence he needs." She traced the edge of her napkin with her index finger and recalled her desire to trace Barrett's jaw. The same urge attacked her now, and she was glad her napkin was spread across her lap so he couldn't see her fidgeting. "Have you noticed your uncle's spending habits changing recently? Did he suddenly buy a new car or a high-definition TV?"

"He's a frugal Yankee." Barrett drank some beer and shook his head. "He's not a thief, Alana. He and Aunt Marge have been married for twenty-eight years, and they've raised two kids. Bobby is in dental school now, and Emily is a senior up in Burlington, at the university. This is not a family you'd associate with embezzlement."

"Do you think maybe someone's conned him?" Alana asked. "Is there someone else who has access to the school department's accounts?"

"How would I know?" He took a slice of bread and spread butter across it. "You're plugged into the local scene. I'm not."

"What kind of law do you practice in Boston?" she asked.

"Labor law, mostly." He smiled sheepishly. "Uncle Bob isn't exactly my specialty, but I'm as qualified to offer him legal assistance as anyone around here. Probably more qualified."

His arrogance amused her. What else could she expect from a Boston legal eagle? "And you're doing it pro bono, I'm sure. Such a noble gesture."

He laughed. "What can I say? I'm a good nephew."

"Do you live right in the city?"

"Back Bay," he told her. "Nice neighborhood. Grossly overpriced." He shrugged and took another swig of beer. "Tell me, does the peace and quiet up here ever get to you? Do you miss the din of traffic? Fresh sushi? Decent cell-phone service?"

She missed all those things, but not all the time. "If I could afford it, I'd keep my house here and have a city apartment, too, so I could enjoy both. I grew up just outside Philadelphia and went to college in Manhattan. My grandmother lived there, so even after college I spent a lot of time in New York."

"This is the grandmother who gave you the menorah?"

Alana nodded, waiting to speak until the waitress delivered their salads and left. "She died last spring. She and I were very close, especially when I lived in Bridgeport. I could just hop on the train and go down there for lunch, and be home in time for supper." She poked at her salad with her fork. "She always made a party out of everything. Passover, Hanukkah, birthdays, the Fourth of July. She loved being a hostess."

"Do you?"

"Love being a hostess?" She snorted. "I'm not sure. I've never hosted a party like this open house before. My grandmother always hosted the parties." She speared an out-of-season tomato, pink and mealy, then changed her mind and dropped it back into the salad dish. "I've got all her recipes, but I'm not as good a cook as she was."

"Do you need help? I'm no great cook myself, but I can peel potatoes."

The hotshot Boston lawyer was offering to peel potatoes for her? Was that some new strategy sophisticated urbanites used to pick up women? Actually, any guy willing to peel potatoes would have an inside track with her. And a guy with Jeff Barrett's sex appeal…

On the other hand, maybe this was a sleazy legal ploy. Maybe he'd say he would peel her potatoes if she'd agree not to write any more articles about his uncle.

But when she lifted her wine and caught him watching her, and his gaze met hers over the rim of her wineglass… She couldn't help thinking that something more *was* going on. She wasn't sure what, but something was definitely going on.

Chapter Four

Jeff Barrett showed up at ten Sunday morning, looking surprisingly eager to peel potatoes.

It wasn't as if Alana had expected him to renege on his offer of KP services. Last night's dinner had been too pleasant, the conversation too easy, the drive back to the library for her to pick up her car too friendly. His car, one of those pricey all-wheel-drive BMW models, had handled beautifully on the wintry roads. She bet he never got stuck on an ice patch in a parking lot.

After pulling into the space next to her old clunker, which was the only vehicle parked in the lot at that hour, he'd climbed out of his car in some misguided gesture of chivalry. He couldn't have walked her to her door; it had been only inches from the BMW's passenger-side door. Maybe he'd just wanted to survey the lot, to make sure no creeps were lurking in the shadows. As if anyone would want to lurk outside on a December night in Crescent Cove, when the air was cold enough to freeze tears.

For one insane moment, she'd thought he had gotten out of his car to kiss her. But he'd only watched her fiddle with her keys and unlock her door, and once she'd settled herself in the driver's seat, he'd closed the door behind her. Then he'd waved, circled his own car, gotten in behind the wheel and waited for her to back out of her space—probably concerned he might have to rescue her again. He'd followed her to the parking lot's driveway and turned right when she'd turned left.

No kiss.

Just as well, she thought as she bent over and gripped Nellie's collar so the dog wouldn't charge out onto the front porch and knock him down. Nellie weighed only about thirty pounds, but she was fast and solid, and she could blitz like an NFL lineman.

Jeff stomped the snow off his boots before entering her house. "Your peeler has arrived," he announced with a grin that was just mischievous enough for her to consider the different connotations of the word *peeler*.

"Are you sure you want to do this?" she asked as he removed his coat and hung it on a hook of the coat tree in the entry.

"As opposed to what?"

She shrugged. "Driving back to Boston?"

He followed her down the hall to the kitchen, Nellie scampering alongside him. "I'm not going back to Boston until I'm sure Uncle Bob doesn't need me anymore."

Alana had a strong suspicion Uncle Bob would need a good lawyer soon enough, but she kept that thought to herself. "If you'd really rather peel potatoes than go home, I won't complain," she said, crossing to the loose-leaf binder that held her grandmother's recipes. It lay open on the counter, beside a couple of large bowls and Alana's food processor. The bags of potatoes she'd bought on Friday sat on the kitchen table.

"Can I ask a question?" Jeff spotted the trash can beside the back door and lugged it over to the table.

"Sure."

"Your party isn't until next week. Why are you making your latkes today?"

"I'm going to freeze them. I won't have time to make them fresh the day of the party. My grandmother's recipe says they freeze well." She skimmed the latke instructions in the loose-leaf binder one more time to make sure she hadn't misread that detail.

Nodding, he lowered himself onto one of the chairs, positioned the trash can between his legs and held out his hand. "Peeler?"

She removed one from a drawer and passed it to him. His fingers closed around the utensil and grazed her palm. She ignored her instant reaction to his touch. He hadn't kissed her when he'd had the chance last night. And he *would* be returning to Boston sooner or later, regardless of his uncle's fate. Besides, at the moment he seemed more interested in her potatoes than in her.

She watched him open the bag closest to him, remove a potato and attack it with the peeler. He wore a thick flannel shirt with a dark blue T-shirt under it, and softly faded jeans. He could almost pass for a Vermonter, she thought, ruggedly male yet undaunted by what some might consider a menial task. The peeler looked good in his hand. So did the potato.

And her brain must have turned to latke batter if she could admire him for his prowess at stripping the skin off potatoes. She got busy cracking eggs into one of the bowls.

"I have another question for you," he said.

"Fire away."

"What breed is Nellie? Or should I say, what breeds? I'm guessing she's got some beagle in her."

"Probably," Alana said. "But she doesn't howl like a beagle. She's probably part collie, too, because she's very smart and she likes to herd squirrels. I adopted her from the pound. She didn't come with papers."

"You think she's smart?" He eyed Nellie, who sat patiently at his feet, peering beseechingly at him. "She's begging for a potato peel. That doesn't seem smart to me."

"She's flirting with you," Alana said. "She figures if she makes big goo-goo eyes at you now, you'll come up with a real treat for her later."

"Oh, so she's a flirt, huh." He grinned at the dog, who flicked her tail back and forth. "Sweetheart, I'm not your species," he told her.

He's my species, Alana almost blurted out. She was used to discussing things with Nellie, who was certainly smart enough to listen, whimper sympathetically and cuddle up to Alana when necessary. Once Jeff left for Boston, Alana was sure she and Nellie would have plenty to talk about.

"Did you get Nellie up here in Vermont? Or did she come on board in Bridgeport?"

"Bridgeport," Alana answered. Poor Nellie had stood by Alana's side through that whole mess. She'd done a lot of listening, whimpering and cuddling then.

"So…" Jeff was already on his third potato. "You're not willing to tell me the real reason you left Bridgeport, are you."

"I told you—"

"The *real* reason." He regarded the potato in his hand as though it was infinitely more important than anything Alana might reveal. "I've read some of the articles you wrote for the *Bridgeport News*. They're available on-line. They were good. Well written and powerful. If you'd wanted to climb the ladder at the *News*, I'm sure you could have."

"No, I couldn't have," she snapped, then sighed, realizing she'd given herself away. He couldn't have missed the resentment that underlined her words.

He scrutinized her, obviously awaiting an explanation.

What the hell. She wasn't ashamed of what had occurred, and if she didn't tell him, he'd probably assume something worse than the truth. "I became involved with my editor there," she said.

Jeff glanced at her, apparently surprised. "And the bastard broke your heart?"

"It wasn't so much that," she explained, touched that he automatically assumed her boss had been a bastard. "He just wouldn't let me advance. He said people would accuse him of playing favorites if he promoted me, even though I deserved those promotions. I asked to be transferred out of his department, but he wouldn't let me do that because he didn't want to lose me as a reporter. The longer this went on, the more I felt he was taking advantage of me. He had me writing great stories for him, he wouldn't put me in for raises, he steered plum assignments to other reporters—and he kept saying it was because he loved me. The whole thing seemed so manipulative." She gathered the potatoes Jeff had peeled and sliced them into chunks for her food processor. "He never got along with Nellie, either," she added. "And when my grandmother died, he was anything but comforting. He got bored when I talked about her, he refused to come to the funeral—he couldn't be bothered. Nellie and my grandmother were a hell of a lot more important to me than he was, so..." She shrugged. "I left."

Jeff didn't seem disgusted or appalled by her story. He simply accepted it, without judging. She appreciated that, even more than she appreciated his skills with the peeler.

She ran the peeled potatoes through her food processor. Once the motor stopped whining, she said, "Now that you've heard my life story, I think you should tell me yours."

"Was that your life story?" He laughed.

"My life-in-Bridgeport story. Come on—I've shared my biggest mistake with you. You've got to share your biggest mistake with me."

"I don't make mistakes."

She tossed a plastic measuring spoon at his head. Laughing, he ducked, and the spoon bounced off his shoulder and onto the table. She joined his laughter as she stretched across the table, grabbed the spoon and tossed it into the sink behind her. "You made a big mistake by trying to intimidate me in Chet's office."

"I wasn't trying to intimidate you," he said with exaggerated earnestness.

"Of course you were. You used the word *libel*. Using the word *libel* in front of a reporter is like using the word *water* in front of the Wicked Witch of the West. It's a threat."

"In other words, you're the Wicked Witch of the West."

She reached into the sink to grab the measuring spoon, fully intending it hurl it at his head again, but his grin melted the icy silver from his eyes, turning them a warm, sweet gray. "So, you've never made a single mistake in your life," she said, dumping the shredded potatoes from the food processor into the empty bowl and reaching for more peeled potatoes. "I ought to do a front-page story about you. Perfection is definitely a newsworthy quality, especially in a man."

He laughed again. "Okay. My mistakes. Let me think. I might remember something." He struck a pose like the Rodin sculpture *The Thinker,* his chin resting against his fist and his brow furrowed from exertion.

"Have you ever lost a case?"

"Yeah, but not because I made mistakes." Abandoning his pose, he picked another potato from the bag and scraped the peeler over it.

"No romantic missteps?"

"I've dated women and broken up with them, but I don't consider any of those relationships mistakes. I did have a great rent-controlled apartment in law school. I had the option of buying it, but I didn't have the money. After I moved out, it stopped being rent-controlled. I could have sold it for a huge profit. But I couldn't afford it at the time, so I don't think that counts as a mistake."

"I guess you're perfect after all."

"And look at how perfectly I'm peeling these potatoes," he added, holding the starchy white lump for her to admire. "Tell me these aren't the most perfectly peeled potatoes you've ever seen."

She laughed. He tossed her the potato, and she cut it in half and ran it through the food processor.

"Are they supposed to look like that?" he said, his smile fading as he studied the shredded potatoes in the clear plastic base of the processor. "I thought they were supposed to be more...I don't know. Smooth. Grated."

"I don't have a grater attachment for the processor," she admitted, then frowned. "How would you know? Have you ever made latkes?"

"I used to hang out in my grandmother's kitchen sometimes. If I helped her, she'd reward me with special treats. We're not talking apricots, either. Rugelach, or a chunk of chocolate-covered halvah. The good stuff."

"The apricots and marshmallows taste delicious," she argued.

He made a face. "Thanks, but I'll take my grandmother's treats over yours any day." He studied the potatoes in the

bowl of the food processor and shook his head. "My grandmother used to hand-grate the potatoes when she made latkes.
She always had a bandage on a finger because she'd rubbed
it against the grater. She used to joke that blood added something special to the flavor."

"You're kidding! My grandmother used to say that, too.
She always had a knuckle bandaged, and she always made the
joke about blood adding to the flavor."

"Oh, my God!" Looking shocked, Jeff leaped to his feet
and pressed his hands dramatically to his chest. "Are you my
long-lost cousin?"

"Do you have a long-lost cousin?"

"I've had a few cousins I wished I could lose," he joked,
moving around the table so he could study the shredded potatoes more closely. "Have you got one of those blade
thingies? Maybe if you process the potatoes with the blade
it'll make them pastier."

"I don't want them pastier. Shredded is fine," she said with
more conviction than she felt. As if she were any sort of expert when it came to making latkes.

"Do you think we should add a little blood?" he asked.

"For flavor. Of course."

"Yours or mine?"

"Mine's probably sweeter," she teased.

"You think so?"

He was standing awfully close to her, close enough that the
merest movement on her part would cause their shoulders to
collide. Close enough that she could feel the heat of his body
filling the narrow space between them.

Close enough that all he had to do was turn his face slightly
and their lips were touching. It was a light kiss, a kiss sweeter
than blood, sweeter than food, sweeter than anything she'd
ever tasted.

It barely lasted a second. He drew back and searched her
face with his gaze.

"What was that about?" she asked. Not the most romantic
thing she could say under the circumstances, but this wasn't

exactly a romantic encounter. They were standing in her glaringly lit kitchen, with her dog wandering around the room now that Jeff had abandoned her, and bowls and utensils scattered about. They'd been discussing potatoes and blood and their grandmothers. Romantic? Hardly.

Yet Alana felt light-headed and short of breath and—damn it—romantic. She wanted to grab Jeffrey Barrett by his broad, strong shoulders and haul him to her, and kiss him again. That notion was so scary she'd had to say something blunt and down-to-earth just to shoo it away.

"That," he answered, using his thumb to trace her lower lip, "was about the texture of the potatoes in the food processor. *This*—" he slid his hand along her jaw and under her hair, which she'd pulled back into a ponytail to keep it out of her way while she cooked "—is about kissing you." He covered her mouth with his in a way that was anything but sweet. It was dark, aggressive, shamelessly erotic. His tongue took her mouth, his other hand slid around her waist and he drew her against him. Her hands alighted on his shoulders, just as they'd wanted to, and she held on tight—and kissed him back.

Maybe his kiss wasn't sweet, but the yearning that flooded through her was as luscious as warm syrup. She felt it in her fingertips, in her toes, her womb, her heart. It bathed her nerves, her cells, her soul. This was about blood after all—her blood pounding hot through her, demanding, thick with desire. From the moment she'd seen Jeff Barrett in Chet's office and been staggered by how handsome he was…

That was what this was about: Alana wanting Jeff Barrett. Who was a Boston lawyer. Who would be leaving town soon. Who never made mistakes—God, how obnoxious!—who implied that she should censor herself in her reporting about his uncle, and about whom she knew pathetically little. Wanting him wasn't enough. Sometimes what a woman wanted was best left untouched.

Reluctantly she leaned back, breaking the kiss. He closed his eyes for a moment and let out a long breath. She felt his arousal through his jeans and hers and realized she must have had as strong an effect on him as he'd had on her.

"Bad idea?" he murmured, opening his eyes and gazing down at her.

It was an irresistible idea. A spectacular idea. But also a bad one. She nodded.

"Not a mistake, though." His fingers tenderly stroked her nape, sending hot shivers down her back. "I don't make mistakes."

"I do," she said, a reminder to herself. Getting involved with this man was one mistake she had no intention of making.

He opened his mouth, perhaps to argue his case like the lawyer he was, but before he could speak, a muted jingling filled the room. He released another breath. "My cell phone," he said, his hands falling from her. "I left it in my coat."

It jingled a second time. "You'd better answer it," she advised.

He lifted his hand back to her face and caressed her cheek, then pivoted and strode out of the kitchen. The third jingle was interrupted by his voice: "Hello?… What's up?… They did?"

She inched toward the door to the hall. A good journalist knew when eavesdropping was appropriate, and the edge in his voice told her it was appropriate now.

"No…listen, Aunt Marge. Don't panic. Tell me, did they charge him, or was it…"

Alana's phone rang. Just as Jeff's end of the conversation was getting juicy, too. Marjorie Willis had called him and she was panicked. Who else would have been charged but Robert Willis?

Her phone rang again. She darted around the table and yanked the cordless off its base. "Hello?"

"Alana? It's Jason Farrar, down at the police station. I promised I'd keep you posted on the school funds investigation, and we've had a development."

"Thank you," she said, glancing toward the empty doorway and wondering whether Jason would tell her something different from what Jeff's Aunt Marge was telling him. "I appreciate your calling. What happened?"

"We brought Bob Willis in for questioning," he said. "We haven't arrested him, but he's been implicated."

"Really? Who implicated him?"

"I can't give you that, not yet. And we haven't gotten a word out of him so far. We just brought him in a few minutes ago."

"I'll be right there," she said.

"Look, I'm not at liberty to—"

"I understand," she cut him off. Jason couldn't tell her anything yet. But by the time she got to the police station, things might have changed. Willis might be singing like an opera diva. Whoever had implicated him might be holding a press conference in front of the station house—although in Crescent Cove, a press conference would probably amount to the person giving the press conference and Alana, period. At least she'd get an exclusive. "I'll be there in ten minutes," she said into the phone. "Thanks, Jason. I owe you."

"Don't I know it," he said, then hung up.

She set down her phone and turned to find Jeff entering her kitchen.

"I've got to go," he said. "I'm really sorry, Alana—"

"I've got to go, too." She emptied the shredded potatoes from her food processor into the bowl, covered it with a sheet of plastic wrap and slid it into the refrigerator. "Jason—Police Chief Farrar—just called me. I think Uncle Bob needs you."

"That's an understatement."

"And Crescent Cove needs me," she said rather grandly. But it was the truth. She was a reporter, and the citizens of Crescent Cove had a right to know what their school super-intendent had done with their tax dollars.

Chapter Five

The taste of Alana's kiss lingered on his tongue even as he entered the police station. He'd figured kissing her would be fun, hot, arousing—but he hadn't expected to react on such an emotional level. They'd been joking around, hadn't they? Talking about candles and latkes and his mocking boasts of perfection. And then he'd kissed her, and...*whoa*. Her kitchen could have disappeared. Her whole house. Her recipes. Her dog. The entire universe. And he wouldn't even have noticed, because the moment his mouth fused with hers, his entire universe seemed to exist right there, within the kiss.

Kissing a woman had never turned him into a poet before. What the hell had Alana done to him?

Whatever she'd done was irrelevant once he stepped through the front door of the station house. She'd followed in her own car. Before they'd left her house, she'd refused to divulge what Chief Farrar had told her, which was reason enough for Jeff to forget the damn kiss and stay focused on reality which, in this case, was that his uncle was knee-deep in crap and Alana couldn't wait to trumpet the news all over the front page of the *Crescent Cove Chronicle*.

On a Sunday afternoon, he'd expected the police station to be subdued, and it was. This wasn't Boston; folks around here apparently restricted their criminal activity to regular business hours. He strode to the counter, and the same clerk who'd sent him to Mort's Diner yesterday rose from her desk to meet him. "I'm Jeffrey Barrett. Robert Willis's attorney," he identified himself, in case she didn't remember him. "I'd like to see him."

He sensed disapproval in her as she eyed him up and down. Maybe he should have detoured to Aunt Marge's house and changed into his suit, but he'd wanted to get here as soon as possible—before Uncle Bob started talking. Bob would have to tolerate an attorney in blue jeans, and so would this clerk.

Alana swung through the door, her cheeks pink and her eyes glistening from the icy air outside. Her cheeks had flushed when he'd kissed her, too, and her eyes had glowed— from heat, rather than from cold. If Uncle Bob hadn't chosen that moment to get jammed up, Jeff would have persuaded her to kiss him again, kiss him until she realized that the chemistry flaring between them wasn't something a person ought to say no to.

His eyes met hers for a moment and he felt the chemistry again, a reaction fierce enough to shatter glass. His gut tightened and his hands itched to cup those cold cheeks of hers and guide her lips to his, and then to slide down her back and lift her legs around his waist, and...

Damn. *Forget chemistry,* he ordered himself. *Today's subject is criminology.*

The clerk recognized Alana. "Hey, you heard?" she said.

Alana unzipped her parka as she walked to the counter. She cast Jeff a sidelong glance and he could have sworn her cheeks grew a shade or two darker. It pleased him to think she hadn't quite put their kiss out of her mind, either. She inched away from him and addressed the clerk. "Yes, I heard. Is Jason around? I need to talk to him."

"He's in his office. I'll let him know you're here." The clerk reached for her phone.

Jeff cleared his throat. "First you'd better take me to Robert Willis. Unless you want me to search for him myself."

The clerk and Alana exchanged a glance. "He was here before me," Alana said, not quite graciously.

Nodding, the clerk emerged from behind the counter and

said, "Follow me." She led him down a hall to a door and pushed it open.

Uncle Bob sat at a scratched oak table in the center of the small room. He wore a V-neck sweater over an oxford shirt, and a pair of twill slacks. His thinning hair was mussed, as if he'd been raking his fingers through it. But his expression brightened at the sight of Jeff. "Thank God you're here!" he cried, pushing to his feet.

Jeff touched his index finger to lips to silence Bob. Even a greeting was more than the guy should say in front of a police department employee. He thanked the clerk tersely, glared at her until she left the room, and shut the door behind her. "Have you said anything to anyone here? Officers, the police chief, that clerk, anyone?"

"Of course I said hello," Bob told him. "I know these people, Jeff. I live with them."

"As long as it wasn't more than a hello." Jeff gestured toward the chair Bob had occupied, and Bob resumed his seat. Jeff settled into the chair across the table from his uncle. He removed a small leather-bound notebook from a pocket of his coat and pictured Alana wielding a similar pocket-size notebook, filling it with quotes from the police chief for her next article on the missing school funds. "All right," he said. "I'm not your nephew now. I'm your lawyer. Anything you tell me is strictly confidential. You understand?"

Bob nodded gravely.

"Aunt Marge told me they haven't charged you with anything yet."

"That's right."

"But here you are." Jeff gazed around him at the faded green walls and the dingy window, which was covered with chain-link mesh. The wall across from him held a mirror—one-way, he knew. Cops could watch him interview his client. But Bob had his back to the mirror, so they couldn't see his face—which was good. "You have to tell me the truth, Uncle Bob. What do they have on you?"

Bob buried his face in his hands for a moment, and Jeff

prayed he wouldn't start crying. "I took it," he finally whispered. "But it—"

"Damn." Jeff kept his voice down, but anger strained it. "Why didn't you tell me?"

"I was hoping…" Bob sighed. "I didn't want Marge to drag you into this. I was figuring I could work it out quietly and avoid all this. Everyone knows me in town, Jeff. They know I'm an honorable man."

"An honorable man who stole money from the school budget?"

"I didn't steal it," Bob argued. "I *took* it, but I planned to return it."

"All right—we'll deal with what you planned to do later. First, tell me what happened. *Everything.* The whole truth and nothing but."

"I think…" Bob sighed again, his words slightly muffled by his hands. "I think Eleanor must have told them."

"Who's Eleanor?"

"My secretary. Eleanor Chase. I did it for her, Jeff. It wasn't for me—it was for her."

Oh, hell. What a cliché—the middle-aged boss and his secretary. Jeff suffered a pang of sympathy for Aunt Marge. Did she know about Eleanor, or was she about to have her simple small-town life torn apart by her philandering and thieving husband?

"You stole the money for your secretary," he reiterated, just to make sure he hadn't misunderstood.

"Not stole. Borrowed. We're going to replace it, I swear. Every dollar."

"When are you planning to do that? After you and Eleanor fly off to some secret hideaway? Some romantic escape? The Caribbean is nice this time of year."

"What?" Bob let his hands fall. He looked shocked and angry. "You think I'd run off with Eleanor? What are you, crazy?"

"You just told me you stole the money for her."

"*Took* it, not stole it. For her daughter."

Great. Now there were two "other women" in the picture: Eleanor and her daughter. "You were going to run off with the daughter?"

"Katie isn't even two years old. And I'm not going to run off with either of them. I'm a married man!" Bob said indignantly.

As if married men never ran off with one—or sometimes even two—women. "Okay. Eleanor's daughter Katie is a toddler."

"She's got a cleft palate." He rubbed his upper lip in sympathy. "She was born with it. She needs surgery to repair it, so she can grow up with a normal-looking face. But Eleanor's health insurance—I swear, the town gives us such substandard coverage. I've fought with them about getting all the school employees a better health plan, but the school board can be so shortsighted—"

"Let's try to stay focused," Jeff urged him. "Eleanor's daughter needs surgery."

Bob nodded. "The insurance company said this procedure Katie needed was elective cosmetic surgery, and they refused to cover it. The child is still in diapers, Jeff. It would break your heart to see her little malformed mouth."

Maybe it would. But he was here to help Bob, not Eleanor's daughter.

"The surgery costs about seventy-five grand," Bob continued. "Eleanor's good-for-nothing husband walked out a year ago, because of their daughter. He called Katie defective and he disappeared. Eleanor can't even serve him with divorce papers, because she doesn't know where he is. But in the meantime, she's still married, and she's employed, so she doesn't qualify for Medicaid. Which would probably consider the repair elective cosmetic surgery, too, so they wouldn't cover it." Bob shook his head before returning it to rest in his hands. "That baby deserves better, Jeff. She deserves to look normal. And the longer you wait on surgery like this, the longer the healing time. Plus the psychological damage. I don't know if you can imagine what that little girl must feel like."

"Stay focused, Uncle Bob."

Bob drew in a deep breath. "I didn't have the money to lend

Eleanor—with Bobby in dental school and Emily in college, things are tight. So we took some money from the school budget. Not enough to affect any of our programs—just a little here, a little there. Some from the janitor's budget—I figured Eleanor and I could pitch in and do a little sweeping and mopping after hours. A few bucks from the maintenance budget. So we won't repaint the bathrooms this year—the walls will survive. A little from the office expenses budget, because we never come close to running through the full amount. We can use the same math textbooks another year. And Eleanor intends to pay it all back. She figures ten, fifteen dollars a week…"

Jeff didn't bother to calculate how many years it would take Eleanor Chase to pay back seventy-five thousand dollars at that rate.

"Jeff, try to understand. Eleanor's daughter is her whole life. Katie has reached the age where she's becoming aware of the stares she gets. She's learning to talk, but she has trouble pronouncing words. She needs to have this surgery. Eleanor wanted it to be a Christmas gift, a way to start the new year. The surgery's scheduled for the second week in January. It'll give that precious little girl a chance at a good life. Every child deserves that."

"No argument, Uncle Bob—but come on. You couldn't think of any other way to raise money for the kid's surgery?"

"Sure, I thought of other ways. Eleanor didn't qualify for any loans. She rents her house so she couldn't borrow against that. And I'm tapped out with the loans we took for Bobby's and Emily's tuition. Last summer, St. Elizabeth's Church sponsored a carnival. By the time all the accounts were settled, they'd raised a grand total of not quite six hundred dollars for Katie. A lot of teachers made donations. That brought in another two hundred or so. I contacted every state agency I could think of, and they all said it was cosmetic surgery. They might have provided assistance if she'd had something life-threatening, but not for this." He let his head sink back into his hands. "To Eleanor—and to me—Katie's condition was life-threatening. That kind of birth defect can destroy a child's life."

Jeff skimmed the notes he'd been jotting. "You said the surgery's scheduled for January, right?"

"January tenth."

"Then Eleanor must still have the money."

"I would assume so," Bob agreed. "You don't prepay for surgery."

"Which means the money can be returned."

Bob looked appalled. "But then Katie can't have the surgery."

Jeff leaned across the table until his face was just inches from his uncle's. "Listen to me. The money was stolen. The law doesn't care about what it was stolen for. All it cares about was that it was stolen, which is illegal. If you and Eleanor give the money back now, we might be able to straighten this thing out without criminal charges being brought. It's your best shot, Uncle Bob. And it would be the right thing to do. You can't just steal money, even if you've got a good reason to."

"But what about Katie?"

What about her? Jeff's problem wasn't saving little Katie Chase's mouth; it was saving his uncle's butt.

"If you and Eleanor return the money and I can get the local D.A. not to press charges, you might even hang on to your job. I can't promise that, of course. That'll be up to the school board. They might be so moved by the plight of Eleanor's daughter that they'll spare your job. Who knows, maybe they'll contribute toward the cost of the kid's surgery. But if you *don't* return the money, losing your job will be the least of your troubles. You could wind up spending years behind bars."

Bob swallowed hard.

"This is a small town where everyone knows everyone else. If you and your secretary could make immediate restitution, maybe your neighbors would forgive you."

"What if Eleanor doesn't give back the money. It's her *daughter.* She promised her this surgery."

"If Eleanor doesn't return the money, then Eleanor will

wind up in prison. How does that help her daughter?" He shoved his chair away from the table. "Let me talk to the police chief and see where you stand with him. While I'm gone, you are not to speak to anyone. Not a word. Do you understand? If you have to go to the bathroom, pantomime the request."

"I don't have to go," Bob said, his voice tremulous. With relief or anguish, Jeff couldn't tell.

He stood, patted his uncle's hunched shoulder and left the room. Was Eleanor Chase behind another closed door on this hall? Had she already given everything up? Did she have a decent lawyer to walk her through this?

And what about her daughter?

Jeff wasn't a father, but he knew his own father would have robbed to save his children's lives. His mother would have killed for them. It was the way parents were. And Uncle Bob, being a parent himself, had empathized with Eleanor— perhaps a bit too strongly, but Jeff couldn't blame him for his compassion.

Through an open door he heard Alana's voice. He slowed to a halt and listened. "So, you're okay if this runs tomorrow?"

"You can print anything I told you on the record. You know the drill."

"Thanks, Jason," she said. "You're a sweetheart." For some crazy reason, hearing her call the police chief a sweetheart irked Jeff.

He heard footsteps approaching the doorway, and he quickly resumed his stroll down the hall so Alana wouldn't emerge from the office to find him hovering outside the office, eavesdropping. She swung through the doorway and nearly collided with him.

His gaze met hers and he felt his gut tighten again. She'd had her hair tied back while they'd been in her kitchen, but now it fell loose, spilling past her shoulders in gold-tinged brown waves. He wanted to plunge his fingers through it, to feel it brush against his cheeks, his chin, his body.

He also wanted to find out what would appear under her

byline tomorrow. A damaging story? Or one that emphasized Eleanor Chase's maternal angst and Uncle Bob's kindness?

"Hi," she said, her voice slightly breathless. From her chat with Farrar, Jeff guessed. The police chief must have told her some exciting stuff.

He took her elbow and steered her down the hall. "We have to talk," he murmured, searching for an empty room. He found an unoccupied lavatory, guided her inside, followed her in and locked the door behind them.

It was a one-seater, small and crowded. She eyed the toilet and arched an eyebrow. "I hope all you've got in mind is washing your hands," she said. "More than that I don't want to see."

In spite of himself, he laughed. The room was so tiny that with their bulky coats on, they seemed to take up every cubic inch of space. The paper-towel dispenser jutted out of the wall and into his spine. His face and hers were reflected in profile in the mirror above the sink. Her mouth was much too close to his, those sweet full lips just a breath away, tempting him.

He leaned back into the towel dispenser. "You've got to hold your story," he said.

She watched him, skepticism mixing with curiosity in her eyes. "And why do I have to do that?"

"It's a lot more complicated than you think."

"How do you know what I think?"

He sighed. Was this intractable journalist the same woman who not too long ago had been, for a few heavenly minutes in her kitchen, so pliant in his arms, so soft and receptive? "What did the police chief tell you?"

"Read tomorrow's *Chronicle* and you'll find out."

"Don't do this, Alana. You could ruin the lives of a couple of decent people."

"People who stole money? I'm not sure I'd call them decent."

"Did Farrar fill you in on the little girl and the surgery she needs?"

Alana frowned. "What little girl?"

Jeff hesitated. If he told her about the girl, he'd have to tell her his uncle had admitted to taking the money. If he confided in her off the record, then she wouldn't be able to write about Eleanor's daughter. She could investigate further, though, maybe go back and press Farrar about Katie Chase. If Farrar was even aware of the kid.

Farrar trusted Alana to publish only things he'd told her on the record. Did Jeff trust her?

Just like her, he was in a profession where ethics and trust didn't always overlap. Professional ethics for her meant telling a story in the most readable way to inform and entertain her readers. Professional ethics for him meant aggressively advocating for his client, protecting him and winning him the best possible outcome. The best possible outcome for Uncle Bob would be Alana's holding her story. Jeff was sure she wouldn't do that.

"There's a little girl who needs surgery," he said, then yanked open the bathroom door and stormed out of the cramped room before Alana's beautiful eyes lured another word from him.

WHAT LITTLE GIRL?

She stared after Jeff as he stalked down the hall to one of the interview rooms and vanished inside. That must be where Robert Willis was being held.

Jason hadn't said anything about a little girl needing surgery. But apparently, Robert Willis had mentioned this girl to Jeff. Which meant Willis knew about the theft. Which implicated him in it, since he hadn't gone to the authorities with his knowledge. If someone else had been embezzling school funds and Willis found out, he should have reported the theft. But he hadn't. Clearly, he was in on it.

So who the hell was this little girl?

Alana wandered back to Jason's office. He stepped through the door just as she reached it. "Sorry," he said with a smile, then motioned with his head toward the door Jeff had vanished through. "This part isn't open to the press."

"I understand—but can you tell me if some sick little girl is involved in this?"

"A sick little girl?" Jason looked genuinely perplexed.

"You don't know anything about it?"

"Nope."

"Okay." She forced a smile and backed off. "Thanks for everything you gave me. If you pick up anything more—"

"With his nephew in the room, I doubt I'm going to get much out of Willis," Jason said. "But if I learn anything you can use, I'll give you a call."

"Thanks. I'll be at the *Chronicle* building for a while, if you want to reach me," she told him. "You have my cell number too, right?"

"Go write your story," Jason said, before turning and heading down the hall.

Writing her story was exactly what she would do. But first she needed to be sure she *had* the story. If a sick little girl was part of the story, then she didn't have it, not yet.

Jason had told her Willis's secretary, Eleanor Chase, had admitted that she and Willis could explain about the missing money. According to Jason, that was all she'd admitted before bursting into tears and demanding her lawyer—who'd gone to Smuggler's Notch for a weekend of skiing. With Eleanor refusing to say another word until her lawyer dusted the snow off his skis and returned to Crescent Cove, Jason planned to see what he could get out of Willis.

Probably not much, Alana surmised. Not with Jeff Barrett keeping his uncle muzzled.

Where did a little girl fit into the picture? A student in the Crescent Cove school district, perhaps?

Or was the little girl a ruse? Had Jeff invented her to distract Alana? If reporters were often likened to bloodhounds, maybe this supposedly sick child was Barrett's way of tossing a steak at Alana, throwing her off the scent.

He was an attorney, after all, and he didn't want Alana to publish a story about his uncle's legal predicament. But the guy was in hot water, and so was his secretary. Alana owed it to her readers to report the truth.

Chapter Six

At eight o'clock, the police chief ordered everyone to go home. Apparently, Eleanor, who was shut up inside her own interview room, refused to talk until her lawyer got back from his ski weekend, and Jeff refused to let Uncle Bob talk until he'd talked to Eleanor's lawyer. Farrar must have figured neither Bob nor Eleanor was a flight risk, so he suggested they get a good night's sleep and come back tomorrow.

The guy seemed reasonable; Jeff had a good feeling about him. After asking Bob to wait for him in the entry, he cornered Farrar alone in his office. "One quick question," he said. "Strictly hypothetical."

Farrar flashed him a grin. "Shoot."

"Hypothetically, if all the missing money was returned within a day or so, could we view this entire thing as a major bookkeeping error and let it go at that?"

Farrar's face registered surprise. "A bookkeeping error?"

"Yeah."

"Hypothetically." He ruminated. "The auditor's been through the financials. She didn't like what she saw."

"Right, but—hypothetically—if there was an explanation for the way the budget got a little twisted around, and all the money was restored, what kind of charges would you be looking at?"

Farrar ruminated some more. "I haven't talked to the D.A.'s office yet. No charges have been filed. On the other hand, if a crime has been committed, we've got to act accordingly."

"But if it's not a crime—if it's just a really major bookkeeping snafu... The D.A. doesn't need to be brought in to adjudicate a bookkeeping snafu, right?"

"I guess not. Hypothetically."

"Hypothetically." Jeff smiled. "Thanks." He shook Farrar's hand and left the office. Bob hovered near the entry, gazing dolefully through the glass door at the darkness outside. Flurries danced through the air, looking like white dust. Jeff clamped a hand over his uncle's shoulder and steered him down the sidewalk to where he'd parked his car. "I'm going to get you off the hook," he said. "But you have to give back the money. You and Eleanor both. I'll need to talk to Eleanor so we can work this out together, but I think we can pull it off. *If* you give back every last dime."

"What about Katie?"

"Eleanor will have to pay for her surgery some other way."

"If she could have paid for it some other way, we would never have borrowed the money from the school accounts," Bob protested.

Jeff unlocked the passenger door of his BMW and opened it for Bob. He didn't speak again until they were both strapped into their seats and the engine was warming up. "There's always another way," he said. "I bet I could find a charitable organization in Boston that would kick in some money. I've got good connections."

"Really?" Bob's face brightened. "You could do that?"

"I can try. On the other hand, if you and Eleanor don't return the money, you'll both wind up in jail. Even if you avoid jail, you'll lose your jobs. Explain to me how that would help Eleanor's little girl."

"If you can raise some money—"

"I'll do my best." His best meant he'd have to drive back to Boston tonight. Returning to Boston was a good idea in any case. He had paperwork to finish up on the age-discrimination suit, mail to wade through, Christmas presents to buy. He didn't have time to stick around Crescent Cove, peeling potatoes for Alana.

Of course, if she ran her damn article tomorrow, Bob would be toast even if the police dropped their investigation. A conviction in the newspaper was in some ways worse than a conviction in court. The court of public opinion could be unforgiving.

Still, avoiding a criminal charge would count as a huge victory.

He handed his cell phone to Bob. "Call Aunt Marge and tell her you'll be home in a while," he said, "and then give me directions to Eleanor's house."

He and Bob spent an hour at Eleanor's house, a modest ranch cluttered with toys and other baby items. Jeff met Katie, an energetic tyke who preferred running to walking and whose speech was even harder to comprehend than that of most toddlers. She had pretty blue eyes and a cute button nose. With a properly shaped mouth, she'd be gorgeous.

Eleanor looked ragged, her cheeks tearstained and pale with worry. While she wasn't overly receptive to Jeff at first, she obviously respected Bob. "If we give the money back," he said, "Jeff will get the funding for the surgery from his friends in Boston."

Jeff was uncomfortable with his uncle's making such a risky promise—but he needed Eleanor to believe her daughter's surgery wouldn't be jeopardized if she returned the money. And damn it, watching the little girl push a toy lawn mower across the worn living-room rug, listening to her squeal, feeling her chubby little arms squeeze around his calf as she gave his leg a hug…he *wanted* to find the money for her operation.

"We can say we set up a rainy-day fund for school department employees," Bob suggested, impressing Jeff with his creativity. "We can say we were trying to see if we could wring some money out of the current budget for employee emergencies."

"But what about Katie's surgery?"

"Jeff'll take care of that. Come on, Eleanor. We'll give the money back."

"But that story, about setting up a rainy-day fund—it's a lie, isn't it?" She eyed Jeff dubiously.

"I'm not going to tell you to lie," he said, mindful of his professional obligations. "However, it seems to me that you actually *were* setting up a fund for employee emergencies. One employee's emergency, anyway."

"So it's not a lie?"

"I'm not saying that. I'm saying you put the money into a fund with the idea that this fund could cover an employee's emergency."

Eleanor scooped Katie into her arms and carried her off to change her diaper. When they returned, Eleanor said she'd back Bob up on his story. "Because it really isn't a lie," she asserted. "I realize that now. It's what we did."

Jeff left his business card with Eleanor and wrote down the name and phone number of her lawyer, a fellow named Burt Ammond. Then he drove Bob home. He entered the house only to grab his suitcase and say goodbye to Aunt Marge. From there, he cruised across town to Alana's house. It was dark.

Swearing under his breath, he U-turned and drove back to town, to the *Chronicle* building. He saw Alana's car parked in the lot—not in the space where she'd gotten stuck, he noted—and pulled into an empty spot nearby. After raising his collar and yanking on his gloves, he climbed out into the frosty, flurry-white evening.

The building's main entry was locked, but he saw plenty of lights on through the glass walls of the vestibule. He found a doorbell on one side of the door and pressed the button.

After a minute, the inner door was opened by the skinny guy with the geeky eyeglasses who'd helped Jeff search the *Chronicle*'s computerized archives in the basement last Friday. He cupped his hand above his eyes to peer through the glass, then opened the outer door.

"Is Alana Ross here?" Jeff asked. "I have to talk to her. I'm Jeff Barrett."

"Um…wait here, okay?" the guy said, abandoning him in the vestibule.

Jeff shook off a shiver as the heated air surrounded him. His body temperature rose a few more degrees when he saw Alana approach the inner door and ease it open. How could a woman with such a steely spine have such gentle eyes, such soft, sweet lips?

She seemed surprised to see him, and a little wary. "Jeff?"

"Don't write the story," he said.

SURE. SHE SHOULD STOP work, just because he said so. She should quit her job and crawl into a hole because Jeff Barrett, the high-powered mistake-free lawyer from Boston, told her to.

A small, treacherous voice in a corner of her brain whispered that any woman would gladly do whatever a man like Jeff Barrett asked of her, a man with snow-bright eyes and a leanly muscled physique and hands that knew how to hold a woman, how to touch her face…a man who knew how to kiss a woman on the mouth and leave her feeling she'd been kissed all over. *I'll do anything you say, Jeff,* that wicked voice murmured inside her skull.

She'd spent the past three hours pursuing his lead about the child who needed surgery, though, and finally she had her story. God bless chatty small-town neighbors, she thought. No one in Bridgeport would have gossiped as cheerfully about her next-door neighbor the way Agatha Lewis had. "Oh, that wonderful daughter of Eleanor's! Such a sweetheart, and it's so sad about her face. But she's going to get the surgery, finally. Eleanor scraped together the money for it. Right after the holidays, Eleanor is taking Katie down to Dartmouth-Hitchcock to have the surgery done."

Alana could guess how Robert Willis's secretary had scraped together the money for her daughter's plastic surgery. Now she had a motive—a heart-wrenching one—to go along with what Jason had told her in his office. She couldn't cross the line and accuse anyone of anything, but she could report a solid story about what the police chief believed had happened to the school's budget.

"Jeff—"

"Listen to me." He gripped her shoulders, holding her motionless in front of him, his face just inches from hers. "There was no theft. The police chief is going to reach that finding. It was all a misunderstanding. Not a crime."

That wasn't what Jason Farrar had told Alana. Why should she accept Jeff's word over that of the town's chief of police?

Because Jason never looked at her the way Jeff Barrett was looking at her, as if he could see through her doubts, through her skin, as if he could peer into her eyes and find her soul lying open for him. Because Jason had never kissed her. Because he'd never made her feel as if she had a candle burning inside her, heating and illuminating her, making her glow in the night like the flames of her ancestors, celebrating the triumph of life itself.

Jeff made her feel things she'd never felt before, made her want things she'd never wanted before.

And he was asking her to kill her story. He was asking her to ignore her work and her responsibility to the *Chronicle,* to Chet, to Crescent Cove.

"I found out about the little girl," she told him. "The one who needs surgery."

"The story's changed," he said.

"The *story?* What about the truth?"

"The truth is, by tomorrow Jason Farrar will determine that no crime was committed."

"By tomorrow? I'm writing my report today."

"Nothing happened today. Your pal at the police station brought my uncle in and then sent him home."

"And the little girl you told me about?"

"Hopefully, she'll have her surgery."

Which would be paid for how? Had someone set up a counterfeit machine to print seventy-five thousand dollars in the basement of the police station? Or maybe over at the school department's offices?

In the dim light of the vestibule, she stared into Jeff's silver eyes. His fingers moved on her arms, gently, coaxing. She wished she could forget about his uncle and the school money and her job and his, and just go home with him, back to her cozy house and her dog and her latke recipe. She wished they could spend the evening getting to know each other better, and letting that knowledge lead them where it would.

But he was here, holding her, pleading with her in his low, seductive voice because he wanted her to sit on her story.

"Trust me," he said. "There's no crime."

She didn't believe him. But not believing him wasn't the same thing as not trusting him. And foolish though it was, she wanted to trust him.

She wanted to kiss him.

She wanted *him*.

Slowly, ruefully, she eased out of his grip. "You'd better go," she said, turning from him and walking through the door, out of the vestibule and back into the newsroom. She didn't wait to watch him leave. She couldn't. She had too much work to do, more calls to make, more people to question. She had a story to report.

Chapter Seven

He'd been exhausted after arriving home from Vermont after midnight, but fueled with adrenaline and caffeine, he started the work week with an eight-in-the-morning phone call to Burt Ammond, Eleanor Chase's attorney, to bring him up to speed. To Jeff's great relief, Ammond was already on top of things. Eleanor would return the money. She and Bob would make a statement about their attempt to set up a special emergency fund. Ammond would help them draft it. They'd negotiate for nothing more than a reprimand. Ammond promised to keep Jeff posted.

Jeff's next phone call was to a woman he knew from the charity circuit who sat on the board of a foundation that funded medical care for uninsured children. She was moved by his description of the little girl whose plastic surgery was deemed a luxury by the insurance company. An hour after his call to her, she called back and told him her foundation would supply the money to cover Katie Chase's surgery, contingent on the board's meeting with Katie and Eleanor and granting its approval.

'Tis the season, Jeff thought as he sipped his fourth cup of black coffee and gazed out the window of his office on an upper floor of the John Hancock Tower. Below him, Boston was dressed for the holidays. The Common was blanketed in white, the shops of Copley Plaza were decked out with enticing holiday displays, lights sparkled like stars on the

branches of leafless trees and Salvation Army Santas rang their bells on every street corner. And a little girl was going to get the surgery she needed.

Would his uncle get what he needed? His name cleared, his job preserved, his lesson learned? Or would a stubborn reporter insist on reporting that Robert Willis had done something illegal? Even if ultimately no harm was done, would she ruin Jeff's uncle's life?

Would she ruin Jeff's life, too? Or would his memory of her eventually fade? Would he someday meet another woman who made him laugh the way Alana did, who challenged him, whose convictions he couldn't help but admire even though they stood in the way of his goals for his uncle? Would he ever stop thinking about her lush hair and her even lusher lips, and all the sexual promise in that one amazing kiss they'd shared?

"This fax just arrived for you," his secretary said as she swept into his office and placed several sheets of paper on his desk.

He tore himself from the window and dropped into his chair. The cover sheet indicated that the fax was from Aunt Marge. "From today's *Chronicle*," she'd written.

He pushed the cover sheet aside and scanned the fax of the front page of the *Chronicle,* reduced to print so small he had to squint to read it. There, below where the fold would be, he read a headline: Police Locate Missing School Dept. Funds. "After a long weekend of active investigation, including an extensive audit by Town Comptroller Dorothy Callahan, Police Chief Jason Farrar has announced that the funds missing from the school department's accounts last week have been recovered. School Superintendent Robert Willis and his administrative assistant, Eleanor Chase, admitted responsibility for shifting the funds to a new account in a bookkeeping experiment. Although proper procedures were not followed in the manipulation of funds, Police Chief Farrar said he did not believe the actions of Willis and Chase rose to the level of criminal activity."

Jeff released his breath in a long sigh. Alana had rewritten her story. He wasn't sure how much she knew about what Bob

had done, but she must have realized it wasn't quite so innocent. She'd written the innocent version, though. She'd let
Bob off the hook. Jeff closed his eyes and sent a silent prayer
of thanks skyward, although he suspected Alana was the one
he ought to be thanking.

He skimmed the rest of the article, which included reac-
tions by several members of the school committee, who felt
Willis should receive a two-week suspension without pay.
"We set the budget," the chair of the school committee was
quoted as saying. "If the superintendent has a problem with
the budget, he should come to us. He shouldn't be playing
games with the money behind our backs."

Two weeks without pay sure beat two years in the slam-
mer. Uncle Bob and Aunt Marge ought to be celebrating.

He flipped the page to read the continuation of the article.
Alongside it was another article: Surgery a Holiday Gift for
Chase's Daughter. Under Alana's byline, the article described
the particular challenges Eleanor Chase faced as a single
mother with a daughter in need of surgery. "The *Chronicle* has
set up a special fund to help defray the costs of Katie Chase's
surgery," the article reported, along with an address where donations could be sent.

Alana had done that, too. Not only had she spared his
uncle, but she'd talked her boss into collecting donations for
the little girl. She'd come through with more generosity than
Jeff could have hoped for.

His gaze shifted from the fax to the files awaiting his final
review on the age-discrimination suit he'd settled last week. He
could get through them by the end of the day if he worked non-
stop. Tomorrow morning he'd have them ready for the final sig-
natures. By the afternoon he could submit his hours to the
billing department and congratulate himself on a job well-done.

And then…he could drive back to Crescent Cove and
plead his own case.

"I'M FINE," Alana told Nellie as she wiped a tear from her
cheek. "I'm missing Grandma, that's all."

Nellie issued a cheer-up bark and rubbed her head against Alana's shin as they stood in the living room, admiring the menorah. Alana had lit the white candle she'd gotten at Burning Bright, and used its flame to light the candle marking the first night of Hanukkah. On Saturday, she'd have a house full of guests to share the holiday with—and hopefully, she'd have all her food prepared by then—but tonight, the first night, she was alone.

She did miss her grandmother. When she'd lived in Bridgeport, she would take the train down to New York the first night of Hanukkah to light this menorah, which stood on the sill of her grandmother's living-room window. She and Grandma would eat dinner and then she'd go back to Bridgeport and return on the weekend, when Grandma hosted her annual open house. This year Grandma was gone and Alana was far from her family.

At least she had Nellie, who seemed transfixed by the teardrop flames dancing atop the two candles in the menorah.

"I wonder if the woman who gave me this candle is celebrating Hanukkah tonight," Alana asked.

Nellie barked again. When called upon, she could hold up her end of a conversation. Her barks were expressive, too. This one sounded disbelieving.

"All right," Alana conceded, lowering herself to the rug and giving Nellie a thorough behind-the-ear scratching. "It's not just Grandma I'm missing." Nellie nodded, as if pleased that Alana was admitting the truth. "I miss Jeff. I don't know why. He was only using me, trying to keep me from writing negative things about his uncle. And I'm not going to apologize for what I wrote. I could have slanted it differently—I still think Jeff's uncle got away with something. But restitution was made. No one was hurt. I think Jeff saved him from his own stupidity, but that's between Jeff and his uncle. All I did was write the story.

"Jeff played me, Nellie. He kissed me, he acted like he cared—and even though I knew all along that it was only about clearing his uncle's reputation, I fell for it. I'm an idiot."

Nellie barked in enthusiastic agreement.

"Thanks. See if you get any gravy on your kibble tonight." Alana's voice was wistful rather than scolding.

Nellie rested her head in Alana's lap and made a suitably sad sound, half a whimper and half a doggie groan. Together, they stared at the menorah. The candles offered the only light in the room other than the glow through the kitchen doorway behind her. The two flames were reflected by the window's glass. Every year, Grandma used to remind Alana of the importance of placing the menorah in the window. "This is a holiday you share with the world," she would say. "With your burning menorah you tell the world, 'I'm a survivor! I can't be defeated! Life is full of miracles!' Because Hanukkah is the story of the Jewish people surviving miraculously. And just like our ancestors, you and I—we can't be defeated, either, right?"

If only, Alana thought sadly. For eight days, she would have to light candles—assuming they continued to fit, which she wasn't at all sure they would—and declare to all the world, or at least to her neighbors on the block, that she could not be defeated. Maybe by the time she'd lit all the candles, one for each night, she would feel like a survivor.

The doorbell rang, startling her. Nellie leaped to her feet and raced toward the door, yapping exuberantly. Alana wondered if one of her neighbors had stopped by to comment on the menorah in the window.

She swung open the door.

Jeff Barrett stood on her front porch, tall and solid and breathing white puffs of vapor into the cold night air. "Hi," he said.

"What are you doing here?"

"Freezing my tail off. Hey, Nellie Bly, how's it going?" He hunkered down and greeted the dog with a few well-placed rubs. "Tonight's a holiday, isn't it? Is Alana going to pour a little wine into your water dish?"

"Nellie is a teetotaler," Alana informed him.

"So, are you going to let me come in?" he asked, straightening up.

She tried to think of a reason to say no. He'd used her. He'd manipulated her. He'd wooed her to get the story he wanted her to write, and then he'd left. And she still wasn't sure whether she should have written the story her own way, rather than his.

But it was cold and dark, and Grandma would have said a person should never bar her door on Hanukkah. So she stepped back and waved him inside.

He carried a small duffel. Why had he brought that here? Why hadn't he dropped it off at his aunt and uncle's house?

"I've got a present for you," he said, bending to unzip the duffel. He pulled out a square gift-wrapped box. "Happy Hanukkah."

"Is this some old Unitarian tradition?" she asked, managing a smile. He laughed and she tugged at the pretty blue ribbon on the box.

"Don't tell me you're one of those fussy types who won't rip the paper."

"Oh, I'll rip it," she said, tearing the white tissue off the box while Nellie ran in circles around her. In the dark, she could barely make out the picture on the box. She carried it toward the kitchen doorway. "Oh!" She grinned as the picture became clear: food processor disks, including one designed for grating.

"I hope you've still got some potatoes left," he said. "I think you'll need that grating blade if you want to make the latkes properly."

"I have plenty of potatoes left," she said as she led him into the kitchen. The bags of unpeeled potatoes sat in a pile on a counter. She'd been figuring she would make her latkes tonight, since it was Hanukkah and she didn't have anything better to do.

Now Jeff was here. He could peel while she grated. "Is it the right size for my machine?" she asked, sliding the grating disk out of the box.

"It's the same brand. The store had your model and I checked the disks out. It should work fine."

"Oh, Jeff." She put the box on the table and turned to him. Surely someone had given her a more thoughtful present in her life, but she couldn't remember a single gift that meant as much to her as this one did. "Thank you," she said.

His smile waned and his eyes grew intense as he gazed at her. "Thank *you*."

She wasn't sure what he was thanking her for. "I didn't get you a present," she admitted. To be sure, she'd assumed she would never see him again.

Without being asked, he removed his coat and tossed it onto a chair. "Thank you for writing a fair article about my uncle. Thank you for showing him such compassion."

"I didn't—"

"You did, so accept my thanks. Thank you for setting up the fund for Katie's surgery."

"The newspaper did that."

"You did it, Alana. Stop being a hardheaded reporter for a minute, and admit that you're a softhearted woman."

She wanted to argue, but all that emerged was a sigh.

"Thank you for being home tonight," he continued.

"Where else would I be? It's the first night of Hanukkah."

"Thank you for having those candles burning in the window. They made me feel…safe. Welcome. I don't know…it's so cold outside, but I saw those candles and they made me feel warm."

"Candles can do that," she noted.

"It's not the candles," he said. "It's *you*. You make me feel safe and warm." He arched his arms around her and pulled her into his embrace. "Thank you," he whispered, then covered her mouth with his.

The last time he'd kissed her she'd backed away. This time she didn't. She couldn't. She wouldn't. Jeff Barrett made her feel safe and warm, too. He'd come all this way not to save his uncle but to thank her. To give her a grating disk. To share the light and heat of her candles with her.

So she kissed him back. She flung her arms around his waist and held him tight, and opened her mouth and her soul and her soft, womanly heart to him.

He surprised her by lifting her into his arms. "Where's your bedroom?" he asked.

"Down the hall." She brought her arms around his neck, amazed that he could carry her so easily. If she'd been pigging out on latkes, he would never have been able to lift her, so it was probably just as well she hadn't made any progress in her Hanukkah party preparations. He strode past the den, past the laundry alcove where she'd dried his socks, past the bathroom where she'd dried his shoes and into her bedroom.

Nellie bounded in as Jeff lowered Alana to her feet. He shook his head. "Sorry, pup. You aren't invited," he said, pointing to the door. She pouted and slunk out of the room, and he closed the door. "She won't knock over the menorah, will she?"

"No," Alana assured him. "She'll probably just chew on your duffel."

"I'll get it," he said, opening the door. He raced down the hall, as though he believed Nellie would destroy his bag if he didn't rescue it immediately, and she grinned at his eagerness, his energy. She knew he wanted no journalistic favors from her now. She knew a man didn't drive all this way just for a one-night fling. She knew—because her heart told her, because Jeff's eyes and his smile and his kiss told her—that he'd come here only for her love. She could no more stop herself from giving him that precious gift than she could keep the flames from melting the wax of the candles in her menorah.

She switched a bedside lamp on low and turned in time to see him reenter the room and shut the door. He dropped his duffel on the floor next to the bed and crossed to her, his steps purposeful, his arms open. He kissed her brow, the tip of her nose, her chin. "I wanted you the moment I saw you," he confessed.

"In Chet's office?"

"Right there."

"You were threatening to sue me for libel at the time," she reminded him.

"Not really. Just trying to scare you a little." He touched his lips to the edge of her jaw. "Then I went downstairs to the archives and read every damn article you'd ever written for the *Chronicle*. If I couldn't have you, I'd take your words. They were almost as good."

"Almost?" His comment was almost unbearably romantic. "My words are the best part of me."

"No, they're not." He stroked his fingers through her hair. "Then again—" he smiled wickedly "—I haven't seen all your other parts yet."

In less than a minute, he'd rectified that situation. One brief kiss on her lips, and he got busy removing her clothing. She did her best to keep up, tugging at his sweater, grappling with his belt buckle, losing her balance and tumbling onto the bed when he reached for her shoes, and then drawing him down onto the bed with her. His jeans fell to the floor. Her sweater snagged on the knob of the closet door. Her bra landed on the dresser...and then they were naked.

Jeff's body was as magnificent as his face. He was lean and sleek, his skin a healthy golden hue that contrasted with her own winter pallor. His chest was tautly muscled, his legs graceful, his back broad and strong. His lips were magic. Wherever they touched they ignited her, and they touched her everywhere. So did his hands, gliding over her breasts, across her belly, between her legs until all she could think of was him, wanting him, wanting.

And then she had what she wanted, all of him. Each deep, sweet thrust gave her more and took more from her. Each sigh, each moan—did they come from her or him? She didn't know and it didn't matter. All that mattered was the sharing, the one-ness, the love.

They peaked together, their bodies shuddering, pulsing, clinging. She closed her eyes and tightened her arms around him, not wanting to lose him. "I'm here," he whispered, as if he knew. "I'm here."

SOME TIME LATER, when her brain began to function again, she noticed the open box of condoms on her night table. "Where did that come from?"

"My bag," he said, gesturing toward the unzipped duffel beside the bed.

She'd been so transported by his lovemaking, she hadn't even considered protection. If he'd brought condoms with him, he must have come to Crescent Cove with sex on his mind. Smart man, she conceded, not at all offended. Every time she saw him, she admitted, sex wasn't far from her thoughts, either.

Moving stiffly, shaking off odd little aches in her thighs and the small of her back, she rose and wrapped herself in her bathrobe. Jeff donned his jeans and sweater. "Are you hungry?" she asked.

"For food, you mean?" He grinned lecherously and pretended to take a bite out of her neck.

"Yes, for food. I haven't eaten dinner yet."

"Neither have I. Have you got a festive Hanukkah meal on the menu?"

"Not until Saturday," she told him. "But I'll rustle something up."

She opened the bedroom door to find Nellie sitting guard outside. "So," he said, wrapping an arm around Alana as they strolled down the hall with the dog, "am I invited to this party of yours? Last time the subject came up, you refused to extend an invitation."

"It's an open house," she said. "If you want to come, I won't stop you."

"I want to come."

The living room was dark, and the scent of wax wafted through the air. She crossed to the window. Her candles had burned down. She suffered a tiny pang that the special white *shamas* candle no longer existed. Maybe tomorrow she'd stop back at Burning Bright and see if the woman had another one.

Jeff moved behind her, ringed his arms around her and eased her back against him. He kissed the crown of her head, and she saw their reflections in the glass, where just an hour ago she'd seen the reflection of the candles. Outside, snowflakes fell silently from a black sky. "It's beautiful," he murmured.

"Yes." Alana turned in his arms and hugged him, thinking it was the most beautiful Hanukkah of her life.

THROUGHOUT THE NIGHT, snow piled up outside Alana's house. Inside, she and Jeff slept, their limbs intertwined, her head cushioned by his shoulder. They woke up around two in the morning and made love again, and then fell back to sleep in each other's arms. Alana would have happily spent the entire day in bed with Jeff if Nellie hadn't started whining and scratching at the door—and if Alana didn't have a job to go to.

Reluctantly she hauled herself to her feet, grabbed her robe, rubbed the sleep out of her eyes and shuffled to the door. Nellie's complaints grew more intense; the poor dog obviously had to pee. Jeff rolled over, his eyes still closed, his breath deep and even. Lucky man. He didn't have an editor expecting him at his desk by nine in the morning.

"Okay, okay, I'm coming," Alana mumbled as she left the bedroom. Nellie let out a relieved bark and Alana shushed her. She ushered the dog to the kitchen door and let her out into the backyard, where piles of fresh snow lay in curving drifts.

She closed the door against the chill, prepared a pot of coffee and kept an eye on the window to make sure Nellie didn't vanish beneath a drift.

"Hey." Jeff's voice floated into the room. As sleepy as she was, the mere sound of it recharged her.

She hurried to the hall. "I'm sorry, did I wake you?" But he wasn't walking down the hall from the bedroom. She spun around and checked the living room. There she found him standing in front of the window, clad in only his jeans, his broad back exposed and tempting. She moved toward him, eager to press her cheek against that warm, tan expanse of skin, to hug him and face the morning with him.

But just as she reached him he stepped aside, and she saw what he was staring at: her menorah.

The white *shamas* candle stood in its holder, tall and graceful, its wick fresh.

What had the woman in the candle store said? *This is all*

you need…. It'll burn down, it'll burn out, and then the next day everything will be fine.

Frowning, Jeff looked at her, then at the menorah again. "Last night, didn't that candle—?"

"Yes," she said. "It did."

"And now—"

"Yes." She touched his hand, and his fingers closed possessively around hers. "Hanukkah is about miracles, you know."

"Is it?" He gave her a hesitant smile, clearly still suspicious of the mysterious new candle. "I thought it was about latkes."

"Latkes, too. Miracles and latkes and light."

"If that's what it's about," he said, brushing her lips with his, "it's a damn good holiday."

Epilogue

The party was a success. Alana's latkes—made with potatoes grated using her new food processor disk—were crisp and not too oily, and they tasted wonderful slathered in applesauce. The brisket was tender. Her guests even seemed taken by the marshmallows sandwiched between apricots and skewered on toothpicks.

She must have had more than fifty people crammed into her house, munching on food, playing with dreidels and catching up on town gossip. Jason Farrar and a few of his fellow officers showed up. Chet and his wife were there, along with Patsy and everyone else from the newsroom and their assorted spouses and partners. Jeff asked if his aunt Marge and uncle Bob could come, and Alana told him to invite them. She set up a bowl to accept donations to the newspaper's Katie Chase fund—even though Jeff had secured financing for the surgery, the local fund would cover incidental expenses—and people added coins, bills and checks to the collection.

Five candles plus the *shamas* flickered in her menorah on the night of the party. Alana had stopped by Burning Bright yesterday to invite the proprietor to her party, but the store was closed. She slid a note under the door, but the woman who reminded her so much of her grandmother didn't come.

Still, she felt her grandmother's presence throughout the evening. The food, the high spirits of her guests, the joy that infused the air during this season of holidays, and most of all the beautiful antique menorah, all gave Alana the sense that her grandmother was close by, nodding and saying, "Yes, Alana, this is how you find happiness in life. You celebrate every occasion worth celebrating, and you surround yourself with friends and loved ones, and your home will be warm and safe."

Warm and safe. She smiled as Jeff sidled up next to her. "I've got a surprise for you," he said.

"Another disk for my food processor? I could use one of those French-fries blades."

He laughed, took her hand and tugged her down the hall, away from the crush of party goers. Several people had a hot-and-heavy gambling game going with a dreidel and a stash of gold-foil-wrapped chocolate coins in her bedroom, so she and Jeff ducked into the laundry alcove, as private a place as they could find in her crowded house tonight.

"You once told me," he said, "that your ideal would be to have a house in the city and a house here in Crescent Cove. Remember?"

She nodded.

"Well...as cities go, Boston isn't bad."

"Boston?"

"I've been negotiating with my firm. Since I'm their labor specialist—and I'm so damn good at what I do—"

"I know, I know," she cut him off, then rolled her eyes. "You never make mistakes. You've told me."

He grinned. "Anyway, they're willing to allow me to work for them as a consultant, one or two days a week, unless a big case comes up."

"And the rest of the week?"

"Remember Burt Ammond? Eleanor Chase's lawyer? He wants to cut back on his hours so he can spend more time on the ski slopes. I talked to him, and he seemed to like the idea of having someone to share his practice with."

"You're moving to Crescent Cove?" she blurted out, then clamped her hand over her mouth. Not that anyone could have heard her, with so many other noisy conversations churning the air.

"I figured we could spend some time here and some time in the city. Isn't that what you want?"

What she wanted, she acknowledged, was a man willing to turn his life upside down to give her what she wanted. What she wanted was a man who loved her enough to make her dreams come true.

"What I want," she said, "is you."

"Well, that's an easy one," he said, giving her a sexy smile before he gave her an even sexier kiss.

Closing her eyes, she lost herself in his embrace for one blissful moment. A chorus of rowdy laughter from the living room reminded her that she had a house full of guests, and she ended the kiss. But she couldn't let go of him quite yet. She wrapped her arms around him and tucked her head against his shoulder.

Her grandmother's voice floated through her head—or maybe it was the voice of the woman from the candle shop, the one Alana wished had been here tonight. *This is the one you need,* the voice said. *Trust me.*

"Yes, Grandma," Alana whispered, so softly even Jeff couldn't hear her. "This is the one."

HARLEQUIN®

AMERICAN *Romance*®

**A Baby to Be is always
something special!**

SANTA BABY

by Laura Marie Altom
(November 2004)

Christmas Eve. Alaska. A small-plane crash—
and nine months later, a baby. But Whitney and
her pilot, Colby, are completely at odds about
their son's future. Until the next Christmas!

THE BABY'S
BODYGUARD

by Jacqueline Diamond
(December 2004)

Security expert Jack Arnett and his wife, Casey,
are getting divorced because she wants children
and he doesn't. But—and Jack doesn't know this—
Casey's already pregnant with his child....

HARLEQUIN®

AMERICAN *Romance*®

A COWBOY AND A KISS
by Dianne Castell

Sunny Kelly wants to save the old saloon
that her aunt left her in a small Texas town.

But Sunny isn't really Sunny.
She's Sophie Addison, a Reno attorney,
and she's got amnesia.

That's not about to stop cowboy
Gray McBride, who's running hard for
mayor on a promise to clean up the town—
until he runs into some mighty strong
feelings for the gorgeous blonde.

On sale starting December 2004—
wherever Harlequin books are sold.

HARLEQUIN *Super*ROMANCE®

A six-book series from Harlequin Superromance.

WOMEN *in Blue*

Six female cops battling crime and corruption on the streets of Houston. Together they can fight the blue wall of silence. But divided, will they fall?

Coming in December 2004,
The Witness by Linda Style
(Harlequin Superromance #1243)

She had vowed never to return to Houston's crime-riddled east end. But Detective Crista Santiago's promotion to the Chicano Squad put her right back in the violence of the barrio. Overcoming demons from her past, and with somebody in the department who wants her gone, she must race the clock to find out who shot Alex Del Rio's daughter.

Coming in January 2005,
Her Little Secret by Anna Adams
(Harlequin Superromance #1248)

Abby Carlton was willing to give up her career for Thomas Riley, but then she realized she'd always come second to his duty to his country. She went home and rejoined the police force, aware that her pursuit of love had left a black mark on her file. Now Thomas is back, needing help only she can give.

Also in the series:
The Partner by Kay David (#1230, October 2004)
The Children's Cop by Sherry Lewis (#1237, November 2004)

And watch for:
She Walks the Line by Roz Denny Fox (#1254, February 2005)
A Mother's Vow by K.N. Casper (#1260, March 2005)

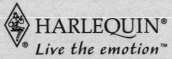

HARLEQUIN®
Live the emotion™

Revisit Trueblood, Texas, with a thrilling NEW novel of romantic suspense!

DEBBI RAWLINS
A Family at Last

It had been more than a one-night stand for Brazilian heiress Terry Monteverde when she had made love to FBI agent Mitch Barnes. So when danger threatened her, she tracked him down and left her most precious possession with him...their baby. She didn't count on Mitch searching relentlessly for her—his soul mate!

**Finders Keepers:
Bringing families together.**

Available in November 2004.

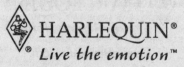

Visit Dundee, Idaho, with bestselling author

brenda novak

A Home of Her Own

Her mother always said if you couldn't be
rich, you'd better be Lucky!

When Lucky was ten, her mother, Red—the
town hooker—married Morris Caldwell,
a wealthy and much older man.

Mike Hill, his grandson, feels that Red and
her kids alienated Morris from his family.
Even the old man's Victorian mansion, on the
property next to Mike's ranch, went to Lucky
rather than his grandchildren.

Now Lucky's back, which means Mike has a
new neighbor. One he doesn't want to like...

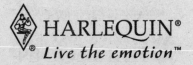

HARLEQUIN®
Live the emotion™

www.eHarlequin.com

HSRH001204